Knowing Yourself
A Medieval Romance

The Sword of Glastonbury Series

Book 1

Lisa Shea

Visit my website at LisaShea.com

First Printing: December 2011

~ 14 ~

Print ISBN-13 978-0-9798377-6-0
Kindle ASIN B006JDEK0I
Lulu 978-1-312-46592-3
SmashWords 9781310392207

Follow your heart.
Let your actions speak louder than words.
Every day,
Express your love for those you care for.

Knowing Yourself

Chapter 1

England, 1174

If you cannot find the truth right where you are,
where else do you expect to find it?
~Dogen

Kay's mouth fell open at the deliciously sinful display of stunning male physiques, her eyes thoroughly examining each man in turn, admiring the thick, corded muscles of their arms; the finely chiseled lines of their jaws; the finger-twiningly-dense hair dancing in the autumn wind - red, blond, brunette, black, tawny gold. A sensual thrill coursed through her, flushing her with tingling warmth. She could choose any man in that group to be her husband and he would instantly, willingly, loyally come to her side. The awesome power intoxicated her to her very core.

She turned to Em, nudging her blonde sister with playful delight as they peered through the thick tapestry curtains of the coach window. "Are you sure I can only keep *one* of them?" Kay joked in a low voice. "It might be useful to have a spare husband around, in case of trouble." Her eyes were drawn to the tawny mane of hair a second time, her gaze sliding down from his shoulders; her breath caught as she sized up the thickness of his biceps.

Her voice grew hoarse. "I am sure I could find *all* sorts of uses for a back-up knight with *that* kind of build."

Em put a hand over her mouth to muffle the flurry of giggles that began to erupt. She adjusted her position slightly to account for her large, round abdomen, visible evidence of the child she had been carrying for the past six months. "It took our father long enough to convince you to use this process in the first place," she chuckled in merriment. "If he realized you were now enjoying it, I am sure it would put his mind at ease."

Kay shook her head. "I still do not agree with the principle of it," she commented more quietly. Her eyes drew slowly along each man who stood on the keep steps, the group being presented with a final set of instructions by an elderly man with sparse grey hair, his elegant brown cloak concealing a frail frame. She knew her father, Lord Weston, was doing his best to present a strong front to his future sons-in-law.

Kay kept her eyes on his slowly moving figure. "I turned down the previous suitors because I found them sadly lacking. For father to force me to choose from one of these five men seems outrageous. What if *none* of them end up being what we need to defend Serenor Keep?"

Em's mouth grew into a wide smile. "Surely, my dear sister, you have to believe *one* of those men would be suitable to stand by your side?"

Kay had to admit that the group had far exceeded her expectations. Her father had sent word the length and breadth of England in his search, bringing in five worthy, eligible bachelors who were interested in control of the seaside tower. All five men had agreed up front to put themselves in the hands of this selection process – to vie against each other for Kay's hand in marriage. Now they were being told the particular rules of the game.

Suddenly all five men's heads turned sharply to stare at the coach, and both women instantly pulled back into the dark interior, their hearts pounding, looking at each other before bursting into a fresh round of laughter. Kay had to take several deep breaths before she could bring herself to speak again.

"I think they have just been told they cannot see what I look like until I have made my final decision," she chortled merrily. "By their reactions, they were none too pleased at that little tidbit!"

Em's shoulders were shaking with mirth as she leant back against the embroidered seat. "Still, you have to admit Father hit on a stroke of genius there," she countered. "By having me play at the shy target of their attentions, you can roam free as my maid servant, watching the men close up. You can observe how they talk about the keep and each other behind my back."

Kay's voice became more somber "Are you sure you are ready for this, to be sequestered in the top level of the keep for perhaps several weeks? If none of the men can see you, but they need to occasionally speak with you, it is the only way to maintain the charade." She took her sister's hand. "Surely you will get claustrophobic after a few days in that tiny apartment."

Em shook her head. "I am looking forward to it," she confided to her younger sister. "Between Eric's whirlwind courtship, and our wedding, I have not had five minutes by myself. I am about to become a mother - a full time task if ever there was one." She smiled and shrugged her shoulders. "This may be the only quiet time I get for decades; the only time to be by myself, to luxuriate in quiet, to sit, to read, to just think. I am going to enjoy every second of it."

"Will you miss Eric?" asked Kay, pressing.

A wistful look came over Em's face. She looked toward the thick, dark curtains which shaded the window, laying a hand against them for a moment. "Yes," she admitted quietly. "He has been my rock, been by my side for so long now that it was extremely hard to part from him." A faint smile lit her face. "Still, it is only for a few weeks, and as they say, absence makes the heart grow fonder. I will keep a journal for him, and he is doing the same for me. It will be interesting to share those once we are reunited."

She drew her gaze tenderly to her sister. "Besides, this looks to be our final outing as siblings. I will have my home here, with Eric, and you will have yours out at Serenor. I am going to enjoy spending time with you for these next few weeks and will find it hard to be separated when the time comes."

Kay gave her a nudge. "I am sure we can visit, once we are both old, married women, but I agree completely. This will be our chance to play at dice, to share confidences, and to have one last gasp of freedom before we are both chasing after children."

Em offered a wink, then reached beneath her seat, drawing out a stoppered, blue glass bottle. "Then, I think it is time for us to celebrate," she chuckled, pulling out the cork and handing it over to her sister. "A toast to our futures!"

Kay took a long pull, and suddenly the coach gave a gentle jerk as it moved into a quiet rhythm. The sound of numerous men on horseback swelled around them.

A tremor of nervousness shot through her. It was all in motion now. There was no turning back; no second thoughts. By nightfall they would be at the keep, and the games would begin. She would have to give herself over to one of these men.

She thought back to the line of strong shoulders she had examined. Perhaps things were not so bad. She took another swig and smiled. Not so bad at all.

* * *

The hours drifted by in a lethargic haze of merry expectations and teasing. By the time the coach pulled in for an afternoon stop, the women were flushed with laughter. A familiar low growl sounded by their window.

"Ladies, it is Leland," he called through the curtain. "I have sent my lad, Eli, to escort the five gentlemen over the ridge and a ways up the road. He will ensure they stay there until we catch up with them. You will have a chance to stretch your legs unseen."

Before he had finished speaking, Em was up and moving, throwing open the door of the coach. She took his proffered hand and stepped out into the sunlight. Kay was only a moment behind her, and they stretched with relish, gazing around them at the rolling meadows with the blue-grey mountains in the distance.

Kay smiled in amusement as she turned and looked over Leland. He was wearing a priest's restrained habit – a long, black, simple tunic without any adornments. His ever-present sword was nowhere to be seen. She shook her head in merriment.

"How are you going to survive the weeks up at that small chapel, Leland?" she asked, her eyes sparkling. "This is quite a demotion from captain of the guard!"

Leland's thick brown brows came together over a well-weathered face. "I consider it a duty of the highest order to look after you two," he responded, his eyes moving between the two women. "Serenor will have only a skeleton staff on hand. Your father wants the potential lords to be able to settle in without having many there to contest their orders and ways. We need to see how they will act when they feel like the *man in charge*." He smiled fondly at the two women. "Still, I will be glad to be watching from the hill, keeping an eye on things."

Kay found her eyes scanning forward, over the rise to where the men were waiting. "They will be like five stallions, fighting for control of the herd," she mused with a chuckle. "It will certainly be something to see."

The women spent another few minutes stretching and enjoying the fresh air, then Em gave a long, loud yawn. "I think I am about ready for an afternoon nap," she admitted. "How are you feeling?"

Kay rolled her shoulders. "Like I want to meet these men for myself," she grinned. She moved to the back of the coach, unhitched her horse, and threw the reins over his head. She mounted smoothly, tucking her loose skirts around her with well-practiced ease. She then drew up alongside the vehicle. "Rest well."

"You behave yourself," smiled Em back at her. "Remember, you are a maid servant now. None of that sassy backtalk, or I shall have to punish you."

Kay grinned widely. "I will be the epitome of quiet grace," she promised serenely. Both sisters burst into peals of laughter, and then Em climbed into the coach, drawing the small wooden door shut with a solid *thunk*. Leland pulled up alongside Kay, and with a nod the coachman shook out the reins, getting the horses into motion again. The group slowly made its way along the peaceful dirt road, the hoofbeat keeping time with the warbling of birds and the gentle whisper of the autumn breeze.

Kay found herself unconsciously smoothing down her simple burgundy over-dress, and she wondered if the dark braids of her hair were still neatly in place. She grinned wryly as they crested the hill. It did not matter, of course. To the five men waiting down in the valley she was naught but a serving girl. They were anxiously awaiting the woman in the coach, not this slender horsewoman who rode with the middle-aged priest. Still, she had her pride, and she wanted to make a good impression. It would serve her best if the men tolerated her presence so that she could overhear their conversations and learn more about them in their unguarded moments.

The men had remained mounted and were lined up along the side of the road, watching her approach with interest. She nudged her horse with her calves, moving into a trot, and Leland matched her action, staying at her side until they reached the quintet.

Leland nodded to the group. "Gentlemen," he rumbled, "This is Kay, the lady-in-waiting to Keren-happuch. As Lord Weston has indicated, Kay here will be your main means of contact with Keren-happuch other than your allotted daily half-hour of conversation with his daughter through a curtain."

Leland turned to face the woman at his side. "Kay, let me introduce you to the men vying for your lady's hand."

The red-head spoke up immediately. "I am Uther," he announced, sweeping himself down into a flourishing bow. He wore a flamboyant turquoise tunic with yellow piping along its edges, and his emerald cloak was pinned at his massive neck with a broach with five different colors of gems. His eyes slid down her form with interest, and his grin had widened by the time he met her gaze again. "I am looking forward to spending time with you."

"I am sure you are," agreed Kay with a gracious smile, turning her gaze easily to the next man in line.

"Alistair is my name," stammered the brown-haired man, nervously brushing down his neatly tailored grey

tunic. Kay wondered if he had spent time in front of a
mirror with a ruler, his creases were so sharp and perfectly
aligned. He sat up straight in his saddle, holding his reins
at an exact right angle. "I heard from the soldiers at the
keep that you will be taking daily prayer with Father
Leland each morning at the chapel?"

Kay's eyes flashed to Leland's, and she bit back a
smile. She would certainly be visiting him each morning to
bring news, as well as to get in some sword training away
from prying eyes. The prayer story seemed a perfect cover
for her activities.

"Yes," she confirmed, her eyes dropping in demure
propriety. "Rest assured that I will be back in ample time
to chaperone the morning talks you each have with Keren-
happuch. I would not let my personal time interfere with
that."

"I find it admirable that you set aside time for prayer,"
continued Alistair, color rising to his cheeks. "It is a mark
of quality in you, and reflects well on your Lady."

"I will be sure to let her know that," promised Kay with
a quick nod, desperately holding in her merriment at the
likely reaction her sister would have to the news.

"I am Jack," stated the third man sharply, his eyes
moving from Kay up to the coach which was slowly
drawing close to them. He wore a well-tailored white
tunic, and the crisp cut of his blond hair matched the frosty
gaze in his eyes. "I am not sure I like the rules of this
game. I like to know exactly what the prize is I am playing
for."

The man at his side grinned. "You are welcome to
resign, if you do not enjoy the odds," he suggested.
"Galeron here," he added to Kay, his eyes twinkling. His
black hair lay in curls against his head and his bright
crimson tunic was matched by a long, flowing cloak of the

same color. He gave a gentle bow to her. "I, for one, am intrigued by the conditions and look forward to our contest."

"Glad to meet you," welcomed Kay with a smile. She turned her gaze to the final man.

He waited quietly, patiently, his green-grey eyes a peaceful pool, and yet she could see the strength in his arms, the firmness in his thighs where they pressed against his horse's flank. His tawny hair fell to his shoulders in thick waves, and the sword on his left hip seemed both well used and well cared for. He wore a leather tunic, a simple design tracing along the edges.

She found herself speaking first. "I am Kay," she murmured, subdued by his presence, by the calm way he held himself. It was as if he had all the time in the world, and speaking with her was the only thing on his mind.

"I am pleased to meet you," offered the man with a smooth bow. "My name is Reese."

The coach had reached them, and the men automatically fell in before it, setting into easy motion. Kay and Leland tucked in behind them, with Eli moving to Kay's other side, his fresh blond curls bouncing lightly around his young face.

Kay turned to the lad with a smile. "So, what do you think of our adventure?" She had known the page all her life, and while he was a few years younger than her, they had spent many enjoyable hours sparring together.

"Are you kidding?" he responded in incredulous glee, his wiry frame tense with excitement. "To spend several weeks as the sole pupil of Leland? I could not have dreamt up a better assignment!"

Alistair's quiet voice echoed faintly back from the group ahead. "Now there is a lad with his priorities straight," he intoned with relish. "You hold with your religious ideals, boy, and you can achieve great heights."

"Absolutely," agreed Eli, giving Kay a wink. "I will do my very best."

"More boys should be like him," continued Alistair, turning to Uther, his voice growing slightly louder. "Too many waste all day solely on physical achievements; they neglect their mind and their spirit." He glanced on either side of him. "Not only the men. I hear tell that some women in this region are familiar with the use of a blade. Can you imagine?"

Uther gave out a loud, guffawing chortle, throwing his head back, his red hair shining in the autumn sun. "A woman, using a blade?" He glanced down the line of men, his smile wide. "There is one use for a woman in regards to a man's blade, and she would be the sheath!"

The line of men chuckled at the joke, and Kay saw a twinkle even in Reese's quiet calm. Her spine stiffened. She and her sister had been training in both dagger and short sword since they were young, and were quite able to defend themselves if necessary. The skill had been expected of them, between the bandits roaming the mountains and the nearness of their rivals, the MacDougals. A dozen retorts sprang to her lips.

She cut them back with sharp effort. She was a maid servant now, not one to be reprimanding the men.

Her head snapped to the side. "Leland, I am going to ride ahead. I feel the need for some fresh air."

Leland nodded across her to Eli, and in a moment she and the blond were cantering down the road, then stretching into a liberating gallop. The wind rushed through her hair, pulling the braids loose, and she was swept away in the motion, in the sure reaching of her steed's muscles beneath her, feeling his joy in the race.

Beside her, Eli's face was wreathed in smiles, and they thundered toward the horizon, toward the meeting of the pale blue sky and fresh green carpet beneath.

She was going home. Not the home where she had been born, not the sturdy, large, noisy castle of her youth. She was heading toward the final outpost against the tossing waves, where she had been conceived, where she had spent every spare holiday and chance of escape. The round tower high over the ocean. The sturdy encompassing walls with their walk. The quiet bailey within, holding all one could need during a snowy winter or a languorous summer. She loved every season there, every time of day, every second. It was waiting for her, up ahead, if only she could ride more quickly.

Eli reined in alongside her, and she reluctantly pulled in to match.

He looked back over his shoulder. "We really should not get too far from the main party," he pointed out quietly. "You know as well as I do -"

Kay nodded in understanding, wheeling her horse in a circle and heading back toward the caravan at a gentle canter. Time drifted by as they rode; it seemed too soon when they saw the group ahead. They pulled up into a trot, then moved past the five men to wheel easily in place alongside Leland.

Leland looked over their flushed faces. "Have a nice ride?" he asked Kay with mild curiosity. "See anything interesting?"

"No bandits; no MacDougals," reported Kay with a wide smile, giving her steed's neck a pat. "Just a nice chance to stretch the legs."

Jack's sharp voice came back to her. "You rode well, for a girl," he snapped, turning his head with a crisp motion, his blond hair ruffling in the wind. "It is important for women to handle themselves rationally in case of trouble. I assume your lady can ride as ably?"

"She rides just as well as most men I know," retorted Kay, piqued by the tone of the comment. "My lady is an avid horsewoman."

"Good for her," agreed Jack, nonplussed by her reaction. "Unfortunately, I will not have a chance to see her in action myself before this little game has played out. I will have to rely on your word for it, assuming you speak truly."

Kay's throat tightened in outrage. "My word is my honor," she growled, her spine stiffening. "You would dare imply -"

Galeron shook his head, his black curls dancing. "My, you are feisty for a maid servant," he interrupted, glancing back at her. "It speaks well for Keren-happuch's nature, that she has such an able companion at her side."

Kay pursed her lips, taking in a long, deep breath as she settled back into her saddle. Galeron was right. She had to draw a tighter rein on her feelings and emotions if she were to get through this ordeal. She glanced at Eli and saw the twinkle of amusement in his young eyes. She nodded with a quick movement to the left. In a moment the two had drawn their horses aside, circled them around and come up behind the coach, where they could no longer hear the men talking.

Eli flashed a bright smile at her. "Before we left, Leland wagered that you would not last ten minutes with them before one of the men riled you," he teased. "They certainly seem an arrogant bunch."

"Not all of them," pondered Kay. "They do seem to be quite different from each other. I suppose I will have to see, over time, what their strengths and weaknesses are."

"Maybe, if you do not spend the weeks in shouting matches," smiled Eli. His eyes sparkled. "You may yet find yourself spending more and more time in 'prayer' with us up at the chapel."

"I may at that," agreed Kay, her face brightening. "I suppose there is always that option, to hide out with you and Leland."

Eli shook his head in merriment. "If your father heard about that, he would tan all of our hides for stretching this process out longer than it needed."

"He made the rules, not me," countered Kay with a laugh. "I can take as long as I wish – and my decision is final."

"Well then," mused Eli, giving his steed's mane a fond pat, "I will enjoy every moment of this break!"

Kay found herself relaxing into the ride. She and Eli stretched out into a canter several more times over the afternoon, racing ahead with the hawks, then returning reluctantly to the slow-moving group.

Soon the road came up along the cliffs against the ocean. She took in a lung-filling breath, relishing the salt air, the crisp freshness, and the even rhythm of the swells as they moved out as far as the eye could see. She could not hold back – she spun out into a gallop, Eli at her side. Together they rode until she felt that familiar jolt of pleasure, coming over the ridge and seeing the keep's tower in the distance. Its protective curtain wall was secure. Strong. Safe.

Home. She was home.

She thundered ahead, her heart soaring, an absolute sense of peace filling her with every hoofbeat. A lone white birch came into view, planted to the right side of the path, and she drew in, slowing to a canter, then finally a walk. She settled into a stop by the tree's side. Her horse edged alongside the slender trunk, nibbling at the grass tufting at its base. She patted the birch's bark fondly, her hand tracing the numerous small indents in its leathery skin, her eyes looking forward to the keep before her. Several men were on the walls now, and one swept his hand in a long wave. She put both hands up above her head, returning the welcome, her heart filling with joy.

She sat gazing at the keep for a long while, a sense of calm filling her while slowly the sound of hoofbeat grew behind her, infiltrating into her being. She waited patiently as the group drew up alongside her.

"Serenor," she stated simply, gazing at the keep with love. She drew her eyes reluctantly from its grey walls, turning to look across the men at her side.

Uther's eyes lit up with delight, his red face flushed, and Kay's breast sparked with hope. Maybe the men would adore the land as much as she did!

The red-head licked his lips with relish. "They have a feast laid out for us, surely," he commented with growing interest. "I am starved!" He spun his eyes to meet Kay's. "Tell me that all the serving wenches are as comely as you, and I shall be forever in your debt."

"They say the way to a man's heart is through his stomach, so you should be all set," she snapped in disappointment, her eyes moving toward his protruding belly.

Uther guffawed, patting the roll with a smile. "A pillow for the head, my lass," he teased, giving her a sly wink.

Alistair nodded in approval. "The keep," he observed in a thin voice, "is much like the monastery in Aird Mhór, Ireland where I spent many years in training. Aloof, isolated. I like that."

Kay relaxed slightly, her eyes moving along the line of men. She did enjoy the quiet here, although … aloof? She found her home to be well settled in its landscape, not held apart from it. She would have called it snug … safe …

Jack's icy eyes swept the rolling hills which surrounded the keep, his eyes resting on the white birch trees which lay ringed in a loose semi-circle every few hundred yards. "Good defensive layout, and these trees …" He rode over to the one Kay had stopped at, eyeing its trunk. He nodded in satisfaction. "About two hundred yards."

Alistair looked more carefully at its bark. "The tree is diseased," he scoffed. "It should be taken down immediately, before it can infect the others with its wasting."

Galeron chuckled in amusement. "No, my dear monkish friend," he corrected gently. "Those are arrow marks."

Alistair looked back at the keep again, shaking his head. "An arrow, from that distance? Unlikely." His eyes came back to the trunk again. "Besides, those are not simply gouges in the bark. They look like black mildew."

Reese had been staring at the keep, a distant look in his eyes, and only now did he turn his head to gaze at the birch. "Flame arrow," he remarked easily, glancing at the marks. "Someone enjoys night shooting, I imagine."

Uther rolled his eyes. "It matters not," he grumbled, turning away. "Let us get going, dinner is waiting!"

The group ambled into motion again, and Kay's eyes were glued on the keep; she could see nothing else as they rode down the slope, the structure growing ever larger in her vision. There were the top floor windows, looking into the private chambers which would be Em's only world for the coming weeks. Below that were the public rooms – the main hall, the study, the sitting room. The ground floor held the barracks, the pantries, the rooms the men would be occupying. Then down below ground, the storage chambers, the cell or two where drunks would sleep off their intoxication.

As they drew near the moat, Leland waved the men back, and they pulled aside, allowing the coach to move forward with Kay on one side, Eli on the other. The main doors of the curtain wall were pulled closed behind them as they passed into the bailey, and Kay was off her horse in a moment, running lightly up to the coach and pulling open its door.

Em blinked sleepily at the evening light, stretching wearily before taking Kay's hand and descending out from the coach. "That was blissful," she sighed with a smile. "The gentle rocking, the peace and quiet, I could not have asked for better." She rolled her shoulders and looked around her. "Now I am starving," she admitted.

"We will get you up to your quarters, and see about sending up food right away," promised Kay, tucking her arm beneath Kay's. Eli came promptly around to Em's other side and together they escorted her toward the main gate, offering friendly waves to the guards and servants who they passed along the way. They turned right at the main barracks, taking the spiral stairs at one side of the room, moving slowly upwards.

A buxom blonde with long, cascading curls met them in the main hall. "Greetings, ladies," she welcomed, dropping a curtsy as they paused for a moment. Her smile widened as she looked over Em's rounded belly. "Why Mary Magdalene, you look ready to pop!"

Em gave her an amused look. "Now, Anne, you know for the coming weeks I must only be referred to by my sister's name – Keren-happuch. If this is to work -"

Anne blushed deep crimson, and she put her hand over her mouth in dismay. "Oh, and we were told that repeatedly over the past days, too!" She looked between the two women. "I promise, I will not make that mistake again."

Kay's eyes twinkled. "You better not," she teased gently. "With all the effort we are putting into this deception, it would be a shame to have it ruined by a stray word."

Em smiled. "In the meantime," she added, "I am in fact ready to eat a horse. Could you bring up some food to the solar?"

Kay nudged her sister. "*Not* horse meat," she corrected. "With all the trouble I put into raising them, I hardly want them ending up on our menu."

Anne giggled. "Tonight is rabbit stew," she informed the duo. "I will have a large bowl up to you in just a moment!" She turned and scampered down the stairs, and was lost to sight in an instant.

Kay and Eli retook their positions on either side of Em, and moving slowly and steadily, made their way with her up the second flight of stairs toward the top floor. An alert guard was waiting on the landing, and smiled in greeting as she came up to the small space. He pulled open the door for her, and in a moment they were securely closed into the solar.

Kay immediately went to the bank of windows overlooking the front gates and gave a large wave with her arms. There was an answering motion from above the gates, and with a shuddering movement the wooden doors pulled open, allowing the six men to ride in and dismount. Kay turned from them, watching as Eli helped her sister settle onto one of the couches in the large, well-appointed room.

Em pulled off her boots, then her socks, stretching her toes languorously before lowering them to dig them into the thick fur carpet. "Ah, here we go, my secret hideaway," she smiled, looking around her at the tapestries, the many windows, the shelves with codices and musical instruments. She turned to Eli. "You will bring up my clothes and journals? Normally, I would be fine to handle that myself, but ..." She looked down at her stomach wryly.

"Of course, M'Lady," confirmed Eli with a smile. "It is no problem at all. You just relax; I am sure your food will be up to you shortly." He headed out toward the stairs.

Kay plunked herself down alongside her sister, stretching out her own feet and looking around. Em was right. The solar was peaceful and quiet - a perfect resting spot. The three bedrooms behind them were warm and comfortable. This would work out quite wonderfully.

She sat for several long minutes, unwinding after the day on the road, watching as the sunset sent long fingers of dusky hue in through the tall windows.

Em finally turned to smile at her younger sister. "I will get the curtain set up for our morning talks later," she mused, "but in the meantime, you should probably head down to enjoy dinner with our honored guests."

"I was thinking I could keep you company up here," murmured Kay, her shoulders dropping slightly. "I am worn out by the newcomers already and would appreciate a few hours of your peaceful isolation."

Em shook her head in amusement. "Duty calls," she reminded Kay. "It is time for you to start learning just what makes these men tick. Knowledge is power, after all!"

Kay sighed, but she stood. Em was right. The sooner she began sorting out the men, the sooner she could start deciding who to eliminate from the list. She gave her sister a fond pat on the shoulder, then moved over to the sturdy door. Pushing through, she nodded to the guard, then made her way down the spiral toward the great hall.

Anne was just heading up with the meal as she reached the hall, and Kay smiled at the blonde, then headed through the maze of tables. The servants and soldiers all waved in friendly greeting as she moved across the busy room. She gave an inward sigh of relief that any spoken greetings were of her nickname, "Kay." While her sister might still be treated formally by the staff, she had been at the keep for so long, and gotten to know the inhabitants so well, that her familiar Kay nickname was the only name ever used for her. It would serve her well in the coming adventure.

Her throat tightened as she came up to the head table. The five men had already taken their seats along its length. Uther was sprawled in her father's chair, his red hair shining in the torchlight. He was tugging on Jessica's arm, pulling the brown-haired serving maid against him, whispering something into her ear.

Alistair was staring around him with wide eyes, his gaze going to the high ceilings above, across to the tapestries lining the walls, the trio of windows opening out over the bailey below. He took a cautious sniff of the mug of ale, then drank in a long draw of the brew, his face relaxing into a smile.

Jack looked up sharply as she approached, his eyes scouring her. "Should you not be with your mistress?" he snapped, his voice rich with condemnation. All five eyes went to meet hers with varying degrees of interest and curiosity.

Kay found herself blushing at the implied accusation of wrongdoing and bit her tongue to hold back on her initial feisty response. She carefully arranged her features into a quiet, dutiful look. "My mistress requested that I consume

my dinner at your side. In that way I can answer any
questions you might have and familiarize you with the
keep and its environs."

Galeron nodded in approval. "Of course my dear," he
agreed, running his hand idly through his dark curls. "I
have countless questions to ask you." He withdrew a small
wood-framed wax tablet from a pouch at his side, as well
as an iron stylus.

Reese pulled out the chair at his side. "Perhaps she
could get some food into her first," he suggested in a low
murmur. She nodded her thanks, moving into the spot,
sighing as she sat at the far end of her own table.

It was only for a few weeks. She could get through this.

A mug of ale was set down before her and she reached
for it with weary relief.

"Let us say grace," intoned Alistair in a monotone. Kay
let the air out of her in a long, soundless sigh, but dropped
her head, lacing her fingers together.

Alistair's voice carried out over the hall. "Dear Lord,
let us be thankful for our safe journey today and our arrival
in this place of godliness. We seek every day to do our
duty to You - to act with honor and courage. Let us always
find the peaceful solution to problems and act within Your
wishes. Amen."

"Amen," echoed Kay, picking up her tankard again,
draining down half of it in a long draw. Then Anne was at
her side, laying down a bowl of rich stew, and the scent
was heavenly. She dug into it with enthusiasm, its warmth
filling her; nourishing her.

"So, tell us about the keep," instructed Galeron, placing
his wax tablet carefully on the table before him, taking up
his stylus. "Four floors with a round tower construction.
Good defensive structure. The curtain wall can be walked
along its entire circumference?"

"Yes," agreed Kay between bites, watching as he wrote. Reese reached over to pass the basket of rolls, offering her one, and she took the warm bread with a smile, nodding her thanks. "The round tower was put in about eighty years ago; it is harder to undermine, and more easily able to deflect projectiles. We are on the central floor here."

She tossed her head toward the spiral stairs at the front of the room. "Your rooms are down below, on the ground floor. Tomorrow morning you will see the top floor, when you have your meetings with my lady."

She still found it hard to call her sister by her own full name, the unwieldy moniker of Keren-happuch her father had saddled her with. She and her sister had barely been able to talk when they had agreed to call each other simply by their initials, K and M.

"How many soldiers are in residence?" continued Galeron in a friendly tone, making notes.

"We have a constable, then four shifts of five men each for the walls," listed Kay, taking a bite of her roll. "Three men to guard the solar and four shifts of four men to ride the roads."

"You knew that rather easily," offered Galeron, his eyes rising to meet hers.

She ate another mouthful of her bread, savoring the melting butter. "I like to know who is ensuring my safety," she responded with a smile. "I make it my business to be aware of what goes on around me."

He nodded. "So that makes … thirty nine men?"

Reese shook his head. "Forty," he corrected in a low tone.

"Oh, right," agreed Galeron, re-checking his notes. "With the constable, of course."

Jack took a pull on his ale, his eyes cold. "That seems rather light for such an important outpost, does it not?"

The muscles in Kay's jaw clenched. *Patience*, she reminded herself. She let a deliberate breath out, relaxing by force of will. She could do this. She gave the excuse, as her father had instructed. "As we are in harvest season, a portion of our men have been sent out to guard the villages while their crops are being gathered and brought to safe storehouses."

Reese chuckled at her side. "I am sure the excess men's departure was hastened by our impending arrival here," he murmured under his breath.

She glanced over and caught the twinkle of amusement in his eyes. "Yes," she admitted, a smile growing on her face. "That did have something to do with it."

Alistair's face wrinkled in confusion. "What? Did you think we would be so foolish as to launch an attack on someone, if we had troops at our disposal? We are peaceful men!" He began nervously fumbling with his mug, turning it in place.

Galeron glanced up from his writing. "No, Alistair," he corrected with a lenient smile. "Kay means that we are already five powerful dogs battling for the lead of a pack. Lord Weston undoubtedly wanted us to have as few external challengers as possible. That way we would only have each other to crash up against."

Uther gave out a merry shout, raising his tankard high. "Less competition for the wenches!" he triumphed, drawing Jessica down onto his lap as she passed, laughing as she pulled from his arms and scampered nervously back toward the stairs.

Kay looked down, taking in a spoonful of stew, then another, focusing on her food. It was only the first night. She would get used to them, used to their way of acting, and grow more tolerant of their questions.

Galeron's voice needled into her thoughts. "So," he prodded, "on to the beasts. Do you have any horses of note here?"

Kay's resolve dissolved in an instant. She could not take any more. She was quite proud of her steeds, and to hear them flippantly dismissed as *beasts* ... she swallowed one more spoonful of stew, grabbed another roll from the basket, then stood.

"I think I will retire for the evening, gentlemen. I will be out at the chapel at dawn, but I look forward to spending time with you and Keren-happuch starting at nine. Each of us will spend a half hour together."

Jack's eyes were sharp on hers. "Who goes first?" he snapped, his blond hair seeming to bristle in the firelight.

Kay's mouth folded into a wolfish grin. "I leave that to you five to work out," she chuckled, her spirits lifting. "That should keep you busy for a while."

She turned and strode to the far end of the room, her feet moving lightly down the spiral stairs. In a moment she was crossing the dark courtyard, reaching the curtain wall, and walking carefully up the stone steps which ran along the front left edge. A heartbeat or two later she was on top of the wall, leaning against the crenellated edging and taking in a long, deep breath of the fresh night air. A large moon hung glowing in the sky, sending a silvery light across the landscape. It illuminated the ring of occasional birch trees, the scattering of scrubs, and sent a glint off the small stone chapel high on the hills to the far left.

A few minutes drifted by in quiet calm, and her shoulders finally lost their tight tension. Footsteps came from along the wall, and in a moment Jevan was alongside her, his dark guard uniform nearly blending in with the shadows.

He leaned against the wall at her side. "There you are," he greeted. He gazed down at her, his eyes sparkling with delight. "Had enough of the suitors?"

"You know it," agreed Kay, looking at him with fond tenderness. She brushed a stray leaf from his short, blond hair, verging on silver in the moonlight. Jevan had practically raised her in this place, and seemed more a favored uncle than a guardsman to her. "It does not matter. I am just happy to be home again."

He wrinkled his short nose, looking back out over the rolling hills with a steady eye. "We are happy to have you back, Kay, even with your rowdy entourage."

Slow footsteps sounded on the stairs, and they both turned to look. Reese came up to the landing, then stopped in surprise as he saw the two standing along the wall.

"I am sorry," he apologized in a low voice. "I did not mean to intrude."

Jevan swept his arm in a welcoming gesture. "Not at all," he offered. "We are always happy for another pair of eyes."

Reese came up to the other side of Kay, leaning against the granite, looking out over the misty landscape. Kay could almost feel his muscles relax as he gazed out over the undulating grass.

He let out a breath. "I had not expected this," he murmured, his eyes sweeping out toward the mountains in the far distance.

Kay turned her eyes to his in idle curiosity. "Expected what?"

Reese glanced up in surprise, flushing slightly. "The beauty," he admitted after a moment. "My father led me to believe this a barren corner of the earth, a rocky promontory of grey bleakness."

Kay nodded, turning to look back out at the quiet distance. "I am sure some would see that," she agreed without censure. "There are some who would consider it a burden to be assigned for duty out here."

Jevan's eyes shone with enthusiasm. "Those we send back," he chimed in. "We would not have any on our walls who did not share our passion for this keep."

Kay smiled, nudging him. "There is a truth," she vowed.

She continued to sweep the hills with her eyes, and suddenly she stiffened. At her side Jevan was instantly following her gaze, peering out into the blackness with a steady frown.

Reese leant forward. "What is it?" he whispered, his eyes searching the shadows.

After a long moment she relaxed, smiling. "A sign of good luck. A stag with a pair of does."

Reese glanced at Jevan. "Do you see them?"

Jevan shook his head, continuing to gaze out into the mists. "If Kay says she sees them, then they are there. She has better night vision than anyone here. We are always glad to have her with us on the wall at night."

Reese continued to stare out, and in a moment he tilted his head to one side. "Wait, I think I hear …" His turned his gaze toward the north, and nodded. "There they come," he added, pointing.

Jevan followed his finger, and a broad smile came across his face. "Good luck indeed," he congratulated. "Shall I get the bow?"

Kay put her hand on his arm. "Let them be," she requested. "They bring us blessings, and we should let them pass in peace for the night."

Jevan's grin widened. "Jessica will let us have it when she hears we allowed a venison steak to wander past untouched."

Reese's face was carefully neutral. "I think Jessica has her hands full with Uther for the evening," he observed.

Kay shook her head, her mood darkening. "Men," she snapped in disgust.

Jevan nudged up against her with familiar playfulness. "Not all of us are like that, Kay," he teased. "Do not lump us all in as one. You would hardly want to be considered 'just a woman.'"

"*That* is for sure," agreed Kay with a smile, shaking off her clouds. She gave Jevan a playful tweak on his short nose, then took one long last look across the darkened hills before turning. "I have an early rising ahead of me, so I am afraid I have to call it a night. Good watching, Jevan." She turned to face Reese. "So, shall I see you first tomorrow after breakfast?"

A smile grew on his face. "I would not give away our decision," he countered with a playful glint in his eye. "You shall find out soon enough."

"O-ho," she chuckled, nodding. "Well then, until the morning."

He bowed low to her.

Her cheeks flushed with heat. Unfamiliar feelings coursed through her, and she turned away, moving lightly down the stairs.

She was just passing the small chapel when she heard a noise from within. She turned and pressed the wooden door open. The room was in shadows, with streams of silvery moonlight shimmering in through the windows.

A woman was sitting in the front pew.

Kay blushed. "I am so sorry, I did not mean to disturb you."

The woman rose and turned. She was an indeterminate age, with smooth skin, long, dark hair, and eyes as deep as a wolf's. She wore a simple but well-tailored dress of deep green. Her voice was the rolling of the ocean. "I have been waiting for you."

Kay's brow creased. "I am sorry, have we met before?"

The woman shook her head. "No. But I have heard much about you. I have traveled quite a distance to meet you here tonight."

She held out a long, rectangular bundle in both hands.

Kay stepped forward in curiosity. It was wrapped in a forest green fabric, but there was something about that shape …

She took the item and peeled back the fabric, draping it over the pew.

It was a sword.

Not just any sword. It was finely balanced; it seemed almost an extension of her hand. The handle was wrapped with green leather and held in place by a bronze braid. The length sported a keen edge.

It was a thing of beauty.

She looked up at the woman. "Did my father send this to me? As a present, in thanks for my giving in to this arrangement?"

The woman shook her head, her eyes holding Kay's. "No, Kay. You have earned this sword through your own actions. Through your loyalty and dedication to this land. You are now at a fork in your path. During these coming days, *Andetnes* here will stay steady by your side."

Kay looked down at the sword again, murmuring its name. "Andetnes."

The woman's mouth quirked up into a smile. "Do not become too fond of Andetnes. When you have at last found contentment, there will be another whose fate balances on the point of a pin. You will know when it is right. And the sword will have a new mistress."

Kay ran her hand along the blade's length. "But *how* will I know –"

She looked up.

She was alone.

She turned around, but there was no trace of the woman or the green cloth. Only she and the sword remained.

Chapter 2

Kay galloped across the misty meadow, the freshness of the morning sun warming her face. The small stone chapel grew steadily closer. Soon she could make out Leland and Eli standing before it, waiting for her with welcoming smiles. Eli took her reins as she pulled in; the blond held her horse while she dismounted. She retrieved her wrapped bundle from behind the saddle, then waved as he led her steed off to the small lean-to which served as their stables.

Leland pushed open the small wooden door to the chapel. "So, Kay, you survived the first night," he offered dryly.

His eyes moved down to the bundle. "What's that?"

She drew off the fabric wrap without a word, holding the sword before her on both hands.

His eyes widened with surprise, and he reached forward to take it up. He swung it a few times, then shook his head, clearly impressed.

"I know your father felt guilty about subjecting you to this process, but he has truly gone above and beyond with this gift."

Kay gave a small smile. "It's not from him."

He blinked, then his eyes brightened. "Ah, a bribe from one of the suitors? Perhaps one of them knows about your sword skills after all."

She shook her head. "I don't think it's that, either. A woman gave it to me, last night, in the keep chapel. She said its name was Andetnes and that it would keep me safe. That I would know when it was time to pass it on to its new owner."

Leland's brow creased. "Andetnes. That means honor. Mercy."

He looked more closely at the blade, and his breath caught. His voice became reverential. "Andetnes."

He swung it again, and the sharp whistle it made seemed almost a song.

He looked to Kay. "I had heard legends about such a sword. Old stories, from long before our grandparents' grandparents walked this land. Queen Boudica's sword. And to think ..."

He shook his head, presenting the sword back to Kay. "Whoever has brought this to you, the sword is the finest I have seen. It has been entrusted to your care. Tend to it well. I have a feeling it will do the same for you."

Her fingers closed around the hilt, and it was as if it had been made for her.

Leland waved a hand toward the chapel. A smile came to his features. "Well, then, you have a fine, new sword. Let's get you suited up for practice and see how you do with it."

She stepped through the entry and looked around with fondness at the familiar building. There were a pair of short wooden pews on either side of the doorway. A simple wooden altar at the front was topped by a carven statue of Mary. A hanging curtain covered a doorway to the right which she knew led to a small living area, undoubtedly where Leland and Eli were spending their nights.

Leland moved to a small trunk behind the altar, opening it and pulling forth a leather jerkin. Kay put her arms up while Leland slipped the jerkin over her head, snugged it into place. Next he brought out a belt and scabbard, strapping that around her waist. She slid Andetnes into its place.

It felt just right.

She looked up to Leland with a twinkle in her eye. "Well, shall we?" The two made their way out to the small clearing tucked in behind the chapel.

Kay enjoyed her hour of training immensely, moving through blocks, strikes, and guard positions with Leland. He was a man of infinite patience, of great talent, and she counted herself lucky to have his dedicated time for these weeks.

It seemed all too soon when she was stripping off her gear, climbing onto her horse, and riding across the growing golden day back to her home. She threw the reins to Stephen with a smile as she pulled into the stables, knowing the stout, red-headed lad would take good care of her steed as always. His younger sister, Molly, played by the stable walls, her ringlets framing her face as she nuzzled a pair of small, grey kittens.

Home.

Kay ran up the spiral stairs with light feet, coming into the solar with a renewed heart.

A laugh erupted from her lips as she gazed around. Em had somehow rigged up a long rod across the back part of the room, and floor-to-ceiling curtains hung across the full length. The black fabric was pulled shut, covering the entire back wall with their darkness.

Kay grinned in merry amusement. "Are you in there?" she called out to the velvet.

A low, ominous voice oozed from behind the thick fabric. "Oooooooo – I am the blackness, I am the night," intoned Em sonorously before the giggles overcame her. A hand pulled aside one of the panels of fabric, and Kay saw that her blonde sister was lounging back on a thickly cushioned chair, her feet resting comfortably on a plush footstool. A table at Em's side held a tankard as well as a silver platter of cheese and grapes.

"Oh, my," smiled Kay, shaking her head. "You *are* all set for this experience."

Em tossed her head at the plush couch and leather chair set up on the forward side of the curtain, a low wooden table positioned between the two. A large pitcher of mead sat on the table, as well as a pair of mugs and a wicker basket of bread.

"I am looking out for you, too," Em assured, her eyes sparkling.

Kay plunked herself down on the couch, putting up her feet along its length. She reached over and poured herself out a healthy portion of mead, then leant back on the couch arm, stretching in relaxation.

Kay found herself blissfully content with the idea of the coming fun. "So, do we have any idea what order the husbands-to-be decided on?"

"Not at all," responded Em with a shrug of her shoulders. She slid the curtains shut between them again, vanishing from view. "Only time will tell!"

Kay looked over at the tall, red candle resting on a table by the windows, dark lines marking down in half hour increments. It was nearly at the nine a.m. level now. She leant back, closing her eyes, peace washing over her. The moments eased past in quiet restfulness.

A knock came on the door and she blinked herself back to the present. She glanced over at the curtain, ensuring it was solidly in place. The wall of fabric was seamless.

"Come in," she called out with curiosity. Who had snagged the primary position?

The door was pressed open, and Galeron stepped into the room, his black curls framing a smiling face. He wore a red cloak over a black tunic with silver piping. He strode over to the chair to the left of the table, setting himself down with careful grace, staring at the curtains with open curiosity.

Kay composed herself into a pose of quiet respectability. "My lady," she announced, "I would like you to meet your first suitor – Galeron."

"Welcome, Galeron," came Em's voice through the curtain, even and friendly. "I am Keren-happuch. It is nice to finally meet you."

"Indeed, I am glad we have this chance to talk," agreed Galeron cordially, leaning back in his chair. "I find the curtain a benefit, in fact, because it means we must pay more attention to each other's words, rather than be distracted by other less important items."

"Interesting," commented Em in an amused tone. "So, how did you manage to get the opening position in the schedule?"

Galeron's smile widened. "Already you desire for me to give away all of my secrets?" He nodded. "Your wish is my command. I simply told them I wanted to go riding each morning and that by meeting with you first it meant I could be gone for several hours after that."

Kay chuckled. "I am sure they jumped at the chance of getting you out of the keep for as long as possible."

Galeron nodded at her. "Indeed they did."

She glanced over at him, amusement dancing on her lips. "So, are you actually planning on going on those rides?"

He spread his arms out in a helpless shrug. "How could I do anything but, having made such a claim?" He grinned.

"I do enjoy riding, so it is no great hardship. It will give me a chance to get to know the lands."

He pulled out his wax tablet and put it on the table by his side, making a few notes in it.

The curtain rippled for a moment, then lay still again. "I have heard about that journal of yours," commented Em, her voice light with curiosity. "So you record everything on that?"

Galeron glanced down at the wood-framed rectangle. "I find it extraordinarily helpful," he agreed. "There is a lot to learn here, between the keep and its inhabitants. The notes help me to keep everything organized. I transcribe them each night onto parchment, then wipe the wax clean in order to begin the next day fresh."

Kay smiled. "So, you are a man who likes to be in control," she mused. "A man who appreciates order?"

Galeron winked at her. "I grew up the third child in a household of eight boys," he explained. "Our family was run like a military group. Everything was ordered, in line, and precise. I learned the value of negotiating to get what I wanted and in keeping track of everything around me."

"What is it you want out of life?"

Galeron counted each item off on a finger as he spoke. "A home of my own, a life of my own, a family, and my own little corner of the world."

Kay arched an eyebrow. "Eight children of your own?"

Galeron grinned. "I think two or three would suit me fine," he amended. "I do think it important for a child to have a sibling - someone to talk with; to share their secrets with." He glanced at Kay with a nod. "Do you have a sibling?"

Kay's smile grew. "An older sister."

"I imagine she always tries to tell you what to do," encouraged Galeron.

Kay grinned. "Oh, yes," she enthused. "She always feels she is right, too." She took in a long drink of her mead.

Em's voice was rich with amusement. "I have a sister too," she chimed in. "My sister is older as well, but she is a mentor I look up to and admire greatly."

Kay nearly choked on her drink, the laughter bubbled out of her so richly. Her sister was certainly going to take advantage of the situation!

Galeron smiled at the curtains. "Your elder sister must be a woman of great merit," he praised. He leaned down to take a codex from the bag at his side, flipping through its parchment pages with a sure hand. "Ah, here we go. That would be Mary Magdalene, the blonde beauty? The one already pregnant with child?"

Em's voice echoed with pleasure. "Oh, you have heard of Mary Magdalene, then?"

"One of the soldiers mentioned her while we were getting ready to embark on our trip," explained Galeron. "With his high praise of the woman, I see why you admire her so."

"Someday I hope to reach the lofty standards she has set for me," intoned Em solemnly, and Kay took in several deep breaths, willing herself not to burst into laughter.

Galeron nodded in appreciation. "It is good to have a challenging goal in life," he agreed.

Kay's hold on her outraged mirth almost failed her. She took another long pull of her mead before trusting herself to speak. "My lady, I am sure that, with a lot of hard work and frequent prayer, you might some day aspire to be as gracious, kind, and honorable as your inspiring sister," she murmured with gentle tenderness. She was rewarded by a snorting gasp from behind the curtains, quickly muffled.

There was a long pause, and when Em spoke again her voice held the tinkling of laughter in it. "Please, Galeron, do tell us of your childhood and of your life until now," she encouraged.

Kay settled back with her mead, occasionally glancing at the candle as Galeron went through his tales of sibling rivalry and childhood hijinks. His stories were laid out to show him in a good light, but she did not fault him for that. He was courting, after all, and it was expected he would present himself in his best form. She reluctantly stood when the candle reached the half hour mark, and he bowed first to her, then to the curtain.

"I have enjoyed my time with you both," he offered with a smile, "and now I need to be off on my ride. I wish you both good day." He turned, and in a moment he had departed.

The moment they were alone Kay turned toward the curtain. "I *will* get you for that," she chuckled. "Blonde beauty indeed."

There was a solid knock at the door, and Kay sat back onto the couch, still laughing. "Come in!"

Jack strode in with a quick step, his white outfit gleaming in the morning sun, not a wrinkle to be seen. He briefly glanced around the room before moving forward to take a seat at the lone chair. He braced his feet before him, staring at the curtain. "Good morning," he greeted, his voice sharp.

Kay nodded to him in welcome. "My lady, this is Jack."

"Good morning there, Jack," came Em's voice through the curtain. "It is nice to finally meet you in person."

He nodded with a quick motion. "What do you want to know?"

Em's laughter echoed lightly through the room. "Right to the point," she mused. "I like that in a man. Efficiency. Well, tell me about yourself."

"I am an only child, but my father was a gambler – he lost our entire estate," stated Jack without emotion, his eyes not wavering. "I was trained from childhood in fighting, strategy, and management. Also, because my father was often … incapacitated, I ran the day-to-day operations of our home from a young age."

"I am sorry to hear that," commiserated Em, her voice more subdued.

Jack's eyes flashed in anger. "I do not want your pity," he ground out. He took in a long breath, running a hand through his blond hair for a moment. "I had a home, I had a good quality education. Through my own efforts I have stayed solvent. I am looking to find a more stable situation where my skills will be put to good use."

Kay leant forward. "Tell us about your projects," she suggested.

He nodded, and began. Kay was impressed as he went through the list. He had begun small, with bodyguard assignments, work he could handle with little experience. He had diligently built his way up to larger tasks, bringing on men to help with convoy guarding, developing a network of trusted soldiers.

The half hour drew to an end, and Jack stood stiffly, nodding to Kay, then to the curtain. He began to turn.

Em's voice was soft. "Jack?"

He turned back, his eyes tense.

"Thank you," she offered. "Thank you for talking."

He nodded, his gaze softening slightly. "You are welcome," he answered, and then he was striding toward the door, moving through it.

Kay stared at the door. "Interesting," she commented. "I would not have guessed."

"There is always a reason why someone is the way he is," mused Em.

A timid knock came at the door, and Kay's eyes brightened with amusement. She knew before the door was opened who would be behind that feeble effort. Alistair was wearing a brown tunic which matched his brown hair perfectly. There was not a spot to be found on his tunic, and his shoes had been shined within an inch of their lives. Alistair moved slowly across the room, his eyes focused on the black curtain with hesitation. He lowered himself into the chair without changing his look.

Em gave a slight chuckle. "Alistair, I imagine."

A high pitched squeak emerged. "Yes!" he agreed, then winced and cleared his throat. "Yes," he repeated in a lower tone, "I am Alistair. It is good to meet you, Keren-happuch."

"So, please tell us about your childhood," requested Em gently.

Alistair nodded a few times, looking down at his hands. "I was a fourth son, so as soon as I reached my sixth birthday I was sent to the Saint Paul monastery to begin training." His voice became wistful. "After the noise and chaos of home, it was like a dream come true. The quiet room, the schedule, the training, the reading, the prayer. It was everything I could have wanted."

Kay looked over with interest. "Why did you choose to leave?"

He looked up at her in surprise. "Choose?" he replied in a shocked tone. Realizing what he had said, he flushed crimson, then returned his gaze to the curtain. "I mean, certainly, when the head abbot came to me, accompanied by my father, I understood and appreciated all this entailed. It is a great opportunity." He glanced around at the room. "In a way this keep is perfect for me. Its isolation, its quiet, and its routine. I would be very happy here."

Kay nodded encouragingly. "Tell us about your monastery."

Alistair tentatively began his tales. As he talked he loosened up and gained tone in his voice. The time scrolled by, and Kay was surprised when she looked up to see the half hour had gone by.

"Thank you for your time," she offered, standing.

He nodded, smiling, bowing to her and then to the curtain. "Until tomorrow," he agreed, a soft smile coming to his face. He turned and headed out of the room.

"Again, very interesting," commented Kay, looking after him. "I guess there is more to our guests than I would have thought."

"You always were the impetuous one," teased Em from behind her black fabric shield. "This might be a good learning experience for you, to be forced to take your time."

"You just watch yourself," retorted Kay, taking a long drink of her mead. "Remember that you are speaking for me, back in that cloaked lair of yours."

A loud, enthusiastic set of knocks sounded on the door, and Kay glanced around, her smile fading. "If we are learning more about the men this morning, let us see what we learn about Uther. So far I am not overly impressed with the man." She took another long drink of her mead. "Come in!"

The door was flung open, and Uther strode in, tossing his red hair back as he looked around him with enthusiastic interest. His eyes latched on Kay and he strode over with a wide grin. "Ah, Kay, there you are, lass.

It is a pleasure to see you again." He took her hand in his, lowering his head to kiss it with a flamboyant bow. He winked at her, then turned toward the black curtain.

"And you, Keren-happuch, how are you this fine morning?" he asked, stepping forward in interest.

Kay half rose. "Ahem," she cautioned. "You cannot touch that curtain, remember. It is one of the rules."

"Just a small glance?" prodded Uther, his grin growing wider.

Em's voice was stern. "Patience, my man," she counseled from behind her fabric wall. "Have a seat."

He sighed in acceptance, plunking himself back down onto the chair. He poured out the mead into the as yet untouched mug and downed half of it in one long swallow. "Well then, Keren-happuch, how shall we begin?"

Kay sat back against the sofa. "Why not tell us about your background?"

"Of course!" agreed Uther, his eyes twinkling in delight. "I grew up the only son in a household with three doting sisters, all older than me. I was spoiled rotten, surrounded by beautiful women all of my life, and see no reason for that to change any time soon."

His eyes moved wolfishly to look over Kay. "It seems by coming here that I will do quite nicely for myself. The food is commendable. The serving staff, very accommodating. Why only last night I was telling Anna -"

His voice babbled on in a stream of story, and Kay barely had to add in a nod here or there to keep Uther going. She found herself, as a game, counting the number of times he mentioned the beauty of a woman's eyes. When she passed thirty, she switched to lips. He seemed to have met and fallen in love with every female within a hundred miles.

Kay gave a sigh of relief when the candle reached down to the eleven mark, and she stood. "I am afraid your time is up, Uther."

"Ah, already? What a shame," he sighed. He stood and drained the rest of his mug, setting the tankard down on the table with a solid ring. He gave a long flourishing bow toward the curtain, then moved over in front of Kay. He bent toward her, and she offered her hand automatically. He took it in his, lowering his lips, holding them against her skin. She bit her lip, fighting the instinct to draw her hand clear. He waited there a second longer than appropriate, then stood, winking at her before turning and striding to the door with a satisfied chuckle. He flung it wide, leaving it open as he strode down the stairs.

Kay looked after him with disgust, shaking her head at his self-absorption. A flush brightened her cheek as a movement caught her eye, as she realized Reese was standing in the shadows, his tawny hair framing his twinkling eyes.

She waved him in, and he closed the door quietly behind him, coming over into the room.

Em moaned from behind the curtain. "Good God, Kay, I take back any complaints that you exaggerated Uther's faults. How did you survive a dinner with that lout? You are sure you were not tempted to dump his soup on his lap?"

Kay winked at Reese, reaching behind her to fetch a fresh tankard from the shelf against the wall, then leaning forward to pour it full before handing it over to him. "I am a paragon of patience and understanding," she offered with a tone of great humility, refilling her own mug as well.

A loud snort sounded from behind the curtain. "I bet you were on that castle wall in under fifteen minutes to get away from him," she challenged.

Reese gave a low chuckle. "I believe she was," he agreed, toasting his mug toward Kay. She returned the toast, then took in a long drink.

There was a coughing splutter from the black curtain, and in a moment Em's voice snapped in a combination of mirth and pique. "Kay, you could have told me Reese had come in."

"If you did not think to cut eyeholes in that curtain of yours, I can hardly be blamed," countered Kay, her grin growing wider. "Besides, I am sure we are not telling Reese anything he did not see for himself."

"Still, it is not right for us to share confidences with one of the men about the others," reminded Em in a reasonable tone.

"I think we can trust Reese," smiled Kay. "And besides, he is our last visitor for the day, which means we can take as long as we like with him. Although I am curious," she added, turning to gaze at Reese, "just why *did* you take the final spot?"

"Maybe it was for that very reason," he commented with a smile. "It also means there will always be at least one man coming out before me, so I can judge his expression and get a sense of the mood of the day."

"Always, at least until the final day," smiled Kay.

"Yes, until then," agreed Reese, nodding.

Em's voice eased out from behind her wall of fabric. "So, Reese," she encouraged, "tell us about your life."

Reese rolled his shoulders gently beneath his leather tunic, settling back into the chair. "I am the second of two sons, so my elder brother inherited our entire family estate," he explained without a hint of ire. "As with most second sons, I was sent off to be a soldier. I took readily to the life, and have spent most of my adult years around the Mediterranean on one campaign or another."

Kay leant forward on the couch. "How did you find the landscapes?" she asked, intrigued.

"Hot," mused Reese, "and desolate. One could go days without finding a drinkable source of water, with nothing but poisonous snakes to keep a person company." He glanced out the window at the sweep of mountains and hills beyond. "It is why I was surprised to hear this area called barren. It is green and welcoming, I would even say beautiful."

Em's voice was warm. "Tell us about your times abroad."

Reese nodded and began his stories. Kay found them fascinating - enriching. He told of disparate peoples in distant lands, how their cultures clashed and complemented. He explored how their style of dress, their speech patterns, their food and drink changed with the landscapes. She became immersed in exotic music and unimaginable creatures. The time spun by in a drifting dream.

A knock sounded at the door, and Kay looked up, startled. The guard poked his head around the door, his eyes bright with amusement.

"It is after noon, Kay," he commented wryly. "Should I have the others start lunch without you?"

"Oh!" cried Kay in consternation, drawing herself to a standing position. "Thank you, we will be down right away."

Reese rolled to his feet. "I am sorry to have taken so much of your time," he apologized, his face shadowed in contrition.

Kay shook her head, smiling. "It was fascinating, really. Maybe we could hear more tomorrow?"

"Of course," he agreed, bowing. He turned toward the curtain. "Until tomorrow, then," he added.

"Good day, Reese," Em agreed, a smile in her voice.

Kay came around to Reese's side, and together they descended the steps toward the main hall.

Anne was already serving the roast beef out to the men as they entered the room, and Kay's stomach rumbled at the lush aroma. She wended her way through the chairs and people to reach the head table at the far side of the space.

Jack looked up as they approached, his eyes surly. "And where have you been," he grumbled. "Your allotted time ended a half hour ago."

Kay drew up short, flaring at the notion that Jack had any right to judge her on her actions.

Galeron's voice smoothed gently into the tense silence. "Why, my dear Jack, Kay is not a slave. She is free to do as she wishes once her duties to her lady are complete." He turned to her with a welcoming smile. "Come, take a seat; you must be famished."

She blushed at the implication that she and Reese had been alone together somewhere, but she held her tongue. Better to let the moment pass. She dropped her eyes, taking her seat next to Reese.

Anne was by her side in a moment with their drinks. Her pink cheeks were even more flushed than usual, and Kay watched her carefully as she moved down the line of men. When the blonde walked past Uther, his hand snaked up to give her a fond pat on the rump. Anne seemed half pleased, half embarrassed by the contact.

Kay shook her head, focusing on the meal before her, soaking up the gravy with a piece of bread. It was bad enough that he was flirting with Jessica last night, but was he going to steal the heart of every maid during his quest to wed? Was he going to leave a trail of broken hearts behind him?

Galeron's voice poked into her thoughts. "Well, Uther, how did you enjoy your first full morning at the keep?"

Uther beamed, and he downed a long draught of his ale. "Ah, very well, very well," he enthused, glancing back at where Anne watched from the doorway. "The keep's inhabitants are quite welcoming and friendly. I could get very used to this. Very used."

Alistair's quiet voice seemed almost a wheezy whisper in comparison. "I spent time in the small chapel here on the keep grounds," he murmured. "It was expertly built, and was quiet during my morning. I gave thanks again for our peaceful journey."

He glanced down the line of men. "A practice we have in the monastery is to spend an occasional lunch in silence. It helps to settle nerves. Could I ask that we do that today? I find I am not feeling very well …"

With various shrugs and smiles, the other men concurred, and Kay found herself quite pleased with Alistair's odd request. She found her own stomach growing tense with Uther's behavior. Jessica and Anne were both sweet girls, and both had childhood sweethearts who lived in the area. What were they risking with their flirtatious behavior with Uther? Surely they knew that either Uther would stay, and become her husband, or he would leave, never to be seen again. She hoped that they were enjoying a harmless flirtation but not risking anything more than that.

She was just mopping up the last of her bread when a pair of young tow-headed boys came racing down the length of the hall. She put out her arms in delight, and the pair leapt into her embrace, yelling wildly in pleasure.

"Auntie Kay! Auntie Kay!" they screamed with a lungpower which seemed far beyond their five years.

Jack's brows furrowed. "You have a sister here?" he snapped in confusion.

Kay flushed with heat. She buried her face in the young lads to cover herself. It was bad enough to play a 'game,' but she still felt qualms about outright lying. She dodged the direct question. "These two darling boys are the sons of Jevan, one of our most trusted guards," she explained. "They just call me Auntie out of fondness. This is Joey, and this one is Paul. Twins, as you might guess."

Joey tugged at her hand. "The leaves are ready!" he cried out in delight.

"If you would excuse me, gentlemen," she apologized, then turned to follow the boys out into the main courtyard area.

They were of course exactly right. A gigantic pile of leaves – far taller than her head – had been gathered by the front gate, up against the curtain wall. It was swept just beneath the walk which ran along the edge of the wall, some ten feet above.

Kay could barely keep up with the boys as they scampered up the narrow stone steps, their eyes shining with delight. Jevan was standing at the top and chuckled as Kay reached him.

"They have been waiting for this all year, you know," he offered by way of apology.

She smiled, looking down at the leaves. "As did I, when I was their age," she pointed out. "Believe me, I am just as happy to be a part of this as they are!"

Joey stepped forward with glowing pride. "I go first, for I am the eldest," he announced.

"Yes, you are," agreed Kay. "You remember the rules?"

Joey nodded, his pudgy face becoming solemn. "No squirming. No kicking."

"Right," confirmed Kay. "Also, if you must scream, please only half shatter my eardrums. I might need them later on."

"Agreed!"

Kay gathered up Joey in her arms, cradling him across her chest. Jevan stood alongside her, helping her line up with the gigantic, incredibly dense pile of leaves. Her heart pounded with excitement.

A reedy cry came from below. "Are you *completely* insane?"

She looked down. Alistair was staring at her with open mouthed horror, his hands clutched to his chest.

Kay shook her head with a smile. "Did you never leap into a pond in your youth, Alistair?"

The man looked as if she had spoken in tongues. "And risk drowning?" he gasped, aghast.

Reese came up beside him, looking at the depth and breadth of the leaves, nodding in appreciation. "I do not think you could miss that pile even if you tried," he commented. "I am sure this is a once in a lifetime adventure for those tykes."

"Once in a year, anyways," agreed Kay, her eyes twinkling. "And here we go!"

She pulled Joey in close to her chest, then jumped out and away from the wall. They were soaring, flying - for a moment they were one with the birds and the clouds. Joey let loose with an unbridled yell of pleasure.

PHOOMPH!

They landed in the giant pile of soft leaves. It billowed up around them, sinking with them to a soft landing.

Paul's voice sounded eagerly from the wall. "My turn! My turn!"

A hand was offered to her, and Kay gladly accepted Reese's help in extricating herself from the giant leaf mound. She made her way back up the stairs, and in a moment she was flying, soaring, releasing the joy of Paul's soul as he became one with his dreams. Another fountain of leaves, and their safe landing embraced them.

Alistair shook his head in dismay. "I will pray for your souls," he intoned, his voice shaking. "Man was meant to stand on the earth, not to soar in the sky." He turned in a huff, moving off to the quiet of the chapel.

Reese's eyes sparkled. "For someone who looks up to God so readily, he is awfully hesitant to take a step up in that direction," he commented with a grin.

Kay winked in return, then she was back up the stairs again, drawing Joey into her arms.

The afternoon spun by in a mosaic of laughter, leaf explosions, and smiling faces. It was only when the boys were too exhausted to climb the steps for one more run that she bade a fond farewell to the group and moved up the spiral stairs toward her own quiet retreat.

She pushed open the door with a worn out satisfaction. The afternoon shadows tinged the room in glowing embers of light. Em had pulled back the curtain and lay sprawled on the central sofa, a bowl of grapes by her head, lazily reading a scroll. Kay plunked herself down on the chair by her side, letting out a long sigh of contentment.

Em rolled up her scroll and laid it on the table beside her. "So, made a decision already?" she teased with a smile. "There do seem to be several options in this pack of wolves."

Kay shook her head, her thoughts dragging away from the simple pleasures of the afternoon to the far more serious challenges before her. It took an effort, but she went back over the events of the morning, one by one.

"I think I may be able to at least start winnowing out the chaff from the wheat," she commented after a while. "That Uther man -"

Em chuckled. "Now, now, we all know how incorrect first assumptions can be," she cautioned. "Maybe his flamboyance is a front, something the man does when he is nervous. Maybe this is simply an appearance, and his actions will show him to be the most honorable, sturdy man of the group."

Kay grabbed a grape and popped it into her mouth. "I am sure you are right that people who are nervous do all sorts of foolish things," she agreed, chewing. "Maybe it is the case here. Still, sometimes people simply are the way they are and it is not a good fit. Maybe Uther would be the perfect man to -"

"To run a brothel," chimed in Em with a wicked smile.

They both burst out in gales of laughter which echoed across the room and out into the courtyard beyond.

The sun drifted across the room in a gentle progression of gold, peach, and rosy red. Then came a soft knock at the door. In a moment Anne peeked around the corner, her blonde curls pulled back from her face, her arms laden with a heavy tray full of food.

Kay ran to help. "Oh, let me get that for you."

"No, miss, I can manage it," insisted Anne, her voice tight. She carefully balanced the load, carrying it over to the central table. She attentively laid it down, then stood up again.

Her face laced with tension. "Is there anything else you need?"

Kay looked over at Anne more closely. They had known each other since they were children. "Anne, is everything all right?"

Anne flushed deeply, and her fingers twined into each other. There was a long pause. "Truly, miss, I am fine. If you need nothing else, I will be leaving you to your dinner." She turned, almost fleeing the room.

Kay and Em looked at each other in surprise. Kay sat down and took a pull on her mead. "I think I need to poke around the keep after dinner and see what is going on," she commented, her shoulders hunched.

"I would agree," returned Em, and they set to work on their meal in silence.

The meat was long cold before a new knock sounded, and Jessica's brown head looked around the corner. "Are you done with the plates?" she murmured. Kay nodded, and watched with a careful eye as Jessica came in to gather up the items. The maid's eyes were downcast, her movements almost furtive.

Was it her imagination, or was Jessica just as distraught as Anne was? Were they both that roiled about Uther's flirtation with the other? When Jessica left the room, Kay nodded to her sister then quietly slipped out the door after the maid.

Jessica worked her way nimbly down the spiral stairs with her load, balancing it easily down the two flights, bringing it out across the empty courtyard and into the fragrant kitchen building with quick efficiency. Once there she handed the large tray off to the cleaning crew. Then she slipped back across into the courtyard and over to the small chapel.

The deep shadows of night had fallen, and Kay found it easy to slip in the door behind her, to tuck herself into the back corner of the quiet stone building unseen. Was Jessica meeting Uther here? It seemed a location more suited for the studious Alistair.

To Kay's surprise, Jessica dropped to her knees before the statue of Mary, bowing her brown head in abject misery. Kay flushed. She had no intention on listening in on a person's private prayers. She would try to slip out as soon as -

"Blessed Mary," began Jessica, "hear my plight. It seemed easier to humor him than to struggle. I had the sense that, had I resisted, he would have forced me anyway, and I did not want to cause trouble for a guest, not on his first day! It was the keep's peace I thought of - you must believe me. But now he says he wishes me as his mistress, even after he is married!" Her voice caught. "A mistress! I could never do that to Kay. Not when she is as dear to me as -"

Kay reeled in shock, and she nearly cried out when the door flew open and a cascade of blonde curls came swirling into the chapel. Anne pulled up short when she saw Jessica before the altar.

"Jessica! I am so sorry, I thought I would be alone in here," Anne stuttered out.

Jessica stood in an instant, flushing deeply. "I am done," she bit out, "please, the room is yours." She nearly ran as she headed back to the keep proper.

The door fell shut, drawing the room into a leaden silence again, only the two small candles at the back of the altar sending their feeble light into the room.

Kay could hardly breathe as Anne ran her fingers through her thick, golden hair, then moved to kneel in front of the statue.

Anne's voice came out low and broken. "Beloved Mary, my sin is my own. It is one thing to give in to a man who is unattached and free, especially one who is a guest, and one who is stronger than you. But what when he seeks to pursue other women after taking a holy vow? What sort of a man would -"

Kay could hear no more. She scrambled toward the back door, sliding it open only a crack, easing herself out. Then she was running, stumbling toward the thin stairs which led up to the wall. Tears stung her eyes as she reached the top, as she leant against the crenellations, catching her breath, feeling lost in the dark, alone …

"Are you all right?" came the low voice at her side, and she nearly jumped out of her skin. Reese's green-grey eyes were looking down at hers, concern reflecting in them. She pressed a hand to her chest, taking in long breaths, fighting to steady herself.

"I am fine," she responded, struggling to keep her voice even.

The corner of Reese's mouth quirked slightly. "You are not a very good liar," he countered gently.

Kay thought of the elaborate ruse that was being put on, the false role she was playing twenty-four hours a day. A laugh bubbled out of her and her shoulders eased. A smile drew across her face, and Reese's answering smile washed away the remaining clouds.

"That is better," he commented, the corners of his mouth tweaking up. "Surely it is too soon for anyone here to have upset you that badly. I am sure it will take another day or two for someone to truly drive you to the brink of ruin."

"Oh?" asked Kay, "and why is that?"

Reese turned to look out at the deep night, at the scattering of clouds drifting across the star filled sky. "For you to care that deeply about what someone had done, you would first have to have great concern for what they did and said. Have you already formed that level of an attachment, in such a short period of time?"

Kay smiled. He was right, after all. "I suppose not," she agreed. "Any issues we encounter now are with just-met acquaintances, and any hurts will be soon smoothed over."

"Just so," offered Reese. His eyes moved to meet hers. "Unless of course you are unhappy with me for some reason, in which case I offer my abject apology for hurting you."

Kay shook her head. "You have been the epitome of a gentleman," she countered. "You provide wise advice."

She leant against the rough stone wall, drawing in strength from the sturdiness of it beneath her hands, breathing in the cool, fresh air as it rolled down from the mountains. This keep had stood for centuries, and it would stand for many more yet to come. Long after her children and her children's children had passed on, this keep would be here, keeping its inhabitants safe.

Uther was but a temporary problem. And what had he done, really? She could be leaping to wild conclusions based on random phrases heard from two women.

She took in a deep breath and let it out again. How could she really judge him, after all, based on the hurried prayers of two women in a guilty moment? Perhaps they had misunderstood his intentions. Perhaps he had only kissed them, in a moment of drunken passion, and they were racked with guilt as a result.

If she was going to make a judgment against him, she had to see for himself what he was like. She chuckled softly. As a lowly maid, and single to boot, she was in a prime position to do just that.

Reese smiled. "See, you are looking better already," he commented. "The night air has done its magic."

"It is a tonic I take often," agreed Kay, her heart lighter. "I think I will head in now." She accepted Reese's low bow, then moved back down the stairs toward the courtyard, a fresh spring in her step.

Chapter 3

Kay closed the main doors of the keep behind her, stopping for a moment with her hand against the heavy wood. She drew in a deep breath, steeling herself. It was time to find out for herself what Uther was really like. She could not make a decision on the man's honor based on hearsay. She had to see, with her own two eyes, what he was capable of.

She headed up the stairs and strode into the boisterous noise of the main hall. Uther was sitting before flickering flames of the large fireplace, his red cheeks made more rosy by the heat. He was flanked on either side by Galeron and Alistair. As she walked up Galeron rose at once, sweeping into a low bow.

"It is frosty tonight; let me offer you the seat by the fire," he greeted her, moving to one side. "I shall go sit on the opposite end; I am warm enough for now."

"As you wish," she agreed, nodding to him.

Uther grinned in delight as she settled herself down next to him. He leant over past her, reaching for the basket of bread, ripping off a piece and popping it into his mouth.

"How are you tonight, my dear?" he asked in a low, rumbling voice.

Kay forced herself to smile widely. She was on a mission, after all. She had to see just what Uther was saying to the women he was attempting to seduce.

"Much better, now that I am by the warmth," she murmured, giving her arms a quick rub.

It *was* nice by the fire; the dancing flames were soothing after the crisp autumn air. She glanced up at him for a moment, then demurely brought her eyes down to her lap again. She had been short, almost unwelcoming with him before. She knew it would seem far too suspicious if she now launched herself at him full bore. She had to take this slowly, to pretend to thaw under his influence.

Uther's hand moved to land heavily on hers, and she started back in surprise, stifling a cry. A chuckle emitted from deep within her, and she shook her head. Perhaps her concerns about careful change were unnecessary – Uther was already stroking her hand with seductive slowness.

"I knew you would come around," he purred, nudging closer to her. "You were only playing hard to get." He took a long drink of his wine, leaning back with pleasure. He moved his lips to her ears. "Of course you were pretending to dislike me," he added beneath his breath in a knowing tone. "You work for Keren-happuch, after all. You could hardly let her know how you truly felt!"

Kay looked up at him, her eyes sparkling with amusement at how easy this was. "You can see right through me," she whispered, giving her lashes a flutter. "I knew it from the start, from the first moment I laid eyes on you."

"I knew it as well," enthused Uther, his eyes locked on hers, his hand closing over her own. "I could feel it every time we were near each other, that you were the one meant for me. It was torture each time you left the room; sheer bliss when you would return."

There was a loud *thunk* from the end of the room. Kay's eyes flicked across automatically. Reese was standing by the main table and had apparently just put his tankard of ale down on the wood – hard, judging by the wave of foam which had splashed over onto the surface and his sleeve. Jessica rushed forward with a towel, quickly mopping up the spill, her eyes glancing between Uther and Kay with a nervous twitch.

Kay brought her gaze back to Uther. There was enough time to deal with Reese and Jessica later. There were only so many dramas she could juggle at once. Right now she had one focus, and that was the man before her.

Uther raised his glass to hers, and she clinked hers against his before draining her liquid down. She would need some fortification to make it through this night.

Plates of sweets were brought and removed, her glass was filled and refilled, and as the evening progressed Uther's body seemed to inch nearer to hers, his face ever closer to her own. Strangely, despite her doubts about his character, Kay could almost see the allure the man had, the power he had to draw in a woman. He was flattering, yes, but he always found a way to single out the traits she wanted to have attention drawn to. He listened to her, asking questions about her stories which showed he had actually heard what she said.

His voice was a low rumble. "Shall we go for a walk?"

She shook herself, looking around. She had almost forgotten others were present in the room. Galeron was busy scribbling notes on his tablet, while Alistair and Jack were in a heated discussion over something involving a battle in the holy land. Reese …

She blinked in surprise. Reese was looking down the table at her, his eyes hooded, holding what could almost be disappointment. She looked away quickly, taking in a deep breath. In Reese's eyes, she was only a maid servant, after all. She should care little what Reese felt about her. There were more important issues at stake.

"I would love to go for a walk with you," she agreed sweetly, putting her hand into Uther's. His florid face flushed deeper crimson with delight, and he stood, drawing her to her feet, up against him. She stumbled back slightly, then turned, bringing him along with her. In a moment, he had taken the lead, moving them across the emptying main hall.

Kay was brimming with curiosity. "Where are we going?" She knew the castle inside and out, knew every nook, every cranny. Where had Uther decided on for their time together?

His voice dropped low. "I heard there was an area near here named *lover's lane*. That sounded quite promising."

Kay chuckled, shaking her head. "That small valley certainly cannot be seen into from the keep or its walls, but it is rough and rocky, and probably muddy to boot this time of year. The name is more a tease than anything else."

"Ah," responded Uther, a hint of disappointment in his voice. "I suppose things are not always as they seem." He quickly rallied, and he moved closer to her. "In that case, I think we should go to the chapel," he suggested in an even lower voice. "We can talk undisturbed there, I should think."

Kay smiled in agreement, relaxing. Her fear had been that Uther would go with her up onto the walls; that he would expose her to censure amongst the men she cared for the most. She would much rather have this discussion take place somewhere unseen. The chapel did, indeed, seem like the ideal location. As long as it was less busy than it had been earlier in the evening!

They moved down the stairs and out the main door. In only moments he had pushed open the heavy wooden door which led into the small stone building.

She paused for a long moment, allowing her eyes to adjust to the gloom. There were ten wooden pews on either side, and the few flickering candles threw shadows and dancing light into the quiet chamber. The altar at the head of the room bore a simple woven cloth on its top, with the beautifully hand-carved statue of Mary. Kay knew that Stephen, the stout stable boy, made a new idol for the chapel each year, and his talents as a woodcarver were quite impressive.

Slowly, reverently, Uther led her down the pews, stopping for a moment at the end of the row before slipping sideways and sitting on the wooden bench. Kay found herself hushed and serene as she sat beside him.

Uther turned to take both of her hands in his own. "I have always imagined you in here," he whispered. He dropped his eyes for a moment. "I have always envisioned you by my side, trusting in me." He brought his eyes up to hers again and in the candlelight they were liquid pools of azure. "Do you trust me, darling Kay?"

Kay found herself caught up in the mood. "Yes," she answered almost without thinking.

"Kay ..." He took in a deep breath, then blurted out his speech in a quick rush. "I love you, Kay. I have loved you since I first saw you, saw you riding off into the horizon, saw the joy for life in your heart. I knew at once you were the only woman for me."

"We barely know each other," protested Kay, almost overwhelmed by his emotions.

"The way you handle yourself on your horse; the way you are so at ease with your mount. The way you are kind and understanding with the staff. Your windswept beauty. Your obvious love of this keep." He gazed deeply into her eyes. "Is there more I need to know?" He leant forward to kiss her on the cheek.

Kay knew she should be fighting this, but it seemed so honest, from the heart, what he was saying. He was touching on qualities she cherished deeply in herself. His face seemed completely open, as if he were pouring out his deepest soul. He could not lie in a church, could he?

"What about Keren-happuch?" she gasped hoarsely, clinging to sanity.

He shook his head, his eyes glowing with fierce passion. "It was my father's doing, to send me on that quest," he insisted. "Now I see that I must take charge of my own destiny. If his foolhardy directive brought me to meet you, then I call that fate. I will turn my back on my father, on my family, and pledge myself to you. Only to you – if you will have me." His eyes glimmered with pleading, hope, and despair.

Kay could see it all so clearly now. She was drawn by the power of his carefully crafted words, of his appreciative eyes, of his hands which slowly, steadily, pulled her in. She could understand how easily the women of the keep had been cocooned in his web. If she had not been forewarned of those same techniques being used on others, she might have half-believed what he said was true. It would have been so easy to think that he honestly had fallen for her traits, that he had glimpsed the beauty of her inner soul.

But she was not the first. He had gone down this same road with Anne, with Jessica, with perhaps even with several others if she were not mistaken. Once he had corrupted her, he would blackmail her into remaining his mistress, becoming part of his harem.

She had to get away. She had to warn Em.

Kay took in a deep breath. She shook her head with a gentle motion, drawing a few inches away from him.

"I need to think about it," she sighed, tingeing her voice with a hint of sadness.

Uther grew rigid against her, drawing her in closer. "But I love you," he insisted, his eyes becoming even more luminous. "You can feel it, too. We are soul mates. We are meant to be together. We are here in this sacred church. You feel it in your bones. If we are together, here, tonight, then nothing will ever part us." His hands moved slowly, inexorably against her, pulling her tightly in, his mouth kissing gently along her neck, her cheeks. "You know it was meant to be."

His hands did feel like gentle caresses, his lips incredibly tender, but Kay's heart beat faster with panic with every passing moment. She pressed to draw away, but he did not release her, did not let up on his ever-strengthening motions toward her.

Kay began to struggle in earnest. "Let me go," she insisted in a low voice.

"I know you, you are a fighting spirit," he growled, his attentions becoming more passionate. "You know what it is to ride a horse hard. They resist at first, and then they relish the flight, the power of it. You want it. I can feel it in you. I will give you what you crave!"

A snap shook through her as she realized he was serious. She pulled away from him hard, twisting. Instantly he rolled down off the pew on top of her, holding her down with his body, his hands eagerly moving across her tunic top, his face lost in the shadows. Whatever soothing litanies he was now calling out, Kay was beyond hearing them.

Kay lunged her hand down toward her waist, drawing her dagger, flipping herself over and on top of him. She pressed her blade hard against his throat.

Time froze.

In the shadowy dusk of the chapel floor, the eyes that stared up at her were reflected black marbles.

Kay bit out her words, hoarse and guttural. "Get out of this holy place," she snarled. She held the blade against his neck for a long moment, then rolled to her feet, releasing him.

Uther slowly brought himself to standing, rubbing his neck, looking her over. "I should have known you were frigid," he grumbled at last. He turned with a shrug, moving his way down the shadowy aisle. When he reached the main door he threw it open with a push, striding out into the courtyard and leaving the door wide behind him.

Kay stared at the open doorway, at the streaming moonlight, her heart hammering against her ribs.

Suddenly a form was standing there, moving into the light from the back of the chapel where he had been hidden. Reese walked the length toward her with a few quick strides, coming to a stop before her, his eyes lost in the shadows.

"Kay? Are you all right?"

She shook her head, looking down almost in surprise at the dagger still in her hands. "He would not have stopped," she whispered, the enormity of the danger hitting her like a physical blow.

Reese gently took the dagger from her hand, and suddenly she found she had stepped forward, had pressed herself against the safety of his chest. She sighed in relief as his arms came around her and held her tight. A wave of tremors ran through her.

She could barely speak, her throat tightened so. "He would not have stopped," she repeated. "If I had not seen it myself, I would not have believed their reports to be true."

The hand stroking her hair froze for a long moment, and when Reese spoke again, there was a note of understanding mixed with the calm. "I should have known. You did this on purpose?"

"Of course I did," she agreed, her shoulders finally easing, her body relaxing against his. "I had to know for myself. I had to know the truth."

Reese gently pressed her back, looking down into her eyes. "Surely there was another way," he insisted, his voice hoarse. "To put yourself at such a risk -"

She shook her head. "Would I put another into that risk instead?" she asked. "If it was to be found out, I needed to do so for myself."

He compressed his lips, his eyes shadowed. "You take great chances for your lady. I hope she appreciates you."

Kay smiled at that. "We appreciate each other, she and I," she gently corrected Reese.

He glanced at the open door. "Did you want to go out and get some fresh air?"

She shook her head. "I feel like this chapel has been … tainted, somehow," she responded, moving slowly, carefully to the pew she had just been sitting on with Uther. She took in a deep breath, then lowered herself into the pew. "It is like falling off a horse. I need to overwrite those memories with something better, something honorable. I will not have this chapel become a place I have poor memories of."

She put up a hand to him, and he took it without hesitation, moving to sit beside her.

She looked around the familiar room. "Let me tell you of my favorite memories here," she softly offered. "I adore hearing the carols sung in the wintertime, when a fire is blazing in the corner, when the room is snug and warm and full of friends. I love hearing the voices blending together, seeing the snow fall through the windows outside, knowing we are safe and secure. The grey stone echoes our song and sends it up to the heavens."

His eyes held hers. "That does seem a wonderful event to experience," he murmured.

"Then there is springtime," she mused, leaning back, closing her eyes. "Fresh garlands of daisies run down every pew, fragrant flowers are strewn on the altar. The entire room is filled with the scents of heather and rose. Spring is when Stephen brings us his newest version of Mary, freshly carved, to last us the year. It feels like the garden of Eden is around us."

"I suppose summer is even better," he encouraged, his eyes warm.

Kay nodded, peace flowing through her. "Summer is the time of love, of weddings," she agreed with a smile. "My father was married in the summertime, and he has a summer birthday as well. We enjoy delicious feasts, the sun streams in glowing ribbons, fresh breezes waft through the windows, and the world is clothed in flowers. One could hope for no more."

"And then comes autumn," he filled in.

"Autumn is the fruition of all," she sighed in contentment. "The bounty of harvest, the grape-vine wreaths, the lush fruit wines, and the rich honey. It is everything one could hope for. There is much to be thankful for when fall is here."

She leant back, looking around her at the familiar carvings, the flickering candles, and the arched windows. "I love this chapel," she murmured after a long moment. "I love everything about it. I could not imagine another in its place. I am glad beyond all measure that it kept me safe this evening."

"I would have kept you safe," vowed Reese in a low voice. "I was halfway down the aisle before I realized you had the situation well in hand. I could not understand what you were up to. Now I do."

"I am glad you were here," offered Kay after a moment. "I have to admit, I am not used to men who would press their attentions like that. Perhaps it is common in larger castles – but it is not something we have encountered here."

"It is not a habit at my home either," agreed Reese. "However, I have heard Uther boast that the men of his family took great liberties with their staff; that it was almost expected of them."

Kay's voice grew hard. "Well, then, he will find another task expected of him tomorrow, when he has his morning meeting."

Reese's voice grew quiet. "You think Keren-happuch will want him to leave?"

The corner of Kay's mouth twitched up. "I think Keren-happuch will want to see him drawn and quartered, but yes, I imagine she will satisfy herself with having him head back home again."

Reese's brows drew together in concern, and he turned on the bench to face Kay. "He may not go quietly," he warned, his jaw tight.

Kay gave him a gentle pat on the arm. "You wait and see," she suggested with a soft smile. "You may yet be surprised."

Chapter 4

Kay pushed her hair back from her face, taking in a deep breath, looking out the window at the billowing clouds of a gathering thunderstorm. The time with Galeron, Alistair, and Jack had flown by in the blink of an eye. All her thoughts had been on Uther and how this discussion would play out.

She had the greatest faith in her sister; Em could talk a cat into befriending a mouse if she chose to. Still, Kay remembered what it was like to have Uther forcing himself on top of her, insistent that he would get what he wanted. If it got to that …

Kay fingered the dagger at her hip and glanced again at the door. A guard was right outside. Em would pull this off, and the first decision would be made.

The red candle clock flickered in motion; the wax slid past the 10:30 mark. At the same moment a flourish of knocks rained on the door. Kay glanced at the black curtain. "Are you ready?"

Em's voice rang out in a cheerful tone. "Come on in, Uther!"

The door flung open, and Uther strode in, his emerald green outfit highlighted with small metal studs which flashed in the light of the many candles which were positioned around the room. He ignored Kay completely, instead smiling at the curtain and moving to sit before it.

"Good morning, Keren-happuch!" he called out with delight. "And how are we this stormy morning?"

"I am doing well, thank you," came Em's voice smoothly from behind her black wall. There was a gentle rippling of the fabric, and then it fell still again. "You are looking quite dapper today, Uther."

Uther beamed and puffed out his chest. "I am indeed, if I say so myself," he agreed. "I always try to look best for my current group of companions!"

"I am sure you must be quite the center of attention in the halls of London," mused Em thoughtfully.

Uther's smile faded slightly. "Ah yes, London," he sighed, his voice tinged with regretful longing. "Now there is a city one could explore for years and never get enough of. If you knew who to ask you could sample rare lychee nuts from China and lush pomegranates from Persia. There were masked balls and summer soirees." His voice grew hoarse. "And the women ... oh, the women ..."

Em's voice was full of curiosity. "You seem the ideal man for London, and yet somehow you are out here, in the distant wilds of the hinterlands. How did you stray so far from your ideal haunts?"

Uther struggled to slide back into his courting personae. "Ah, but here I would be Lord of the Keep," he stated with vigor, seemingly to convince himself as much as the women in the room. "I would be the top dog, with all at my beck and call."

Em was rueful. "Ah, but you see how few staff we keep on hand," she pointed out. "And in the wintertime I am afraid it gets even more dreary. We are not exactly a sought-out destination."

Uther's gaze dimmed. "I admit when I heard about this opportunity that I had romantic notions of a bustling castle on the sea, of parties all day and song all night ..." He glanced about him, his smile wilting.

"Clearly you are meant for so much *more* than this," continued Em encouragingly. "If we are this quiet now, imagine what we will be like in the dead of winter!"

Uther visibly melted. "And that will be when the parties in London will be at their fullest, during the festivities of the Christmas season." He groaned, his shoulders slumping.

"Uther," stated Em with warm compassion, "You have done me a great honor by coming to court me and spend time with me. The entire castle has benefitted from meeting you, learning from you, and experiencing your style and elegance."

Uther revived slightly, the hint of a contented smile easing onto his face.

Em pressed on. "I think it would be a shame – no, even more than that, a tragedy – if we held you from the world you so rightly are meant to adorn. You deserve to be the shining jewel in London's crown, surrounded by adoring fans."

"I do deserve that, don't I," mused Uther, his eyes growing distant.

"You do," agreed Em firmly. "There are wealthy widows who need consoling and beautiful young ingénues who will never have the benefit of your wisdom and experience. Never mind the dedicated cooks whose culinary endeavors will not be properly appreciated!"

"My palate *was* said to be the best in the northern quarter," reflected Uther, his face regaining its color. "I am sure I am missed in many parts of London. They often said a party would not truly come to life until I arrived."

"I am sure they did," encouraged Em. "In fact, I feel it would be selfish of you to hide yourself away at the prime of your power, to miss this important opportunity to share yourself with the adoring throngs who need your guidance."

"Your wisdom knows no bounds," praised Uther, his eyes sparkling with freshly found enthusiasm. He drew himself up to his feet. "My true calling – my proper place – is in the heart of London, with its marvelous cacophony of fine cuisine, of political intrigue, of clandestine meetings and tumultuous galas. You have opened my eyes, and for that I will be eternally thankful."

He gave a flourishing bow toward the curtain, then turned and strode toward the door. He tossed it open with a pull, then turned back toward the curtain. "Farewell, my dearest Keren-happuch! Any time you venture toward London, know that I would consider it an honor to escort you to the finest establishments and introduce you to the wonders that they hold!" And then with a sweep of his hand he was off, moving down the stairs with a spring in his step.

Kay stared after him open mouthed, amazed as always at the silver-tongued talents her sister possessed. Just how did the woman do it?

There was a movement in the doorway, and Reese moved into view, the shocked surprise on his face mirroring her own. He smiled when he saw her, and she waved him in to his seat.

Em's voice came cheerfully from behind the curtain. "What do you think, will he be on his horse and galloping full tilt toward London in five minutes, or ten?"

Reese accepted the proffered tankard from Kay and settled into his seat. He took a long pull on his ale before responding. "I put it closer to five minutes," he chuckled. "Just how did you do it? I was ready to come in and pull him out by force, if necessary, after the way he behaved last night."

Em's voice took on a sharp edge. "What did he do last night? Did he hurt one of the maids?"

Reese glanced at Kay, and she dropped her eyes. Her voice was hesitant when she spoke. "M'Lady, I did not tell you because I thought it would interfere with your ability to send him away as smoothly as you did."

"Tell me WHAT?" came Em's voice in rising tones.

"I ... I told you about of hearing of Uther's actions chasing after both Jessica and Anne," continued Kay reluctantly, "but I did not tell you that, in order to confirm my theory, I ..."

Em's voice was a low growl. "You *what*, Kay?"

Kay blushed, and when she spoke, she found her throat had closed up. The words emerged in a whisper. "I used myself as bait, to see what he would do once he got me alone."

There was a violent rustle behind the curtains, and Kay was half-afraid that her sister would come storming through the fabric to throttle her. "Are you *insane*?" cried out Em. "I know you can handle yourself in most situations, but what if he had hurt you! What if -"

Her voice caught.

Reese's voice was quiet. "I was there," he assured her, "watching over Kay. She would not have come to any harm."

"Thank goodness *someone* was thinking with his head," huffed Em, "although why you let her do it in the first place is beyond me!"

Kay flushed. "He did not know what my plan was," she quickly defended. "He only knew I was acting oddly, and his sole thought was to keep me safe."

Reese's lips quirked into a smile. "She did not need it," he added. "Your maid is fairly deft with a knife."

There was a long moment of silence, then a low chuckle rolled out from behind the curtain. "That she is," agreed Em. "She has a multitude of talents." There was another pause. "Although, *maid*, let me make it clear that any future adventures must be revealed to me *in full and in advance*. Trust in me to handle the knowledge well."

"As you wish," agreed Kay, pitching her voice to be as meek as she could manage.

Another pause, and then peals of laughter billowed from behind the curtain. Kay found herself joining in, and Reese was smiling as well. Kay could almost imagine her sister wiping the tears from her eyes.

Finally Em's voice came through the fabric. "Well, we are down to four, at least," she commented, "and if nobody has come to blows yet, I count us ahead of the game." She gave another chuckle. "My dearest Kay, the chance of keeping you fully out of trouble is about the same as keeping a cat on a fast in a room full of mice." She sighed. "Reese, will you look after her for me?"

"It would be my honor," agreed Reese with a smile, looking over at Kay.

She smiled back, and found herself captivated by his eyes, by the depths in them. Were they the grey of wood smoke, curling from a winter's fire? Or were they the soft green of a spring moss, just emerging from its wintry blanket? She warmed from within; a sense of peace slid down her chest and wrapped around her heart.

Chapter 5

Kay followed Reese down the spiral staircase and came up beside him as he waited for her at the bottom. It seemed so natural, so comforting, to enter the main hall with him by her side. She smiled when Alistair, Jack, and Galeron looked up with interest.

Uther was nowhere to be seen.

Jack's voice snapped out with sharp precision. "So, is it true? Uther is out of the running?"

Kay moved forward to sit down at the table, looking around for the maids. While this might have been great news for the men in contention, and certainly for her personally, how would it affect her household? Perhaps she should seek out and speak with Anne and Jessica first.

The pair of women came sweeping into the room with platters of roast duck, their faces wreathed in smiles, moving side by side in smooth harmony. The difference in their bearing from the night before to now could not be more distinct.

Kay held her eyes on the two women. "Yes, Uther has chosen to return to London, to rejoin the throngs there," she admitted.

Anne tossed her blonde curls. "And good riddance, too!" she chimed in. "The man was not to be trusted!"

Jessica put down a pair of tankards with a solid ring. "Not at all," she agreed "I think we can all be grateful that lout is on his way!"

Jack moved his eyes along the table of men with careful evaluation. "And so the field reduces," he mused. "I think this occasion deserves a toast."

He raised his mug, and the others did in turn, clicking and downing their brews in unison.

A shiver ran through Kay. The reality of the situation suddenly enveloped her full force. This was not just some kind of game. This was a serious endeavor, and at the end of it she would be tied for life to one of these men. Not only would her own future be set in stone, but also the lives and safety of every person within this keep.

She spent the meal in quiet, pushing the cubes of turnip around on her plate with her knife, suddenly without appetite.

When the meal was over, she excused herself and retreated into the library, taking down the family copy of the Bible, delving into Corinthians. She found the verses comforting; the message strong and powerful. She lost herself in the reading for several hours, the storm brewing outside her window, the candles providing a serene glow.

The door swung open, and she glanced up. Alistair was standing there, a look of surprise on his face.

"I am so sorry," he stuttered, looking at the Bible in her hands. "I did not realize another might be interested in sharing the wealth of the Holy Book. I thought only I drew comfort from its pages."

"Not at all," demurred Kay with a smile. "There are many inspirational passages in here."

"I agree completely!" responded Alistair with growing enthusiasm. "If I could but sit with a Bible all day long, and draw in its message, I would count myself a lucky man!"

"Part of taking in the word is to then put it in practice, do you not think?" countered Kay cheerfully. "If you sat in a room solely reading the word, where would be the time to take action on what you had learned?"

"Is not the knowledge itself enough?" asked Alistair with some confusion. "To become a lamp full of glowing oil, brilliant with the word of God?"

Reese suddenly appeared over Alistair's shoulder, his eyes serious. "Kay, I think you need to come out to the stables," he called, his voice tense.

Kay tossed the Bible down without a second thought, her heart tight, leaping to her feet. She ran out the door, through the hall, across the pelting rain of the courtyard to the open stable door.

A row of torches lit the roomy building, and there was a rustle of noise as the horses moved in their various stalls. Galeron was standing in the middle of the room with his ever present tablet in hand, going over a list. Jack's sharp eyes came up to meet hers as she came to a halt within the doorway.

Jack did not mince words. "Two horses are missing," he reported, waving a hand toward a back stall door which hung open.

Kay's heart dropped. She knew every inch of these stables. She did not have to ask, but she did so automatically. "Which two?"

Galeron's stylus moved methodically down his list. "Heather. Star. Those two are not accounted for."

Kay wavered, and Reese's sturdy arm was behind her, supporting her. She had helped raise Heather from a foal, and when Heather had herself become pregnant, she had been the one to nurse her through the final days of pregnancy. She had been the one to help birth Star that stormy night several months ago.

That these two would be the ones missing?

She moved immediately to the wall, pulling down her saddle and kicking open the door of her horse's stall. "We are going out after them."

There was an incredulous snort from the doorway, and she turned in surprise. Alistair was standing there, slightly out of breath from his quick walk here. "You must be joking," he gasped in horror. "There is a torrential thunderstorm out there, the likes of which only Noah has seen!"

Kay set her lips in a thin line. "Heather and Star are out in that," she reminded him. "They are my charges, and I will not abandon them."

"It is God's will that they be in this storm," solemnly intoned Alistair, his eyes rolling up toward the sky.

"It is God's will that we get our tails in gear and get out to save those horses!" snapped Kay with fury, cinching the saddle onto her steed and swinging up onto his back.

Reese pulled up alongside her, mounted and ready. In a few moments Galeron and Jack were behind them.

Alistair nervously looked between the four, then gave himself a small shake. "I will pray for your safe return," he stated in somber tones.

"You better pray we find those horses alive," returned Kay with a snarl, pulling down a cloak from the wall to wrap around her. She took one last look at the deluge descending from the heavens, then she urged her horse to course out of the stables into the pouring rain. The main gates stood open for her, and she was in a full gallop before they crossed the threshold into the dark night beyond.

Kay knew well the fields where the horses liked to graze this time of year. The clover lingered there long past fall, and the winds were blocked by the edge of a small cliff. She drove the first mile hard. If the horses had lagged somewhere close to the keep, they would have been heard or seen by the sentries. They had to be further back, perhaps in against the cliff itself. She reluctantly drew in on the reins as they moved beyond vision of the wall, pulling her cloak tighter around her. The hammering of the rain against her head made it that much harder to focus on what was around her, to hear anything. The occasional flashes of lightning lit the world, but the resulting darkness was even more challenging to deal with.

She knew this landscape as intimately as the well-worn creases of the reins beneath her fingers, but how could she spot the horses in this chaos? What if they lay injured, mired in the mud?

She drew her horse to a walk, chafing against the slow speed, straining every sense to make out a shape, a noise, a tiny change which might point her in the right direction. The three men moved along with her, their heads swiveling, their eyes seeking in the black night for a sign of the lost horses.

At her right, Reese froze.

She instantly pulled in alongside him, holding up a hand to alert the others.

For a long moment the world stood still. Nothing but the inky black of the storm, the pelting of the hard raindrops against their bodies, against the thick hides of the horses, and there was nothing ...

"There," whispered Reese, pointing up ahead.

Kay followed his finger with her eyes. Her heart sank, felt as if an iron bar had been wrapped around it and cinched tighter, tighter. Reese was pointing to the cliff face. As her eyes readjusted to the black night, she could see the barest hint of a shape halfway up, a small horse's head, a crumpled body.

"No ..." she breathed out in agony. He could not be dead ...

The small head gave a turn.

She urged her steed into action, driving toward the cliff. Her horse gave a whinny as they came toward the base of the cliff. There was an answering cry from nearby as Heather, the mother, came out to join the crew. Her eyes whirled in wild panic, her head pointing up the cliff toward her young foal.

Kay leapt from her steed, giving the reins a wrap around a nearby birch. She worked forward toward the cliff through the brambles, her eyes pinned upwards at the small shape. God's teeth, he was at least twelve feet up there, maybe fifteen, wedged into a crevice. He must have fallen down from above, landing in that nook.

He heard his mother's call and turned his head at that, crying out piteously.

She began to climb.

Jack's voice was tight with exasperation. "For God's sake, Kay," he cried out from below. "The foal is clearly injured. If you make it down without breaking your own neck, we will only have to put it out of its misery. Let us go back for a bow and end this quickly."

"Not on your life," grit out Kay between clenched teeth, finding another foothold. The rock was slippery, but she had lived in these hills all her life. She had tackled climbing these rocks during spring deluges and winter ice storms. No mere force of nature was going to hold her back now.

Galeron's voice came up to her, calm and patient. "I have the mother now, Kay," he offered. "We have saved one of the two beasts. Let us get her back to safety."

Kay strained with her right hand, missed the ledge, cursed as her leg slid sharply against an outcropping, then caught her hand securely on her second try. She pulled herself up. Her left foot found a crack to wedge into, and she pulled herself up level with the slim ledge the foal had been caught on.

She caught her breath. Star's front leg was a mass of blood and brambles. The foal turned to look at her, and she gazed into those big, brown eyes for a moment. He nuzzled her, and she rubbed her forehead into his in return. She had been there for his birth. She would be damned if she abandoned him now.

Balancing herself on one arm, she used her other to gently probe at the foal's leg. He let out a deep, shuddering breath, but held still under her movements. It did not seem that anything was broken beneath the skin. She leant forward against the rock, putting all her weight into it, then carefully used both hands to rip the hood from her cloak. She twisted the fabric and then wrapped it several times around the injured leg. She gave it a knot at the end to hold it in place. That would at least stop the bleeding until they got Star back to the stables.

"It is all right, little one," she whispered to him, her blood pounding in her ears. Again the foal nuzzled her softly, and her heart melted at the trust he had in her. She gently slid her hands beneath his frame, getting a firm grip on his body.

Her blood suddenly ran cold. The reality of her situation sank in with full force. She was balanced – precariously – perhaps fifteen feet up on a rocky cliff. She barely made it up this far with both hands free. How could she possibly make it back down again?

She looked into the brown eyes and felt ripped in two. She would never leave him here. But to climb down with him in her arms was an impossibility. She was lost …

Reese's voice streamed through the torrential deluge like a beam of sunlight. "Kay. Imagine Star is Joey."

Kay shook her head in confusion. Now Reese had completely lost his mind. It was undoubtedly the combination of the inky darkness, the pounding rain, and the jagged rocks. She looked down at him.

Reese was standing beneath her, his arms open in a cradle shape. His eyes held hers and were dead serious.

"Let go," he stated, no hesitation in his voice. "Trust me."

Kay's heart stopped. She felt the hammering of the thunderstorm, felt the soft heaving of the injured foal's body, and yet all that existed was Reese and her.

He had lost a hold on his sanity. There was no way he could catch her and the foal. The ground was littered with sharp shards of rock which would slice open her skull as easily as a sword swung through spring mud. And yet his eyes promised that she would not be hurt, that he would be there, would be there …

She nodded, then took a deep breath and gathered up the foal securely in her arms. If she lost control of the young horse, then all would be lost. She needed to cradle him within her own body and trust in Reese to do the rest.

She closed her eyes, made a mental calculation of the distance back from the cliff face she would need, and pressed off from the wall.

The fall seemed to last forever. She inhaled the warm scent of the foal against her body, resonated with each beat of his heart, and soaked in the comforting assurance that she had done all she could do. It was out of her hands now. Every second seemed to last an hour.

Slam!

She was enveloped in musk and leather, the wind was knocked out of her, and Reese driven down to one knee by the force of the impact. Star kicked her hard in the ribs in panic, scrambling out of her arms, racing to his mother with a triumphant whinny. Kay doubled over in pain, rolling against Reese, moaning in agony.

"Kay! Kay! Are you all right?"

She heard it as if from miles away, and her head swam in a miasma of pain. She would not be sick. Not in Reese's arms.

There were muffled shouts, and then she was up on a horse, Reese behind her, and they were riding through the dark night, her body a sodden turmoil of agony. It took her several moments to draw enough breath to shout out, "Star? Heather?"

Reese's voice came low but sure from behind her. "Both are safe. The other two will bring them back safely."

"Safe ..." repeated Kay weakly.

Then the world swirled into darkness.

* * *

Kay's vision swam into focus. She wasn't in her room. The walls were filled with long shelves of jars, there were hanging herbs ... she winced. She had been in the infirmary enough times over her childhood to know the room by heart. Just what had she done now?

Leland moved into sight, his face tense with worry. "God's teeth, Kay," he reprimanded as he ground a poultice in a mortar on a nearby table. "You should have called me before setting off after that foal. You know how bad those cliffs can be at night, never mind in weather like this."

Kay flushed. She knew she should have waited for help, but the situation seemed too urgent to her. She bit her tongue and nodded. "I should have. I am sorry."

"But you would not do it any differently next time," mused Leland, his eyes gentling. "Well, then, let us see what damage you have brought onto yourself with your new injury of the week."

Reese's voice came from her other side. "So she comes here often, does she?" She glanced up, and he was standing beside her, looking down at her in a mixture of frustration and admiration.

Leland's frown eased. "Not nearly as often as she should," he responded, almost smiling. "Half the time she just tries to tough out the wound."

Kay huffed, crossing her arms. "That is only because you treat me like a baby, when I am barely scratched! Like now, when -"

Reese glanced down. "When the blood from your leg is already soaking through your dress?" he interrupted, his voice tense. He looked around him. "That damn Anne is taking too long," he added sharply. "Prudery be damned."

He pulled his knife from his hip. "I am sorry, this has to be done," he added to Kay. In one long movement, he sliced Kay's garment up to mid-knee, pulling the fabric away to reveal the wound.

A twisted slice of open flesh, oozing blood, snaked up the full length of her calf. Reese let loose a low oath, then in a moment he had a wet rag from the table and was carefully wiping the blood and dirt away while Leland continued to finish creating the poultice.

Kay glanced down in curiosity. She had injured herself so many times in her wild youth that the sight of blood held little concern for her. She wriggled her toes, testing. She felt the pain of the injury, but could discern no other issues. The wound looked superficial – a steady stream of blood, but little danger of permanent damage.

She smiled and lay back against the bed, sighing in relief. "Is that all? I barely needed to bother with the infirmary for that tiny scratch."

Reese looked at her, shaking his head. Leland came over to press down a layer of the green material on the wound. He took some clean rags from the table and tied them around to hold the poultice in place. Done with that, he wiped his hands on his pants, looking up at her with a smile.

"Well, my young mountain goat, is that the extent of your injuries for the night?"

Kay smiled wryly. "I should think so!" She pushed on one arm to sit up in bed. Instantly she was hit with a mind numbing pain in her stomach, and she doubled over, clutching at her middle.

The two men helped to ease her back onto the bed. Reese's knife was at work again, separating her dress in half across the waist, pulling the fabric apart to reveal her stomach.

Leland's eyes went wide. "God's teeth, Kay," he whispered in shock. "What in the world have you done?"

Kay wiped the stream of tears from her eyes and sat up gingerly to take a look.

There, embedded on her stomach, was the perfect shape of a small hoof mark.

"That is *amazing*!" she cried out in joy, her eyes shining with delight. "Is it going to stay that way? Really?" She reached down to trace the design with awe.

Reese and Leland looked at each other for a long moment, then both burst out with laughter, shaking their heads.

Anne stumbled into the room, pulling her robe on around her in sleepy confusion, looking between the two laughing men and the prone patient. "What insanity is going on in here?" she burst out in concern. "Is Kay hurt?"

Kay barely heard her. "I will be fine, Anne," she soothed, still marveling at the beautiful decoration on her belly. "Just look at what I have done!"

Anne turned on Reese. "And you, sir," she snapped, "you should not be in here!"

Reese glanced down at the exposed stomach and leg and flushed. "She was injured -"

Anne bustled him out. "Yes, injured. But now Keren-happuch is coming down to check on her, and you are not allowed to see the lady. So out you go."

Reese held his gaze on Kay. "I will check on you later," he promised.

Kay met his eyes, and the night flooded back onto her in full force. He had saved her life. He had saved both of their lives.

"Thank you," she breathed, awed by the depth of what she owed him.

He nodded, and smiled, and then he was gone.

Chapter 6

The morning had drifted by peacefully. Galeron and Jack had both come and gone from the upper floor, offering conversation to Em and solicitous concern for Kay's health. She had lain quietly, stretched out on the couch with a swaddling of blankets, more as a way to not be drawn into the conversation than for any real concern for her health.

The events of the previous night still swirled in her mind. The calmness of Reese's voice beneath her, the steady reassurance she had that, when she jumped, he would catch her; he would save her. She had never felt that way about a man before. Certainly Leland would give his life for her, would do so for any member of her family. But this was different somehow.

"Kay, are you there?" asked Em for, judging by the sharp tone of voice, what must have been the fourth time.

"Oh sorry, Em, I was just lost in thought."

"It is *M'Lady*," reminded Em with a gentle laugh.

"Oh, right, sorry," apologized Kay again. She shrugged herself up to a seated position.

"I was asking if you were sure about sending away Alistair. Any hidden rendezvous I should know about this time?"

Kay sighed, pulling her blanket closer around her, shaking her head. "No, no hidden meanings, no secret issues. I just cannot bring myself to be with someone who passively sits back and waits for life to roll him over."

"There is something to be said in trusting in God," pointed out Em complacently.

"Yes," countered Kay, "And also, 'God helps those who help themselves.' God does not expect you to lay in bed all day, with your mouth open, waiting for manna to drip into it!"

Kay could hear the amusement in her sister's voice. "You are very right," agreed Em. "If this is your choice, then that is what we shall do."

A timorous knock sounded on the door, and Kay nestled herself into the covers more thoroughly as Em called Alistair into the room. She could not bring herself to look on him. He would have sentenced Star and Heather to death. He would have sat, safely, in his warm and cozy hall, while Star shivered in fear, waiting for rescue, waiting …

Alistair's eyes were serene. "My dear Kay, I see that my prayers have been answered. You have been brought home safe and sound."

Kay did not trust herself to speak. She nodded as he moved around to take his seat.

Em's voice flowed smoothly from the other side of the dark layers of curtain. "You are quite powerful at prayer, Alistair," she intoned. "I am very grateful for the efforts you put forth to bring Kay back to me."

"I am happy to be of service," murmured Alistair, brightening visibly.

Em's voice took on a more thoughtful tone. "It almost seems a shame for your talents to be wasted in menial ways. To be subject to the boring tedium of chores and miscellany, when clearly you have such an amazing talent for working the wonders of God."

"I strive to be humble, but there are times when I would feel that way as well," admitted Alistair, his cheeks pinkening, lowering his eyes. "There is so much I would love to do, if only I had the time."

"We have often dreamt about having a priest available to perform special prayers for us at the monastery. Someone to pray for our departed loved ones and of course for special occasions. However, we never knew a man personally who we had faith in." continued Em.

"I would be proud to intercede for you," beamed Alistair. His face fell. "But of course, I have been sent away from the monastery for now."

"We would not want to waste your talents in the tedious work of a daily life," insisted Em, warming, "when you could be much more instrumental to the entire region's salvation as our intercessor. Perhaps if I became your patron?"

It was as if Em had taken a torch and set Alistair alight with an inner glow. His entire body shone, and his eyes brimmed with tears.

"Would you, really?" he stuttered, almost choking in surprise.

"I could think of no other man I would entrust with our spiritual well-being," responded Em, her voice serene. "If you would be willing?"

Alistair was on his feet in moments. "Would I be willing?" he cried out in disbelief. "It would be my dream come true!"

"The letter to your master is there on the table," offered Em quietly. "I think the best of all possible roles for you would be as our spiritual guide and intercessor."

Alistair grabbed up the letter, scanned it with almost unbelieving eyes, then kissed it fervently. "Thank you, thank you," he whispered, crossing himself, looking up at the sky, then turning to run from the room, leaving the door open behind him.

A long minute passed, and then Reese walked in shaking his head in amazement, looking between Kay and the dark curtain. "I do not know how you two do it, but I am very impressed," he commented, sitting down in the chair and pouring himself a tall tankard of ale. "I assume, given last night's escapades, that you somehow told him he was better off in God's service?"

Em's voice bubbled with amusement. "Yes, we certainly did. And he agreed completely."

Reese took a pull on his ale. "As would I," he toasted to the black wall. He turned to look at Kay. "On a more serious note, how is your leg healing up?"

Kay shrugged off her cover, tossed it to one side, and slid over to sit on the side of the couch nearest him. She took the ale from his hand, downed half of it, then smiled as she handed it back to him.

"I am ready for an afternoon ride. How about you?"

Reese laughed, toasting her with his mug. "Nothing keeps you down, it seems!"

Em chimed in from her curtained nook. "*That* is for sure," she agreed. "There was this time -"

Kay threw a grape at the curtain, shushing her. "No story telling!" she insisted with a laugh. "It would be unfair, because I cannot tell any stories about you!"

Reese leant back in his chair, a wide smile on his face. "You both are quite welcome to tell as many stories as you wish about each other."

"That is not going to happen," chuckled Kay. "Not until this game is a distant memory."

Reese took a long drink from his tankard, then set it down.

His eyes glinted with emotion.

"I am content to wait."

Chapter 7

Kay was almost content as they relaxed during lunch. Anne and Jessica were laughing, joking with each other as they served out the bread pudding. Galeron was working on one of his endless lists, his black curls bouncing as he made another gently teasing comment. Jack's eyes were sharp as they took stock of the quality of the knives and the sturdiness of the table. And Reese …

She smiled as she turned to look at Reese. He was like a second skin to her, like a half of her soul. He could finish her sentences and know what she was thinking before she began. If there was trouble in one of the villages, Reese was the man she would want at her side, to watch her back, to rely on when all else had failed.

He leant over to her ear. "Would you like to go for a walk along the castle wall?" he murmured.

A warm shiver eased down her neck, swirling in her heart, sending ripples out through her body.

Galeron perked up with delight. "That sounds perfect," he chimed in. "I have not yet made a list of the improvements to be made there! Indeed, let us take a walk along the walls."

Galeron was up in a moment, leading the way. Jack was right behind him. Kay and Reese followed, walking side by side out the main door and into the courtyard. In an instant Galeron's tablet was in his hand, and his stylus moved in scribbled activity.

Jack shook his head as they walked beneath the drawbridge. "The drawbridge support is fairly weak on the left side," he commented sharply. "See how the wood bows out in that spot."

Galeron's stylus flew to his tablet, writing out a series of comments.

Reese examined it for a long moment. "Yes, you are right," he agreed. "I could have a timber shaped for that in a few hours with -"

Galeron shook his head. "No, no," he countered. "We do not want to start on any random tasks just yet. The first logical step is to catalogue everything, to break out in detail exactly what needs to be done, and then to prioritize everything. That way what is important to do, we do those first."

Reese glanced at Kay. "But surely, if it would just take me a few hours, I might as well -"

Galeron smiled widely, holding out his wax tablet. "I am almost done with all of my summaries, Kay," he reasoned. "Surely waiting another day or two for Keren-happuch to come to the proper decision about what should be done would make sense? After all, she should have say in what is done to her keep, yes?"

Kay glowed with pride at his words. It would be her keep. She would have a say in what was updated, in what changes were made. She nodded in agreement. "Yes, we can all review the list together," she agreed.

They continued to move through the courtyard area, pointing out deficiencies, noting what needed to be improved. They climbed the narrow stairs up to the wall. Galeron's stylus never stopped moving.

Kay was impressed with Galeron's methodical attention to detail. She wondered, idly, if there would be any way to keep all three remaining men on staff. Certainly Uther and

Alistair had needed to be sent on their way – but the last three? Could she have a perfect keep under their watchful gaze?

A horse became visible on the horizon, and the four watched as he moved at a trot toward the keep.

Kay's eyes narrowed as he came within range. "That is Jeff, from the village off to the east," she murmured. She ran down the stairs, curious what would bring him in to the main building.

Jeff drew rein as he clattered into the courtyard. "Kay, it is good to see you," he greeted as he dismounted. His face was lined – she guessed he was in his mid-forties by now – and his brown hair had faded to speckled grey. "We are mid-harvest, and we are having some issues which we thought -"

Jack snapped into action. "In the middle of harvest? Issues? We are coming out with you immediately." He sprinted toward the stables.

Kay was warmed by a surge of kinship with the man. He cared that much about the food supply of her people? Maybe she had overlooked him over the past few days! In a few moments the group was saddled and riding the short distance toward the town.

A great sense of pride and love swept over her as they rode through the rolling hills and tufts of heather, through the jumbles of rock, moss, and undulating grass. This was her land. These people trusted in her to keep them safe from the MacDougals, to store their grain for the tumultuous winter, and to celebrate the delights of the sultry summer. If they were having a problem, she would help find a solution.

The village was a collection of warm, snug homes nestled into the side of a cliff wall. There were perhaps fifty small buildings surrounded by waving fields of golden grain and a few head of cattle. Most of the villagers were out amongst the ears of wheat, gathering it up by hand.

She glanced around, but there was only one grain cart in the center of the village, already stacked high with wheat. Normally the village had at least three carts to ensure smooth movement between the mill and the fields.

"What happened, Jeff?" she asked, instantly sizing up the situation.

"I am baffled, Kay," responded the man, shaking his head. "I would almost say the faeries were at work here, and not just a plague of bad luck. If it was one cart which threw a wheel, it might seem expected. But for both of them to lose a wheel, and none of our spares are fit for using?"

Jack rounded in fury, his short, blond hair flashing in the sun. "What, you called us out here because of some broken carts? Get your children out there carrying the wheat by hand, and put your back into it! That is what you are there for – to do menial labor!"

Tension corkscrewed her stomach, but she took in a deep breath and let it out. "Jeff, surely there must be some mistake. We have wagons back at the keep. All we need to do is -"

Jack blew out breath in exasperation. "Kay, stop coddling these people!" He waved a hand at the single cart. "They simply do not want to do the work. Their laziness reeks. You need to learn how to motivate them!" He spun his horse to gallop up toward the fields.

Kay's heart leapt in her throat, and she charged her own steed after him.

Jack dismounted in the center of a group of villagers, his movements sharp. Whip in hand, he strode up to them, his body tense with anger. "You! Peons! Stop lollygagging and put your backs into it! Half of you will have to start carrying bags of grain manually over to the mill! March!"

Kay slid off her horse behind him, her face crimson with outrage. How dare he talk to *her* people in such a way! He had no right!

A young girl of perhaps eight stared up at Jack in fright, and Jack raised his whip arm menacingly. "Get back to work!"

Instantly a boy of ten darted between the two, his fists balled. "Stay away from my sister, you hooligan!"

"Hooligan?!" bellowed Jack in fury.

His whip came down.

There was a sickening crack as it landed on the thin outstretched arm of the young boy.

Kay flung herself forward. "No!" she screamed, her cry mingled with that of the boy, and then she was beside him, shielding him with her body.

Her hands raced to pull the sleeve back from his arm. There was no doubt. The break in the arm bone was clearly visible through the skin, in one place, perhaps two.

She stood in an instant, spinning in fury to face Jack. Her voice carried across the field.

"Bring the grain cart; we need to get this boy to the keep," she ordered.

"What, are you crazy?" choked Jack. "This is just one boy! We have grain for the entire village in that cart! It needs to get milled!"

"And if it were not for you, this boy would be whole," snapped back Kay, her eyes flashing fire. "What right had you to harm this child?"

"You stay out of my way," growled Jack, taking a step threateningly toward her. "This is man's work. Who are you, a mere maid, to question me? Your place is to sit and follow orders at the keep. Let the competent adults handle the challenging tasks."

Competent adults?

Kay could barely breathe. "You lay a hand on any one of my people again and I will see you clamped in iron, you bastard," she snarled, her face glowing with fury.

His hand moved faster than she could follow. Her head exploded into a brilliant, multi-colored burst of showering stars. The ground slammed up to meet her body full force, and it was a moment or two before she could make sense of what had happened. She gave her head a soft shake and it sent her world spinning. Looking around more cautiously, she saw that Reese and Galeron had grabbed a hold of either side of Jack's arms and were holding him securely.

Jeff was at her side, helping to roll her up to a seated position. "Are you all right, Kay?" he asked hoarsely, his face taut with concern.

"Fine enough," she agreed, giving him a reassuring pat. She drew herself up to one knee, then pressed hard to regain her feet. It was less than an hour from when they had left the keep, and yet looking on Jack now, it was as if a lifetime had passed. She could not imagine ever having wanted him anywhere near her lands.

She shook her head, and a wave of nausea flowed through her at the action. She fought to steady herself. She had to think. She turned automatically to Reese. "We need to get the boy -"

Reese glanced at Jack with barely restrained fury. "Yes," he agreed, his words tight. "We will get the boy – and you – to safety." He looked across at Galeron. "You can handle Jack?"

Galeron nodded, a half-smile coming to his face. "Certainly, leave this to me."

Reese released Jack's arm, then moved over to where the young boy lay whimpering. Dropping to one knee, he carefully cradled the boy in his arms, smoothly lifting him up.

Jack glared from Kay to Reese, his eyes shining with heat. "I do not need handling," he snapped. "You are spoiling these people. A firm hand is what they need."

Galeron gave Jack a warning shake, then turned to Reese. "I will be fine here," he repeated. "You go on and get those two back to the infirmary."

Kay allowed herself to be helped into the back of the cart; her head was throbbing with pain. The boy was lowered gently into the crook of her arm. She held him against her, telling him long stories of haunted ships and impossible romances as the group made its way back to the keep. After a drifting of light and breeze and pain and weariness they were moving back through the main gates. Then a pair of warm arms lifted her, a rich smell of musk enveloped her, and she was carried back down into the infirmary.

Leland's voice was rough. "God's teeth, Kay, what was it this time?" In moments she was laid back down into the familiar bed. A pair of fingers prodded at her cheek and she winced in pain. "Were you dealing with that drunken lout of a grandfather again?"

Reese shook his head in amusement. "Is this a daily occurrence around here?" he mused in wonder. "No, this mouse is courtesy of one of the remaining courting gentlemen."

Leland's eyes shot up to Reese's in fury, and Reese put up his hands in innocence. "Not me, I swear," he quickly added. "This was Jack's temper flaring, when he saw the wheat was not being gathered quickly enough."

"So he hit a woman?" snarled Leland in anger.

Just at that moment Jeff strode into the room carrying the lad with the broken arm. Leland's face turned a richer shade of purple, and a vein bulged on his neck. "And he injured a *child*?"

Kay coughed. "He will be gone tomorrow, Leland," she promised, her voice rough through the pain. "It is better we find this out now rather than later. His true colors have shown. He will be gone."

"He should be flogged within an inch of his life," muttered Leland, his voice tight. "What kind of a man would do a thing like this?"

"A man we do not want within our borders," agreed Kay wholeheartedly. "We will send word to Lord Weston, send Jack away, and justice will be done." She put a hand to her head. "But in the meantime, can I have a cold compress?"

Leland was bent over the boy's arm, working carefully on the separated bones. "My dear, you know I love you with all my heart, but right now you need to be patient. Unless Reese can -"

Reese spoke immediately. "Reese most certainly can," he chimed in, and he was gone. Only a minute passed before he was sprinting back into the room holding a small cloth soaked in well water. He moved to sit beside Kay, pressing it against her temple. She sighed in relief, the cooling sensation blanketing her pain.

"You can *not* tell ..." Kay paused for a moment, her befuddlement making it hard to remember the right words. What was she supposed to be calling Em? "My lady. You cannot tell my lady what has happened today."

Reese tilted his head to the side, staring down at her in quiet contemplation. "You wish me to lie?"

Kay shook her head and immediately regretted the decision as her whole world spun and whirled. She took in several deep breaths while the movement settled down again. She had to remember *not* to do that.

"I will tell her, soon," she promised. "Please, just wait until tomorrow afternoon. If she knew what happened, she would have him thrown into the holding cells here, and it would spoil everything. Lord Weston's men will get to him soon enough. Her time here should be stress-free and smooth. It is important for her health."

Reese looked at her for a long time. "You really do care about her greatly," he commented at last.

Kay nodded. "I do."

Reese smiled gently. "If that is your wish, then I will abide by it."

Kay put her hand on top of his, drawing in the warmth of his fingers - the strength, the caring. Her worries melted away. It would be all right, as long as Reese was by her side.

They sat that way for a long time, until eventually Leland finished with his task and came over to sit with the two. "The boy will be fine; the break was clean," he reported. "How is this bruise doing?"

Reese lifted the compress back, and Leland prodded experimentally at the tender area. "Nothing you have not seen before, missy," offered Leland with a smile when he was finished. "I think you can head up to get some dinner into you. You must be starving by now."

Reese shook his head. "Just what kind of a life do you lead up here, when maids routinely encounter bruises like this?"

Leland's smile grew wider. "Ah, but Kay is a special case, or had you not guessed yet?"

A jolt of nervousness ran down Kay's spine at Leland's double-meaning jest, but Reese seemed to take it in stride. "She *is* a special woman," he agreed, then offered his arm to her. She moved slowly, but already her world was coming more into focus, and she swung her legs around to ease out of bed. With Reese's help they were soon walking through the main hall and toward the central table.

Galeron offered her a large tankard of mead. "Quite a black eye you have there, Kay," he commiserated. "Here, take a long draw; it will chase away the edge."

Kay gratefully drank down a swallow, and indeed the pain dulled almost immediately.

Reese tensed beside her, and she looked around to see Jack moving to join them at the table. His blond head was held high, arrogantly, and his eyes moved dismissively to the bruise on her face. She met his look without flinching, sitting down at her place, and holding his gaze as Anne and Jessica moved around them to serve the veal and fresh bread.

Jack ripped off a piece of bread and dipped it into his sauce. "Sometimes what a maid needs is a quick rap, to knock some sense into her," he mused with a smirk. "Feeling better now, are we?"

Flames spiraled up her spine, and she forced an icy cool tamp in response. "So you do this often to maids, do you?" she queried with deceptive calm.

He shrugged. "Maybe once or twice," he agreed, his eyes glowing with triumph. "You notice that the blonde one is much more prompt about refilling our ale mugs, after all."

Kay's eyes moved in shock to Anne, who was bringing around a fresh pitcher. Sure enough, a small welt showed at the corner of her face. Anne blushed when she noticed the perusal, quickly tilting her head so the cascade of blonde curls fell across the location.

Kay's hand slid down to her knife before she had conscious thought of the movement. Rage coursed through her. At her side, Reese coiled, his own hand dropping, preparing to follow through on whatever she started. Warmth flowed through her at the thought, at knowing he was so in sync with her. It would be so easy ...

But Em was upstairs, and the last thing her sister needed right now was more high-stakes drama.

She took in a long, deep breath, marshaled her emotions, and slowly replaced her hand on the table. Jack was a belligerent fiend. He needed to be brought to justice, and he would be. There was no need to cause the explosion in the middle of her own home, where her own servants and friends would be hurt. A team of soldiers would be waiting for Jack in the morning, and they would safely take him into custody.

"Actions bring matching consequences," muttered Kay under her breath, willing herself into calm.

Beside her, Reese untensed, his hand coming up off his weapon.

Jack popped another piece of bread into his mouth. "Of course they do," he agreed with a smile, leaning back in his chair.

Kay found herself unable to talk for the rest of the meal. As soon as they were done, she strode out of the hall, through the courtyard, and up the thin stairs to the curtain wall. She was not surprised when, only a few minutes later, Reese was there at her side.

He gazed down at her. "You do not intend to let him go free." It was a statement, not a question.

"We have sent word," agreed Kay somberly. "He will be taken and brought to justice. He will be captured somewhere where he cannot hurt innocent people in the process."

"If you asked me, I would challenge him," offered Reese, his tone serious.

Kay took in the rigid set of his shoulders; the clenched hands. She raised her hand to gently stroke the side of his cheek, her smile soft.

"I know you would," she agreed with appreciation. "I treasure that more than words can say. But I want it to happen far from the keep."

Reese nodded. "Far from Keren-happuch."

Kay turned and looked back out at the dark night, at the ghostly line of trees which encircled the keep. It was almost a stab in her heart, now, to hear Reese refer to Em by her name. She felt wrong in deceiving him, in not telling him the full truth, after all he had done for her. She knew it was part of the game, but it went against her nature, and it loomed like a chasm between them.

"Yes," she agreed, "I need to keep her safe."

There was a long moment of silence, and then Reese moved to stare out into the dark distance alongside her.

"And you stay down here in hopes of preventing her from seeing your bruises until after he leaves?"

Kay blushed, hoping the darkness hid the sign of her reaction. His astuteness continually surprised her. She had not met a man like him before.

"It would be better," she murmured. "She need only know enough to make him go."

There was silence for a moment. When Reese spoke, his voice was tight with concern. "Do you truly think even your lady's silvered tongue can send Jack away in a contented frame of mind?"

Kay's heart fell. If there ever was a challenge to Em's talents, this would be it. She thought of putting on a brave front, but the weight of the day dragged heavily on her shoulders. She clasped her hands on the wall, sighing deeply. "I do not know," she admitted.

Reese put his hand on top of hers, and resolve surged back through her, buoyed by the tenderness and strength of his grasp. "Whatever happens, I will be there."

She closed her eyes, the richness of the words easing through her, wrapping her in their embrace.

"I know."

Chapter 8

Galeron was talking, saying something, going through the list on his tablet, and Kay knew she should be focused, should be paying attention, but she just could not do it. All she could think of was the rage billowing from Jack's face as he turned to launch his fist into the side of her head.

She forced it from her mind. She deliberately replaced the thought with the security, the tenderness in Reese's hand as he held hers.

Her heart skipped a beat as thoughts chased each other pell-mell through her brain. Soon it would be down to two men. Soon, maybe in only a few days, she would have to reveal the truth to Reese, that she had been deceiving him this entire time.

Would he understand? Would he see it was simply part of the game?

And what of the man now sitting at her side? Galeron had been so helpful with his diligence and his note taking. She almost hated to see him go. Would he be willing to stay, perhaps as captain of the guard? Would he be upset with her as well?

Soon her sister would be gone, back to her husband, and raising a family. She would miss Em desperately. Everything was changing so quickly. She just wanted time to hold still, to give her a moment to breathe, to figure out what was going on -

"Kay?" asked Galeron with a hint of amusement. "Are you in there? I will be heading out now for my morning ride. Are you sure you do not want me to fetch you anything?"

Kay shook her head, coming back to the present. At least her head was no longer swimming with every movement. Galeron was standing, smiling down at her.

She ventured a half smile. "I apologize, it was a long night. I am quite set. Enjoy your ride; it looks to be a lovely day."

Galeron chuckled. "Indeed, I would venture to say almost perfect." He bowed again toward the curtain, then turned and headed out the door with a quick stride.

Em's voice came through the curtain the moment the door closed behind him. "Are you sure you are all right, Kay? You are acting quite oddly."

Kay stood and went to the window, making sure her hair fell well in front of her face as she did so. Em might be behind a thick curtain, but she was certainly capable of peering out when they were alone, and Kay did not want her sister getting upset in any way. The situation was almost done with. Jack simply needed to be talked to and then sent on his way. They had already dealt with two of the suitors smoothly. Number three was about to face his end.

"I am just finding it harder each time, that is all," she offered to her sister, which was true. She had thought each suitor would be more and more alike as they got to the end, but to her surprise she was finding their level of malfeasance to be escalating. "With his issues of temper, we do not want him around our people. Lord Weston's men will be waiting to take him into custody."

"It is certainly shocking that he roughed up an innocent child," agreed Em.

Kay winced. She hated misleading her sister, but the woman was pregnant after all. Kay would tell her the full details once the child was safely born and Em was back in the loving care of her husband.

She drew in a long breath, looking out over the courtyard, past the wall and trees to the ridge which ran above the poorly named *Lover's Lane*. A row of covered wagons sat along the ridge, and she nodded in satisfaction. The castle workmen would get the wheels fixed up in no time, and the village harvest could go on without further problem.

There was a sharp rap at the door, and Kay started in surprise. It had begun. She had to trust in her sister's eloquent skills to make this work out properly. Her hand dropped to the knife at her hip. Either that or she had to trust that the guard outside the door, and Reese's ready blade, would keep the situation under control.

The door swung open before either woman could say anything. Jack stepped into the room. "Good morn," he greeted crisply, dropping into his seat without further preamble. "I suppose you heard about my decisive actions yesterday."

Em's voice was cool. "I did indeed," she offered. "You certainly know how to step up when something needs to be done. You see an issue, and you do what is required."

"Your keep is already the better for it," agreed Jack with a smile, leaning forward. "Anna and Jessica are far more efficient now that I have dealt with them."

Kay winced, and immediately her head throbbed. So much for shielding her sister from some of Jack's misdeeds. He was not making this any easier on himself.

Em's voice developed an edge. "So … you 'dealt' with Anna and Jessica?"

Jack nodded in agreement, his face brightening with pride. "Certainly. It will be one of my main tasks, as ruler of this little keep, to make sure the servants are all in line. That they know their place."

Brittleness layered itself into Em's query. "And just what is their place?"

"Why, at our beck and call, of course," stated Jack, a cold steel coming to his face. "It is what they are born and bred to do. They are the servants. We are the masters."

"But surely," responded Em, reforming her voice into a more even tone with effort Kay could clearly hear, "one role of a master is to take proper care of those he is responsible for."

"Absolutely," offered Jack, stretching his arms languorously above his head. "If we break one of their arms, we should make sure it mends reasonably well, so they can go back to work soon. Otherwise we have simply spoiled one of our own beasts."

There was a choking noise from behind the curtain, and Kay had to stop herself from running forward to check on her sister. This was not going well at all.

Em's voice was wound like a spring when it next came through the curtain. "Your precision and tight control would be well commended in the military," she crisply pointed out.

Jack shrugged his shoulders. "In the military they have too many rules to follow, too many superiors questioning your tactics. Here I will make all the rules, and the minions will do as they are told. It is far more ideal for my talents."

"Maybe the mercenaries then -"

Jack's eyes sharpened. "What is all this talk of mercs and soldiers? I am the perfect candidate for this job, far better suited to get the locals in line than either that stylus-pushing fool Galeron or that idiot Reese, who seems not even interested in the keep's head position any more. I say I am the best man here, by far!"

Kay roiled in confusion. "What do you mean, about Reese?"

Reese did not want to stay at Serenor? The thought sent a cold knife through her heart. It could not be true. Jack was simply making his case, in his upset state -

Em's voice came smoothly on top of her thoughts, regaining control of the situation. "Jack, you have many admirable qualities, but I see that we will not be able to come to an agreement on this issue. I am afraid I am looking for something different in a husband. Call it the vagaries of a woman's choice."

Jack rose to his feet in fury. "A woman's choice? What foolish game is this to allow something as important as the control of this keep – and all its servants – to the whim of a woman! You clearly have no idea what you are doing!"

Em was complacent and firm. "Unfortunately, this is the way the game is played and was agreed on by you. My decision in this matter is final."

Jack took a threatening step toward the curtain, and Em's voice rolled out with perfect calm. "Of course, if you violate the terms of the game, then there will be no turning back; no chance of any relief."

Jack's hand balled into a fist, but he stopped in place. "Relief, you say. I will go talk to your father about this immediately," he threatened. "I will tell him exactly what has gone on here, and how your delicate woman's sensitivities have made a wildly wrong decision."

Kay could almost hear the smile in her sister's voice. "Yes, I agree with you completely, Jack. You should tell my father in great detail what has happened. I think it important he knows exactly what you have done here."

"Do not think for a moment that I would hesitate!" shouted Jack in warning.

"I think you should do what you feel is right," insisted Em. "If you feel my father should be told of all occurrences here, then you are the very best person to convey that information. That way you can make sure all information is told exactly as it happened, with no sugar coating."

Jack's eyes lit up in triumph. "I will make sure of that," he vowed, squaring his shoulders. "I will make sure I get there before any messenger you might send, to ensure my version of the truth is the one he hears first. Then he will know the rightness of my taking control."

"As you wish," murmured Em, her tone accepting.

"I will be back soon," promised Jack with heat. He gave one last scowling look at the curtain, then turned on his heel and strode from the room, flinging the door wide on his way out, his boots echoing loudly on the stairs as he descended.

Reese was at the door in an instant, looking between Kay and the curtain. "Are you both all right?" he asked, his voice tense.

Kay became lost in his gaze; her voice choked within her. Did Reese really have second thoughts about staying at Serenor? Had her beloved home failed to seduce him? Had she done something to upset him?

Em's voice was rich with relief. "We are fine," she answered. "He is going."

"I will make sure of that," vowed Reese with determination. He turned and in an instant he was racing down the stairs after Jack.

Kay made her way to the door, closing it firmly, leaning against it for a long moment. The emotions of the day spun within her, and she did not know what to think.

The curtains parted behind her, and Em came up to give her a hug from behind. "There, it is all over now," her older sister soothed into her ear. "I know it was hard, but it is done with." She gave Kay a gentle tug. "Come by the window. We will watch Jack leave together."

Kay allowed herself to be drawn, and the two stood side by side staring down into the quiet courtyard. In a few minutes Jack strode from the main doors toward the stables, a bag slung over his shoulder. It was not long after that he was streaming out through the gates, heading at a gallop in the direction of the main castle.

There was another movement down in the courtyard. Reese had mounted as well, and he headed out in the same direction Jack had gone, moving at a steady canter.

Em patted Kay on the back reassuringly. "See, it is all fine now." She moved over to the couch and picked up the scroll sitting on the nearby ledge. "Come, Kay, let me read to you for a while. We have the keep mostly to ourselves, and I think the passages will help clear the air of the feel of that man."

Kay still felt as if she was in a daze, but she allowed herself to curl up at Em's feet, to close her eyes, and to be lost for a while in another world.

Chapter 9

Kay sat in her room as the sun delicately painted the sky with autumn colors, brushing her hair out for the twentieth time. She knew she should head down to dinner, but the butterflies flitting through her stomach had taken hold and left her with a sense of nervousness. There were no more false contenders for her hand. She was now presented with two quite capable men, each with an important set of skills, each pleasant to be with, intelligent, capable. On her choice rested the fate of not only herself, but of all of the inhabitants of the castle.

She drew the brush slowly through her hair, staring at her reflection in the mirror. She had put on her embroidered green dress, one of her nicer ones. It was still suitable for a maid assigned to a woman of Keren-happuch's rank, but it brought out the highlights of her eyes. She wanted to start to shine in her own right.

But was that fair? Should she choose the man who reacted the most to her presence, at the detriment to the care of the keep as a whole? What if she chose a partner for her heart, and the keep then fell during one of the raids by the MacDougals?

She closed her eyes. She must do the best for all involved. She must make a decision based on the most qualified man, overall, and she must do that objectively. No matter what consequences it might bring for her own happiness.

She put her brush down on the table, then turned and moved into the main room. Em was already sound asleep in the other room, the excitement of the day taking its toll on her. Kay was careful not to make any sound as she slipped through the outer door. She nodded at the guard in the hallway, then made her way down the spiral staircase.

The main hall seemed quiet although the usual contingent of guards and other castle folk were at the various tables throughout the room. The head table was almost empty now. She noted with a smile that neither Galeron nor Reese had taken her father's central seat. Both had chosen to sit in the lower ranking chairs, near the fireplace. Both men were staring at her with interest, and she flushed as she saw the admiration in their gaze, as they looked her up and down.

The men stood as she approached them. Reese's eyes trailed down her form, then back up to meet hers again. "You are a vision," he finally offered, his voice soft.

"Indeed," smiled Galeron, glancing between Reese and Kay. "My dear, why not sit there on Reese's side. It is closer to the fire and will keep you warm. The fall crispness is in the air, I fear."

Kay nodded shyly, moving to take the offered seat. In a moment Anne and Jessica were moving amongst them, setting out circles of veal and a bounty of turnips and onions.

"A toast," offered Galeron, picking up his mug in his hand. "To new beginnings."

Kay clinked her mug against his, then turned toward Reese. Again she felt her breath catch at the look in his eyes, at the steadiness of his hand, at the sureness of his body at her side.

She wrenched her gaze away with an effort. She had to be objective. She had to do what was right. She looked down to the ever present tablet which sat alongside Galeron's plate.

"So, what research do you have for us today?" she asked, striving to keep her voice light.

Galeron tapped the wood frame with a proud smile. "I think my tallies are nearly complete," he reported. "Every security issue to fix, every item of wealth to keep safe, every guard and his state of health. Would you care to hear?"

Kay ripped a piece of warm bread from her loaf, spreading a square of the fresh herb butter onto it, keeping her mind in focus. "Yes, certainly."

She ate slowly while Galeron went through the problems with the main gate, the weakness of the bar on the doors, and the spiral stairs which were a challenge to deal with if an enemy got within. She knew she should feel encouraged that Galeron had been so thorough, but it made her depressed to hear Serenor's beauty whittled down to broken windows and rusty hinges. Her beloved home had been sliced, diced, organized, and slotted into compartments. Her beautiful keep sounded more like an obsolete cottage, waiting to be torn down and rebuilt.

She looked up and saw the enthusiasm in Galeron's eyes. She sighed in acceptance. He truly was enjoying this task. She put on a smile and encouraged him to continue.

Even so, when they were done with dessert, she found herself rising, apologizing, and heading out to the curtain wall. She sat on the cool stone floor, her back to the outer wall, looking in toward the keep proper. The windows shone like jewels in the night; the people within seemed content, warm, and happy. It was more than a collection of stones, hinges, and bolts. It was her home - her beloved home.

There was a movement, and Reese was sitting beside her, giving her a gentle nudge. "Do not let him get to you," he offered quietly. "He means to help in his own way."

"All he can see is the flaws," countered Kay in frustration. "He seeks out the problems and counts them with joy. Can he not see the beauty?"

She turned toward Reese and found he was staring at her with steady regard. She flushed, returning her gaze to the keep. "It is all I want," she added, staring along its sturdy lines, looking up to the top floor where her sister slumbered peacefully. "Just this, nothing more."

"And the hillside chapel too, I imagine," added Reese with a chuckle, "where you go to sequester yourself every morning."

Kay smiled. "Yes, I imagine so," she agreed. "It is a special sanctuary for me."

Reese was quiet for a moment. "I would like to ride out there with you, to see what it is that captivates you up there," he commented in a low voice.

Kay's heart caught. Reese had laughed, with the others, when they had talked of female swordfighters, all those days ago when the party was first riding to the keep. How would he feel when he saw how she spent her mornings?

Her heart raced. She was not ready for that yet; not ready to risk losing him.

"You can ride with me part way," she finally agreed. "The views in the morning are quite spectacular and I would enjoy sharing them with you. But for now, my sanctuary hour must remain mine alone."

"As you wish."

She soaked in the warmth of his body next to hers. Almost of its own accord, her hand slid along the cool stone until her fingers were resting alongside his. Then, with the slightest of movements, she put just two fingers on top of his, the gentlest of connections. He went still beside her, not moving, not disturbing the moment. She resonated with the palpable power in their touch, in the contact which joined them. They sat that way for a half hour, maybe more, the cool night air drifting around them, the keep before them in its glowing beauty.

Finally Kay gave a yawn and drew herself to her feet. Reese stood as well, staring down at her.

"Until morning," he offered, his eyes holding hers.

Kay found herself not wanting to leave, not wanting to turn … but she forced herself to, to move down the narrow stairs, across the courtyard, and up to her room. She tumbled into her empty bed, but she knew she faced a sleepless night where all that mattered was the sun coming up over that horizon again.

Chapter 10

The sun was not quite up yet when Kay made her way into the courtyard the next morning, but Reese stood there at the ready, both horses saddled and fresh. Kay found herself blushing and moved quickly to her horse to hide her emotions. In a moment she had mounted, Reese was at her side, and the horses walked slowly through the main gates.

They rode in an easy silence, the gentle calling of birds echoing around them as the faintest hints of golden light stretched across the dewy grass. The drops of water glistened like a sea of sparkles before them. They made their way up a small hill, and before long they were about halfway between the keep and the chapel.

"Here, stop please," requested Kay, turning her horse to face back toward the keep.

Reese did not question her, but turned to remain at her side, and together they looked out over the landscape.

A rich hue saturated the fields, the mountains, the stone of the long wall, and the trees beyond. And then in an instant the sun slipped above the horizon and the world blazed into color. The rich greens of the earth, the deep blue of the sky, the pearlescent line of grey encircling the keep, it all bloomed into a rich beauty. Although Kay had seen it hundreds of times, it still brought tears to her eyes to look at it.

Her voice was hoarse. "Is that not the most beautiful thing you have ever seen in your life?"

She turned to look at Reese, and found he was staring at her, his eyes looking down her auburn tresses, to her lips, back to her eyes again.

He nodded in agreement, and Kay sighed in relief. Jack had been wrong. Reese did appreciate the keep; did see the beauty in her corner of the world. Everything was going to be all right.

"I need to leave you," she commented finally, glancing up toward the chapel.

Reese's face tensed. "Leave me?" he asked, his voice tight.

Kay gently smiled, tossing her head up toward the chapel. "I would miss out on my sanctuary time if we lingered here all morning."

"Oh!" Reese looked back toward the small stone building, and he nodded. "Yes, of course. I will see you later, then, at our appointed time?"

"I would not miss it for the world," agreed Kay. "Until then?"

"I will be waiting," promised Reese, bowing his head. Kay found herself resisting any motion, but at last she gave her horse a prod, nudging him up the hill and heading toward her morning workout with Leland and Eli.

Eli's young face was bright with excitement as she pulled to a stop, and he stabled her horse in record time. He caught back up with her just as Leland finished strapping her into her gear.

"There are only two left!" the lad called out in excitement. "Do you know which you will choose?"

Kay blushed crimson and focused on the short path which led to the clearing behind the chapel. "I am still deciding," she mumbled half to herself. "Both men seem admirable in their own way."

Leland drew his sword and saluted to her, his mouth quirking into a smile. "I hear Galeron is a mite enthusiastic about cataloguing the keep's faults." He rested his sword against his right shoulder.

Kay brought her own sword angled downward and to the left, its tip skimming the surface of the ground. She nodded at the comment. "I admit it irks me, but it needs to be done. We want the keep to be secure. Galeron is right – these issues need to be fixed if we are to hold off an attack."

Leland swung his sword in a high arc toward her left shoulder. She shifted her weight to her back foot, drawing the tip of her blade up, catching Leland's blade with hers and deflecting his blow off to her right. In a flash she shifted to her forward foot, bringing her sword down with a gentle rap against his head.

Leland nodded in satisfaction, stepped back, and reset his sword to his right shoulder again.

Eli's young voice piped up with laughter. "You had better not tell Galeron about the ocean-side tunnels, then," he advised. "That would fill reams of journals, to document those all!"

Kay smiled in agreement, watching Leland's sword come down at her from her left, retreating back a half step, again deflecting the blow with a sure motion.

Leland reached over to twist her wrist. "Keep that cross guard at an angle, to make sure it catches the blade," he advised. "Try that again." He reset and swung a third time, and Kay focused on orienting the blade properly to counter.

"Better," he agreed, stepping back to reset. "As for those tunnels," he added, glancing at Eli, "those were checked and sealed up decades ago. Lord Weston's grandfather had wild ideas about escape routes, but as you know tunnels can be used in both ways. Long before now, Lord Weston took care of those threats."

Eli chuckled. "There certainly are a lot of them," he commented. "I have spent every day crawling in and out of them, and I swear I could be at it all year and still not know them all."

Kay nodded, deflecting a fourth blow, then a fifth. "I have been in those tunnels for many years myself," she returned, "and I think they get more confusing each time I go down into them. Perhaps they multiply when they are not being watched?"

"That is it exactly!" cried out Eli, his eyes alight with glee. "They are faery tunnels!"

Kay laughed with mirth, and then Leland began his attacks in earnest. She lost herself in the thrill of deflection, attack, and counter-attack under the darkening sky, as billowing grey clouds slid in from the east.

Chapter 11

Em shook her head. "If you keep that up you will wear a path in the carpet," she chuckled, watching her sister. "I know it is raining out, but surely there is something you can find to do to distract yourself from whatever is eating at you."

"A sparring practice is what I need," ground out Kay in frustration. "Unfortunately, my partner seems a bit rounder than usual right now."

Em patted her abdomen in satisfaction. "I am, and I am very happy to be so," she agreed. "I can always spar in a few years, once I have begun the family properly."

Kay turned and headed back down the length of the room again. "If only this cursed rain would let up. It was fine this morning ... but look at it now!"

Em smiled fondly at her sister. "If only there were a practice sword in the keep somewhere, so you could work out your frustrations without leaving the building."

Kay frowned. "The moment I headed into the guard area, one or both of the men would be after me to see what I was up to, and where would that leave me?"

Em shook her head. "I was thinking of a pair of wooden swords, in the basement."

Kay looked up, her eyes brightening. "Do you think they are still down there?"

Her sister shrugged her shoulders. "There is only one way to find out ..."

Kay did not wait for her to finish the thought. She made her way quickly to the door, almost skipping down the stairs, down to the pantry level. Reese was standing in the guard room, talking with Jevan, but she barely saw them as she passed through. She turned left before the workroom, moving to the sturdy wooden door.

With an effort she pushed the massive door open, reaching to the ledge on the right to pull the torch off its hook. She lit it on the storeroom's main fire, and then returned to the cellar door and made her way down the musty stairs into the large room below. She went from torch to torch, creating a ring of light around the cluttered room.

The basement stretched perhaps the whole length and width of the main hall two floors above it; the walls were lined with shelves and boxes of supplies. The central area was kept open and well swept. She and her sister had spent many wonderful hours down here playing together, sparring with each other, practicing while their parents held dinners and social gatherings above. It was their secret retreat; their hideaway from the world. And their swords were normally tucked …

Kay dug into the lowest shelf on the back wall, and her heart leapt in delight. The brown sack was still there, the familiar two shapes nestled within. She pulled them out and laid them on a nearby crate. The wooden swords were proportioned for their height, but were in all other ways identical to the practice swords used by the men upstairs. She traced her hands down the blades with a smile. One had a "K" carved into it, the other an "M." The workmanship was exquisite, and she still remembered clearly when Leland had presented the swords to the sisters several years ago.

She picked up her sword, whirled it around her head for a moment, and a blanket of calm eased over her. This is what she needed. She moved from one guard to another, relishing the security of the sword in her hand, relaxing with the sure sequence of movements. A deflection for a high attack. A counter-cut when both swords were high. The turning thrust. She was safe, she was secure, she was in control. She went through her practice moves and she could feel the tension melting from her shoulders. A twisting leap ...

Her foot landed on a loose ball of twine and she stumbled slightly, landing with her sword hard against the outer wall. The noise rang out in a strange, hollow fashion.

She drew to a stop, confused.

She walked forward toward the wall, putting a hand out to it. The stone was the same cool, grey stone which made up most of the keep structure. It felt just as solid and real as any other stone making up the bones of this building.

She struck it again, and again there was a hollow ring to it. An almost echo.

She moved along the wall, striking as she went, and in most places the wall was sturdy, the noise dying out almost instantly. But not here. Not for about five feet on the side which faced the ocean.

She put the sword down on the crate, and took the stairs two at a time. Maybe Leland would know about this. He had spent many years out at the keep with her father, and undoubtedly the two had talked about the work done on the keep. Could these be the tunnels he had mentioned earlier?

She flung open the cellar door - and ran headlong into Reese's chest. The tankard of ale he was carrying splashed full across her dress, soaking her thoroughly.

"Kay!" he cried out in surprise. "What in the world -"

She grabbed his hand and pulled him back down the stairs. "Never mind that," she responded, drawing him to the bottom and across the room. "What do you make of that?"

He glanced down at the two wooden swords, picking up the one closest to him, engraved with the letter "K." "These are very fine quality," he commented with curiosity. "Quite well made." He glanced at the other one. "K? M? Do these belong to the two sisters?"

Kay flushed crimson and turned her face, hoping the torchlight hid her reaction. "Yes," she agreed. "Keren-happuch sent me down to fetch them. She wanted to put them safely in her room, to keep them out of harm's way."

She grabbed the sword out of his hand, forestalling further investigation, and then swung it hard at the wall. That odd echoing noise sounded throughout the room again. Reese's head swiveled immediately, distracted from the swords, staring at the grey stone.

"Do that again," he asked, focusing intensely.

Kay complied, striking harder, and again the sound echoed through the room with a hollow reverberation.

Reese picked up the other sword and, as she had done previously, began moving along the wall. He struck the stone in various locations, narrowing down the area of interest. Finally he stepped back, staring at the wall.

"About five feet wide," he mused, "and clearly different from the surrounding structure."

"Maybe it is the tunnels Leland spoke of!" enthused Kay.

Reese turned to look at her in confusion. "What tunnels?"

Kay smiled. "Old smuggling tunnels," she confided. "Leland said that … Lord Weston … had them filled in long ago – at least the ones he could find. They were a legacy from Lord Weston's grandfather and his fear of being trapped in the keep without a way to get out."

Reese gave another hard rap to the wall. "It sounds like this one, at least, was not fully filled in." His eyes roamed the wall, and suddenly he dropped to one knee, brushing at the stone. "What is this? Maybe a note about the tunnel?"

"What, let me see," insisted Kay, and she dropped to her knees besides him.

He pointed at a carving in the grey stone.

Kay looked at the stone, and then rocked back, flushing even more deeply. She had forgotten about that.

There, carved into the stone over ten years ago, was a crudely shaped heart. She had done that over the course of several years, making the lines deeper and deeper, leaving her mark on her sanctuary. Within the heart was "Kay", and then a plus sign, and below it … nothing.

"That … that was me," she admitted quietly.

Reese brushed away more of the dirt, and suddenly he was silent. The moment stretched on. Finally, he quietly commented, "I suppose you were interrupted before you could write in the name of your true love."

Kay shook her head, staring again at the carven heart. She could feel the angst and hope and dreams of those years, of coming down to stare at the heart, to wish against all odds …

"No," she responded in a whisper.

"I do not understand …"

Kay reached out a hand and ran her finger along the edge of the heart. "There was never anyone," she admitted, and she echoed with the pain as she put it into words. "There was no man who loved this place as much as I did, who I could trust to stand by my side, to stay with me, to defend its walls with the passion I felt." Her shoulders hunched. "There was never anyone."

She drew her hand back, staring at the heart. "I always hoped that someday, somehow, I would find a man who was content with this rocky corner of the world, who was content with -"

Her throat closed up, and she could not continue.

"Content with you," finished Reese quietly.

Kay found she could only nod in agreement.

Reese was silent for a long moment. He glanced up at the wall before them, then gave himself a small shake. "Maybe we should let Galeron know of this, for his notes to shore up the keep -"

"No!" cried out Kay, grabbing at his arm.

He stilled instantly, turning to look at her.

"Not this," insisted Kay, knowing her feeling was irrational, but she could not stop herself. "I do not want Galeron to see this."

Reese nodded slowly. "As you wish," he agreed. He stood, and offered his hand down to her.

She took it, drew herself up to be by his side, but she could not bring herself to release his fingers from hers, to release the warm touch of his hand in hers.

It was Reese who finally broke the spell. "Do not forget the swords Keren-happuch sent you for," he reminded her. "Undoubtedly she hopes to give her sister, Mary Magdalene, hers back as well." He reached over and picked up the pair of wooden weapons. "K and M," he read, handed them to her.

Kay nodded, then moved through the room, putting out the torches, before heading back up the stairs toward the light.

Chapter 12

Kay looked over Galeron with a careful eye, her feet tucked beneath her, watching as he went over his detailed notes yet again with her sister. She listened as the words rolled out of his mouth, as he detailed the pounds of lard, the quantity of wood beams, the man-hours of effort that would go into making the Serenor Keep come up to his standards.

He was certainly a handsome man, she determined, taking a sip of her ale. His jet-black curls hung almost in ringlets around his face, and his dark eyes were sharp, engaged in their task. His red cloak cascaded over his wide shoulders, catching on one side where his sword hung. His hands were steady and sure as they flipped through the pages in his codex.

Galeron would certainly be good with the details, with tracking the harvest and ensuring every last grain of wheat was accounted for. Logically, this should make her content.

"Kay? I am leaving now ..." Galeron was standing, smiling down at her, and she blushed. Apparently she had lost track of time, become unaware of the goodbyes which had been going on before her.

"Yes, of course," she replied with a smile. "Enjoy your morning ride."

He swept down a bow toward her, then one toward the black curtain, and in a moment he had strolled out the door. To Kay's surprise, Reese did not come sauntering in at the same time, and her heart tightened. She forced herself to laugh, to shrug off the sensation. He would be here soon. With the contest coming down to only the two men, it was natural that the schedule would be off a little.

Em's voice floated through the curtain wall. "So, we have a pair of final contenders," she commented quietly, her usual levity tempered by a note of seriousness. "Things become far more difficult."

Kay leant back on the couch, tension settling into her shoulders. "The two men both have admirable traits; both seem perfectly suited in some ways." She glanced up toward the curtain. "I know you, with your logical mind. You would argue in favor of Galeron."

There was a long pause. "I admit, there is a lot to be said for someone who pays attention to the details, who can ensure that nothing is overlooked," admitted Em thoughtfully. "We are talking about the safety of almost a hundred people, after all. It is an awesome responsibility."

Kay looked down at her metal goblet, turning it slowly in her hands. "And yet," she responded wistfully, "I cannot help but remember that night in the torrential rainstorm. Galeron was logical, analytical, and he would have saved the mother horse while abandoning the foal. He made the calculation and came up with the odds. While Reese -"

Em's voice was quiet, holding a note of caution. "Reese risked your life," she reminded her sister.

Kay shook her head, her gaze lost in the memory. "Reese stood by me," she countered. "Reese was there when I needed him. Reese did not waver, or argue, or quote Bible passages, or count the odds. He simply stood by me." She looked up at the dark curtain, her eyes looking through its thick layers, making that connection with her sibling beyond. "And, God as my witness, when he caught me in his arms -"

There was a clearing of a throat behind her, and Kay felt as if her face had suddenly caught on fire, as if the candles on the shelf had melted their wax and soaked into her skin. Reese walked in through the door, and she turned her head to her ale, taking in a long drink, reaching to refill it. She did not glance over again until he had settled himself into his seat; had faced himself at the long, black curtain wall.

Em's voice was steady when it came out from the ebony depths. "So, Reese, now we are down to two. Galeron engaged us with a thorough listing of what Serenor needs in order to be up to his specifications. What shall we talk of with you?"

His mouth quirked into a soft smile. "I suppose we could talk about the many ways in which Serenor is perfect just the way it is."

Kay's heart leapt, and her eyes automatically went to meet his. Warmth swept through her, imbued her toes, her fingers, soaked into her spine and radiated out until every part of her felt as if she were glowing. She knew it, suddenly, as an absolute reality.

She wanted him to win.

Reese looked away suddenly, and she flushed, confused, drawing herself back to just where she was, what was going on. She could not let emotions cloud her judgment. She *had* to objectively figure out what was best for the keep.

Reese's voice had a tinge of hoarseness as he asked Em, "Can I ask what is likely to happen next? Once you choose one of the candidates, I mean."

There was a short pause, then Em replied, "I suppose that is a fair enough question, now that we are down to the end." Another pause, and when Em spoke again her voice had shades of embarrassment in it. "I will confess that my father is rather stodgy in some regards," she admitted. "Once the engagement is agreed on, he wants word to be sent immediately – that very minute – so he can come and oversee the arrangements. The messenger will leave this keep and arrive back home within the day. That would mean he would arrive – with the remaining Serenor troops as well as his own retinue – the following evening."

Reese's eyes twinkled, and he nodded. "I am not unfamiliar with that mindset," he agreed. "My elder brother has made me swear, on my honor, that, should I be accepted, that I send word that very minute to him. And if things do not work out, I myself must instantly head out to ride home and inform him personally of my failings."

Kay glanced at the curtains for a moment. "Elder siblings can certainly be demanding at times," she huffed.

Reese became solemn. "I do not begrudge my brother his ownership of the estate; it is the way these things go. Zeke has always been a role model for me to look up to. He has managed our home with fairness and compassion." He looked down to the leather pouch which hung on his belt. "And he surprised me beyond words with his generosity."

Kay found herself leaning forward. "Oh?"

Reese nodded, fingering the belt. "My mother passed away when we were young, after a lingering disease. Everything she owned became part of the estate; became the possessions of my brother and his wife. And yet, when he heard I was to come out here to vie for the hand of the Serenor maiden, he gifted me with her most precious possession. An intricately worked necklace."

Kay nodded in understanding. "And that is why he wants to hear the resolution or have you return."

Reese's eyes came up to meet hers, and she was lost in them, drawn inexorably by the depth of their pull. It was a physical loss when he turned away, aligned to face the curtain again.

"Yes," he agreed quietly, "this necklace means a great deal to both of us. It was my mother's favorite item, one she wore daily. If it is not to go on the neck of the mistress of Serenor, it needs to promptly return to a safe location. I swore an oath to my brother, and I will stand by that."

Em's voice was somber. "I would hope none would stand in your way."

A knife twisted in Kay's stomach. Standing in the way of Reese leaving? She launched to her feet, turning to look out the window in consternation.

In an instant Reese was at her side, his eyes gazing down on hers.

"Are you all right?"

Kay starting to shake her head, then caught herself and nodded. "I am just hungry," she deferred, her emotions in turmoil. "Perhaps if we went down early for lunch?"

Reese held out his hand. "Yes, certainly," he agreed, glancing back at the curtain. "Until tomorrow, then, Keren-happuch?"

"Enjoy your lunch," agreed Em's voice, but Kay barely heard it as she moved across the solar and down the smooth stone steps toward the main hall.

Galeron was already sitting at the head table as they moved through the scattering of maids and soldiers. He was scribbling notes on his tablet, but he glanced up as they approached and tucked it away with a smile, putting out a welcoming arm.

"You are down early!" he grinned. "All the better, for the soup is almost ready! Here, sit down and enjoy." He motioned toward the two chairs beside him.

Kay allowed Reese to pull out the middle chair, and settled herself into it as he seated himself on her other side. In a moment Anne and Jessica had brought out fresh bread, dill butter, and a plate of sliced cucumbers.

"To decisions!" called out Galeron with a smile, and Kay and Reese joined in the toast, but Kay's heart tightened with the clinking action, with the long, hard pull she made to her ale. Decisions were getting harder, were threatening to pull her heart and her soul apart.

Galeron's steady voice dripped into her awareness. "So, Kay, what is the nature of a decision to you? What if there are two choices and there is no clear cut answer?"

Kay took another long pull on the ale, and Anne was at her side, refilling her tankard as if by magic. "There is always an answer," murmured Kay, staring down into her dark brew.

"Ah," chuckled Galeron, "But sometimes perhaps there are multiple questions. What is best for Situation X? What is best for Situation Y?"

Kay took up her knife, taking a long draw on the dill infused butter, making a show of smearing every last bit of the bread in her hand with the yellow substance. Galeron was right, of course. If the question was who was the logical choice for managing the exact operations of the keep, she might be forced to say Galeron had the qualifications. She ate deliberately at the bread, then took a handful of the cucumber slices and worked on those. Galeron had tallied the issues to fix. He had paid attention to the weak chains and the worn links. His knowledge would be invaluable.

She reached for another roll. Reese's hand was there, and she glanced up at him, her heart catching. He placed a roll in her hand, and she barely felt it, so lost was she in his eyes. Were they sea grey, or the blue of the sky in winter, the soul of Serenor?

She shook herself, returning her gaze to the table, breaking apart the roll, buttering it with deliberation, eating it piece by piece.

Could she be that selfish, to choose based on the yearnings of her heart, no matter how strong they were? Could she risk the lives of a hundred good men and women, all to satisfy her own childish needs for affection?

Galeron's voice came low in her ear. "It is hard, sometimes, to reconcile between what is best for your purposes and what is best for your needs."

Kay looked up at that and saw he was serious, that his eyes held a glimpse of a hard truth she had not noticed before. She turned to Reese and saw his eyes had the same firm cast, that the discussion had struck him to the core as well.

Kay could not take it any more. She pushed her chair back, and both men stood as she did.

"I need to go to the courtyard," she said without thinking. She flushed once the words had come to her mouth. She craved the exercise, the action that she normally found in her swordplay with the soldiers here and at her father's home. She could not do that here, not with Galeron and Reese attentive, but it was too late to draw back her words. She turned and moved quickly through the crowd, down the staircase, and out the main doors to where the soldiers were moving through their routines.

Galeron and Reese were at her shoulder in a moment, looking over the group of men with interest. Galeron's tablet came to his hand as if by levitation. "Ah, excellent," he commented. "I will be able to enumerate their strengths and weaknesses."

Kay took another step forward, sweeping her hands through her hair. Strengths and weaknesses. She saw none of that. She saw her friends, her companions she had grown up with, swinging their swords in unison, now drawing them high into a guard to the left, now stepping forward to block a low cut. Desire carved through her, to join them, to lose herself in that familiar routine, to shed off the worries and decisions and confusions of the past week and just be as she had always been. To immerse herself in the meditation, to forward step, the lunge to the right, the pivot -

Jevan stepped before the group of men and held up his hands. "Very good," he called out. "Divide up into pairs, and for today we will work on fast, high attacks." In a moment the men were dodging and slicing, shedding blows and spinning to counter-attack. Kay's longing almost overwhelmed her core. If only she could join them for a few moments -

A small, pink shape darted out from the right side, and Kay cried out in disbelief. Molly, her red curls bouncing, had raced into the center of the fighting men, laughing with glee, chasing a tiny fuzz-ball of grey and white.

"Molly!" cried out Kay in panic, diving forward. She grunted in shock and disbelief as a strong, unmoving arm grabbed her hard around her waist.

Galeron's voice was implacable at her ear. "Hold on there, you fool!" he chided her. "This is a man's work."

Outrage filled every aspect of her core, but before she could turn to argue, a blur was dodging through the fighters. In a moment Reese had reached the child, had snagged her and the kitten, and drawn them up in a safe embrace.

Javan looked around in confusion. "Hold!" he cried out. "What is that?"

Reese held up the child. "I have her; you can continue." He worked his way back over to the side of the courtyard.

Kay's heart pounded, and she ripped away Galeron's arm from her chest, a mixture of frustration and fury threatening to sweep her away. She dropped down to one knee, rousing her attention to focus on Molly, to draw her from Reese's protective embrace into a warm hug.

"You silly girl, what did you think you were doing?" she asked, looking down at the innocent face.

"Kitty!" announced Molly with a bright smile, nuzzling the fuzzy ball in her arms.

Galeron shook his head with amusement. "Little girl, you must learn that swords and armor are no place for a female! Stay safe with your dolls and kitties in the keep."

Molly gave a short curtsey. "Yes, uncle Galeron," she responded dutifully, then giggled and raced up the stairs in through the main doors.

Kay glanced from Galeron to Reese, from Galeron's satisfied smile to the twinkle in Reese's eye. She looked again into the large, solid doors of the keep, closing behind Molly's small hand. The women were safely within, the men ringing sword on sword without.

Her heart plummeted. No matter who she chose, she would have to leave her passion for swords and self-sufficiency behind. She was only a girl. There was no place for her to have both a husband and a sword in her hand. Neither of the men would accept it.

She found herself striding, then running. In a moment she was up the steps to the wall, moving along the path, and circling to the back.

She stared out at the ocean, mourning the loss of one of her dearest dreams.

* * *

The sky was tingeing in cascades of oranges and saffron colors when Jevan came up beside her. He offered her a roll, and she grabbed it from him. She wolfed it down in about five seconds, her stomach rumbling.

"I had not realized it was so late," she admitted, as she reached for the second roll he held in his other hand. "Is dinner already over?"

Jevan smiled fondly. "I am sure they put a plate aside for you," he responded. He handed her the skin at his belt, and she gratefully drew down the ale within.

Jevan waited until she had finished before continuing, more quietly, "There is a tough choice ahead; I understand that."

Kay looked out over the ocean, as she had been doing for the past hours, drawn into the ebb and flow of the waves. She thought of the longings which filled her heart – and of the needs of the keep around her. The duties of her station and the desires of her soul seemed at war.

She shook her head and turned to look at Jevan. "Jevan, can we talk a moment of Sarah, your wife?"

Jevan nodded, his face becoming more serious.

Kay looked down for a moment. "I know it is still hard for you, even after two years. We all mourned when Sarah died during childbirth. She was a wonderful friend."

Jevan smiled slightly, holding her gaze. "I have sworn to keep Sarah's memory alive for Joey and Paul," he responded quietly. "They only had a few years with her, so it is my duty to ensure they know what an amazing mother they had. That they know everything there is to understand about her."

Kay leant against the crenellated stone wall, the cool breezes rising as the sun slipped beneath the horizon. Her voice, when she spoke again, was as soft as the wind which slipped along the castle wall.

"How did you know?"

Jevan nodded slowly, his gaze unfocusing. "There were women who were more beautiful, who had hair that shone like burnt gold; whose lips were like ripe plums. But I looked at them and I knew that charms fade, that beauty slips away, and that any attractions of lust of eyes are of the moment only."

His voice became quieter. "There were women who were more adept at alluring talents – who told sweeter tales, who designed snares and nets woven from words. But those talents are made for courting and rarely last beyond the threshold of commitment."

He looked down at his hands, rubbing a finger along the gold band which still adorned his finger, almost caressing it. "What sustains a couple through ice-enshrined winters and through sultry summers, through the parched deserts and the stormy seas, is an absolute trust in each other, and a friendship which backs each other up without question."

Kay felt her friend's loss as a wound in her own heart, and she put a hand on his arm. "It must be hard to be without her," she offered softly.

Jevan's head dropped, and she saw his eyes fill with tears. "It is something you grow to accept, never something you get over," he responded, his voice ragged. "It was months before I gave up hope that somehow she would return to me."

Kay stood holding his arm for long minutes before he drew his sleeve across his face, looking back up at her.

"Your sister would say to go with the logical choice," he commented finally, his voice still rough.

Kay chuckled wryly. "You know her well," she agreed. "And for Keren-happuch, perhaps those are words of wisdom. She needs a man who can fortify the keep, who can detail the ounces of ale and servings of cod."

Jevan's voice was soft. "But for you, Kay, what is it that you long for?"

Kay turned, her heart aching, staring out at the rolling sea, at the movement of waves beneath the mother of pearl moon as it shimmered into life in the onyx sky.

"God, Jevan, it is so much more than a longing, it is a craving, a cascading desire that saturates every corner of my being -"

His arm came around her, and he pulled her close, pressing a fond kiss against her forehead. "Ah, my child," he offered gently, "then you should tell him."

There was a movement behind them, and Kay pulled apart, turning to see who approached. Reese stood there, a pair of rosy red apples in one hand, a jug of ale in the other, his face lost in the shadows.

Kay's heart leapt into her chest. Had she said anything to compromise her sister? Just what had they been talking about? Her mind raced over the topics - Jevan's wife and his sense of loss. Perhaps she was safe?

"Thank you," she choked out, taking the fruit. Jevan accepted the pottery jug, and then Reese was turning, fading into the deep darkness of the night, and was gone.

Chapter 13

Kay cantered down the road from the chapel through the brilliant morning sunshine, her heart soaring, her skin glowing, the dewy trail leading her back to her keep, her home. Today would be the day. Today they would gently ask Galeron to leave, and she could admit the truth to Reese. She could leave behind all the curtains and hiding. She would hold nothing back and give herself to him fully.

A shadow seemed to drift across the sun, and she shook off the cold chill. She glanced over her shoulder at the chapel, a long sigh escaping her. She would have to give that up. She knew Reese's feelings about sword fighting. She adored the exercise, the feeling of control – but all of that paled before her love of Serenor and her feelings for Reese. She could make that sacrifice.

The gates of the main wall moved over her head. She pulled into the bailey as if she were floating, handing the reins off to Stephen with a wide smile, moving with light feet up the main steps and over to the long spiral. It seemed only seconds before she was stepping through the ornate oak door and coming up to stand before Em, her heart pounding in excitement.

But … Em was not smiling. Her face was somber. Her eyes held Kay's with concern.

Kay's breath caught. "What is it?" she cried out in alarm, her eyes dropping immediately to Em's round belly. "Is something wrong with the baby?"

Em shook her head slowly, taking a step forward.

"Kay, it is Reese. He came by to see me earlier, while you were at the chapel practicing."

"What, alone? Why would he do that?"

Em took in a deep breath, then let it out again. "He has withdrawn his name. He is no longer interested in being Lord of Serenor."

Kay felt as if she had been punched in the stomach; she nearly doubled over with the pain. Em rushed to her side, supporting her, and it was several moments before Kay could catch her breath to speak.

"Where is he?" she gasped out in shock, her mind frantic.

He could not leave, could not abandon her!

"Stephen sent word that he has left the keep," explained Em sadly. "I am so sorry, Kay. I wish -"

Kay did not hear the rest of her sentence. She was running, tumbling, racing down the stairs as fast as she could go, taking them two at a time, her breath coming in great heaves. She could not lose him, not now.

Her horse was just being led into his stall as she raced into the stables. Stephen took one look at her face and spun the steed in place, bringing him back out as Kay slipped the bridle over his head and set the bit in place. In a few moments the horse was resaddled and she was vaulting on top of him, pulling hard on the reins, wheeling him out of the doorway, and thundering through the main gates.

Her horse flew across the road at a gallop. She urged him harder, leaning low over his mane. She craved every last ounce of speed, every extra second to get to Reese before he vanished, before he disappeared from her life, left her alone, alone ...

She rode up over the crest of the hill and suddenly a grateful relief washed over her. There he was, far ahead, his horse cantering along the road with steady rhythm. She dug in her calves, and they were flying, soaring, racing down toward Reese as if nothing else mattered in the world. As if her reaching his side was the only thought that existed.

Reese spun as she drew near, standing up in his stirrups, pulling into a halt. By the time she wrenched her reins to a skidding, spinning stop near him, his face was tight with anger.

"What in God's teeth are you thinking, riding like that?" he shot out, pulling alongside her with a snap of his reins. "You could have been killed!"

Kay's voice was ripped out of her in anguish. "Where are you going?" she pleaded, drawing in her breath in long gasps.

Reese's eyes held hers, and the anger softened as he took in her distraught state. "I was heading home, to talk with my brother," he quietly advised her. "I vowed, on my honor, to return the instant I was no longer in the running for Serenor."

"Why did you make that choice?" pleaded Kay, turning her body to gaze back at the keep, nestled in the autumn colors, the mists of morning still gently swirling about its base. "Is this not the most beautiful place on earth?" Her voice caught. "I thought you felt the way I did, that you wanted to stay here forever ..."

Beside her, she felt Reese turn his gaze, staring out alongside her toward the sweep of the meadow, the line of the road. Suddenly he started, and Kay's eyes tracked, following the line of his eyes.

She squinted against the bright sun to make out the tiny figure moving across the greenery. A lone horseman was riding out from the keep, moving at an easy lope. Kay drew her eyes along to his destination and found a cluster of dots waiting down in the hollow of Lover's Lane. She could make out four ... no, five figures on horseback waiting down there, safely hidden from the sharp eyes in the keep.

Swordsmen. MacDougals.

Kay swept her eyes back to the lone figure. Who was betraying them? Could any member of her household be turned by money?

Her breath caught. A flash of red blazed out from the cloak he wore as it swirled in the wind. Fury roiled within her as the full import of the scene took hold.

"The traitor!"

Her hand flashed to her hip and swept open air. She wheeled her horse, preparing to charge out. "I will bring them in myself!"

A strong hand grabbed at her reins. "Kay, think! They are six armed men!" he insisted, pulling her in. "We have to get help!"

"We have to get weapons," snarled Kay, spinning her mount again, kicking him into a gallop, heading toward the chapel, almost at the halfway point between her and the clearing, but higher to the right.

"Where are you going?" cried out Reese at her side, his horse in a full gallop, his gaze sweeping between the chapel and the keep.

"To the chapel," shouted back Kay in frustration. Surely that was evident? She urged her steed to even faster lengths.

"Why?" he insisted, and she shook her head, focusing on the ride. There would be time enough for explanations later. Right now she had to make it to the chapel, to get to Galeron before he turned over his lists, his copious notes, to the enemy. She could not believe how stupid she had been. She had watched him, this entire time, as he recorded every detail of the keep, charted every flaw, every issue while refusing to fix even the smallest latch.

He had been cataloguing for an attack.

The chapel was suddenly before her, and she reined in hard, spinning to a stop. Leland and Eli were before her in a moment, still in their leather gear, their eyes seeking to hers in surprise.

"Eli, get to the keep," she ordered as she leapt off her horse, moving toward the chapel. "Galeron is a traitor. He is at this very moment meeting with the enemy, down in Lover's Lane."

"On it," he responded without hesitation, racing behind the building toward the back shed.

Kay did not break her stride. She moved into the main chapel, headed toward the trunk, pulled out the leather jerkin, and slid it over her head in one smooth pull. She did not pause one moment, putting her hands up over her head once it was settled, allowing Leland to wrap the belt and scabbard around her waist, buckling it into position. He reached over to the wall where her sword hung, tossing it to her, and she slid it into the sheath with an easy movement. She reached under the jerkin, pulling out the dagger and resettling it tucked into her sword belt.

Leland's voice was even. "How many are there?" he asked, giving her a once-over and adjusting her jerkin with a practiced eye.

"Six all together," she responded, her throat tight. "Odds are three to one."

"Two to one," corrected a calm voice from the doorway.

Kay spun, looking up at Reese. Her heart caught as she took in her outfit; the sword at her side. She had failed.

Everything was lost now, and yet she could not pause; could not give thought to it. Everything depended on her intercepting Galeron before he turned over his copious notes.

"This is not your fight," she managed to bite out, her voice tense. "This will be serious; it is the very life of Serenor."

"I will ride at your side," he insisted, his gaze not wavering. His eyes did not move from hers.

Kay gave herself a shake. There was no time for discussion. She launched into motion, and in a moment all three were mounted, riding hard toward the clearing, thundering in a line. The time streamed by in hoofbeat and flying dirt. It seemed only minutes before they crested the ridge and moved down into the bowl. The six men below them spun their horses, gathering around in an opposing guard.

The dust raised and settled.

Kay drew in a long breath, her eyes held firmly on Galeron's.

"You will not turn over those notes to the MacDougals," she shot out, her voice hot. "You will come with us back to the keep."

Galeron's eyes warmly swept her, taking in her appearance and sword. "You continually impress and astonish me, my dear," he complimented her. He glanced at Reese for a moment. "You had not abandoned Serenor after all," he added wryly.

"Never," agreed Reese, drawing his sword, moving to a position at Kay's right.

Galeron's eyes moved across to Leland. "Ah, Leland," he grinned, nodding in recognition as he saw the man now outfitted in leather armor. "So you are the quiet 'priest' at the hillside chapel. I should have known Lord Weston would not leave his daughter unguarded. Still, his Captain of the Guard – I am impressed. So you have been lurking nearby, keeping an eye on his precious valuables?"

"I will guard her with my life," snarled Leland, drawing his sword, moving to Kay's other side.

Galeron's mouth quirked into a smile as Reese looked over in surprise at Leland, then met his own eyes again.

Galeron's voice was light. "I give you one last chance," he offered. "Leave now, and let us go on our way. The odds are against you. If you come at us, we will have no choice but to defend ourselves."

Kay ran her eyes over the man before her, the man she had trusted, had joked with, had almost considered to take as a husband.

"Never."

Galeron nodded in understanding. "I suppose I expected no less," he agreed. He turned to the men to either side of him. "Take down her two companions, but leave her untouched," he ordered. "She is to be mine, after all."

They charged.

The world erupted into spinning hooves, clashing swords, calls of attack, and high whinnies. The enemies split into two halves. Kay brought her sword high above her, diving in at one of the men on Reese's flank. The soldier turned in surprise, driving across at her, swinging a sword down and across to disarm her.

She turned deftly, wheeling her horse and pulling hard on her reins to rear him up. The steed leant back, turning under her command, spinning with raised hooves.

Her opponent cried out in surprise, falling under the striking hooves. His body landed hard on the ground.

Kay's horse sprung forward under her guidance, and she was on one of Leland's attackers in a second. The swordsman engaged her, drawing his attention from

Leland, blocking her swing and immersing into a swift exchange of blows. She dove in toward his side, spinning her horse, and he turned with her, swinging his sword wide to keep her clear. She gave her steed a nudge …

There was a shout from above, and she turned her head sharply, looking to spot the fresh danger. Had reinforcements come to Galeron's aid so quickly?

There was a sharp pain at her thigh, and she cried out in surprise. In an instant Reese was at her side, his sword high, taking out the soldier with one twisting slash and moving to protect her.

Galeron and the two remaining soldiers turned and fled toward the north as the keep's troops thundered down the hill, drawing in around the trio.

Leland drew up by Kay in concern. "How bad are you, girl?" he snapped, shaking his head. "Have I not told you a thousand times to keep your attention on your opponent?"

Reese was at her other side, his eyes sharp on the wound. "We need to get you back to the keep," he murmured. His eyes went up to Leland's.

Leland held his for a long moment, then nodded. "I will trust her in your care, then," he stated at last. "Be sure you are worthy of that trust."

"I swear I am," vowed Reese, his eyes steady.

Leland nodded again, then turned, raising his sword. "After the traitors!"

In an instant the troops had moved with him, thundering to the north after the retreating three.

Reese dismounted in a moment, drew his dagger, and sliced a length off the bottom of his tunic. He bound up the long, jagged slash on Kay's leg.

"Can you make it back to the keep?" he asked in a low tone.

"I will not fall," promised Kay with heat. "I will get that man in irons if it is the last thing I do!"

She waited for him to remount, then she pushed her horse hard, heading back at a canter, wincing in agony with each movement and willing herself not to falter. Reese was aside her at every movement, his eyes sharp on her, keeping time alongside her with easy skill.

It seemed too long before they were pulling into the main gates, before she was falling off her horse, before he was catching her and carrying her into the infirmary. She was laid down on the bed, and Anne was leaning over her, clucking at her in weary acceptance.

"Oh, Kay, what have you done now," she tsked, drawing a knife. She cut the lower dress material away from her leg and removed the makeshift bandage Reese had wrapped around the wound. The long, sharp-edged cut began to bleed freely and the blonde cursed, reaching for a nearby ointment.

Reese moved in to help, taking hold of a fresh dressing and pressing it down on the wound to hold back the blood while he worked.

A woman's voice called from the entryway, the tone strong and steady. "Reese."

He turned in surprise at the familiar sound, then froze, his eyes sweeping down her form in a long look.

Em strode into the infirmary, one hand resting on her swollen belly. Her eyes moved to Kay's jagged injury, her brow creasing in concern. Her eyes flicked to Reese for only a moment before returning to the woman lying, moaning, on the bed.

"Leave us, please," she ordered without looking up.

Reese pursed his lips, cataloguing the clear evidence of Em's pregnancy. He glanced down at Kay with a last, tender look.

And then he nodded, turned, and strode from the room, leaving the sisters alone.

Chapter 14

Em settled onto a stool at Kay's side, examining the injury with attentive eyes. "Oh, Kay, what happened this time?" she sighed, shaking her head. "This is far beyond a minor scrape."

Kay winced in pain as Anne worked on the wound, biting back a cry. "It was Reese who saw them from the high road," she informed her sister, her breath coming in short, shaking draws. "We rode to the chapel for arms, then on to confront Galeron."

"And Galeron attacked you?" snapped Em, her voice harsh.

Kay shook her head. "To be fair, he asked for us to part ways without swords," she explained. "We could hardly allow that, given the knowledge he has about the keep!"

She gasped as something was pressed against her leg, her breath leaving her in a sharp exhale.

Em looked up. "How is she, Anne?"

"She will mend," the maid muttered, focused on her careful wrapping of the cloth bandage. "At least she might, if she would only stay still for a few weeks."

"A few weeks," ground out Kay, shaking her head. "We will be lucky to have a few hours." Her eyes glanced toward the door. She gave a long sigh of relief. "At least I will be able to end this charade with Reese. It has gotten so difficult, these past days."

Em shook her head with a deliberate movement. "No, not now," she corrected in a steady voice.

Kay's eyes shot to her sister's, her face creasing in agony. "What good could it possibly do to keep up the farce now? The game is over! Our keep is about to be under assault!"

Em took Kay's hands in her own, her face somber. "I know how you feel, but think about it," she soothed, holding her sister's eyes with her own. "What if we are overrun? Reese is a man of honor, and you are relying on his ability to deceive with absolute perfection." Her gaze became more serious. "Just one mistaken word will reveal all. Galeron's attention to detail is staggering. One glance, one movement, could alert him."

Em gave a gentle squeeze to Kay's fingers. "If Galeron realizes he has two hostages, and not just one, imagine what he might do."

"I cannot put you at risk," ground out Kay. "If anyone is to be taken for ransom, it should be me."

A slight smile eased onto Em's face. "What, and you will somehow convince Galeron that I am not worthy of holding? Remember, he had been told about the blonde sister, Mary. He had been told Mary was pregnant. The moment he sees me, and you at my side, he might remember those details and guess who we are." She shook her head. "Our only hope is to hold off that knowledge for as long as possible. I need to stay hidden, and you need to stay in place as Kay, my maid. If he thinks he only has one hostage to chase down, it gives us an advantage."

"I trust Reese with my life," vowed Kay, her voice hoarse with emotion.

Em shook her head again. "I am afraid that I do not. Again, it only takes one word, one mistake to undo this. We have been very lucky so far, that everyone has done so well with the names. We only need to keep this up for another two days, until Father arrives. Remember, he is already on his way to us. It is best we stay with the status quo as best we can."

Kay's stomach knotted in frustration. It went against every fiber of her being not to tell Reese the truth.

Em's hands tensed on her own, and Kay looked up. She saw the worry which swirled in her sister's eyes. Her gaze dropped down to the unborn child swelling within her sister's body, innocent and helpless.

Kay's resolve weakened, and her shoulders slumped. If anyone had a right to make this decision, it was Em. Her sister clearly had the most to lose if something went wrong. If this is what Em truly wanted, then Kay would stand by her.

Reluctantly, her eyes still lowered, she nodded her assent. She longed with every fiber of her being to tell Reese, but she acquiesced, pushing away the growing pain in her heart.

There was the noise of running feet from the hall, and both turned their heads in alert attention. In moments Leland burst into the room with Reese hard on his heels. Leland scanned the room as he skidded to a stop, his face relaxing in relief as he spotted Kay leaning back on her bed.

"Keren!" he called out, coming up alongside her. "What is the damage?"

Em stood alongside Kay, catching Leland's eyes with a sharp, penetrating look. "Yes, I am here to look in on my maid. *Kay* will be fine with rest," she snapped.

Leland's eyes flicked between the two women, and he nodded in understanding. "That is good to hear, Keren-happuch."

Em's gaze went down to her sister's injury, and when she looked up at Leland again her gaze was smoldering. "So, tell me, how did my beloved Kay get injured?"

Leland flushed, his eyes holding hers. "I have no excuse," he stated without hesitation. "I should have protected her."

Key drew up to sit. "Hold on," she called out. "I launched us into that fight when Reese would have had us go back for support. I take the blame for what happened." She smiled, looking up at Leland. "Besides, I was only hurt because I looked away from my opponent when I heard hoofbeat on the ridge. If Leland has scolded me about that once -"

Em wheeled on Kay in outrage. "You took your eyes away from someone you were fighting?" she cried out in disbelief. "*That* is why you were hurt? You are lucky you only got your leg ripped open!"

Kay sighed, shaking her head. "I know, I know," she agreed, looking between Em and Leland. "I admit it. I was wrong. I got distracted. I learned my lesson. Can we move on?" She brought her gaze more fully on Leland. "Were you able to catch Galeron?"

Leland shook his head in frustration. "He must have studied every twist and turn of that area around the ravine. We scoured the area for any trace of them, but they were completely gone. I thought it best to come back and make sure word was sent for reinforcements."

Reese stepped forward. "We should send to Lord Weston for support as quickly as we can," he insisted. "We do not have the manpower to defend against a full attack."

Em nodded. "Word had already been sent," she confirmed. "We will have a full contingent of my father's men within two days."

"Which means a full thirty-six hours before anyone arrives back here," mused Kay, running a hand distractedly through her hair. "Galeron knows every problem with this keep - every issue, every weakness. He deliberately held us back on making repairs, so that he could make use of his knowledge." Her eyes went to Reese and Leland. "If Galeron returns with the full force of the MacDougals behind him, how long can we expect to hold out?"

Reese looked to Leland, his eyes somber. "We would be hard pressed to last that long," he admitted quietly. "The men here are willing, but you saw the lists that Galeron compiled, Kay. The main gates are worn. The hinges on the drawbridge are giving way. He is going to know exactly where to hit us."

"We will have to do our best," vowed Kay, glaring at her injured leg before pulling to swing around to the side of the bed. All three people moved forward in alarm, attempting to hold her back.

Kay shook her head in frustration. "I will not lie in bed when we are about to be overrun," she snapped, "leg be damned. Surely there is something I can do!"

Reese's eyes were steady on her. "You can sit in the solar," he advised. "You can act as a look out. If that wound festers, you will not do anyone any good."

"Sit in the solar," huffed Kay, her voice tense. "What, like father would punish me, locking me in my room. So I can sit there, staring out the window, staring out at that tree." She gave a low chuckle. "I suppose now I can stare at the tree and those carts ..."

Her voice trailed off, and suddenly she was in motion, pushing herself up and stumbling across the room.

"Good God, Kay, where are you going?" called out Reese. He came up alongside her, moved his arm around her waist, and caught her as she stumbled hard against him.

"I have to get to the solar," she ground out. "Those carts, those carts …"

She tripped again, and Reese drew her up, lifting her into his arms with a gentle heft. In a moment they were moving across to the stairs, climbing slowly but steadily up the long spiral. Behind her Kay could hear her sister being helped along by Leland.

Reese brought her over to the window and gently lowered her down. Her eyes went immediately to the covered wagons, and beside her Reese stiffened, his arm drawing tightly against her waist. They stood in silence as the footsteps came up the stairs, as Em and Leland came over to stand beside them.

Em looked out at the brightly lit meadows. "The carts are in motion?" she asked in surprise. She pressed forward, peering. "With an escort?"

"Fifty men," agreed Kay, her eyes moving across the tiny forms. "Thirty mounted." She watched them for another moment. "They are taking it slow – those carts must be heavily laden. It was all a ruse. The carts hold their siege gear, and they sat there right under our noses."

She glanced at the trees, then back at the slowly moving group. "I give them eight hours before they get within arrow range."

Reese turned to look at the others. "It will nearly be dark by then," he warned "They will be able to get to our doors by tomorrow dawn without a scratch."

"Not if I can help it," ground out Kay, glancing at Em. "When they reach that tree, we will be ready."

"Ready for what?" asked Reese, looking between the two.

"I have been shooting at that tree since I could walk," nodded Kay, looking back out the window. "I have great night vision. My lady has a strong arm. We would play a game. If I launch a lit arrow at something, and create a target, she can plow an arrow into the spot without fail. That tree was planted as our marker, the furthest we could shoot from this very window."

Leland nodded. "I will fetch your bows and as many arrows as I can gather," he agreed. "This is the best of all solutions. It keeps you two safe up here while the rest of the soldiers man the walls. Even if you can whittle down a few men as they go – or slow them up – it will be a huge assistance to our efforts." He turned and in a moment he was gone.

Kay turned to the window again, then staggered as her leg gave way. Reese was instantly supporting her; guiding her back to the couch. "It will be eight hours before you can do anything, before they are within range" he pointed out. "You should sleep now, to gain your strength. It sounds like it will be a long night."

Kay sat back on the couch, weariness overcoming her. "Normally I would argue, but I have to admit you are right," she sighed. "You just swear to wake me up the moment they are in range. I do not want to lose one moment of effort against them."

"I swear it."

His gaze softened as he looked down at Kay. "You are a woman who is full of surprises," he added quietly. "So much has gone on today. It is hard to know where to begin."

His eyes moved over to Em, to her rounded belly. "For example, I have a few choice words for your father, Keren."

Em's mouth tweaked into a smile. "I am sure you do," she agreed with a chuckle. "I am afraid that will have to wait until after we defend the keep and he reaches us."

Reese nodded. "I will do my best to ensure he finds this keep safe and sound, with all inhabitants equally secure." He bowed to both women, then turned.

Kay listened to his footsteps until they faded from hearing, and then she stretched out on the couch.

In moments she was fast asleep.

Chapter 15

Kay was lost. The cave network seemed to go on forever, an ant maze of twists and turns through the damp darkness. Another fork presented itself, and she looked down each path, desperately trying to sense even the slightest difference in brightness. Perhaps the left fork was slightly more reddish? She plowed forward.

There - yes - there was a lightening of the cave walls ahead, and suddenly she rounded the corner and came out into the cool air of the rocky beach. The dark sky was just tingeing ruby red with the coming dawn. And there, his back to her, looking out toward the horizon ...

Her heart leapt in relief.

"Reese!" she cried out, stepping forward.

But there was no sound at all when she made her call - the air was quiet, stagnant, and Reese did not turn. Instead he stepped forward.

Kay realized there was a long, low wooden boat pulled up to shore, with four pairs of sturdy men manning the oars.

Reese took a few more steps, boarded, and found a place at the aft end. In another moment the men pulled in unison. The boat slowly made its way through the low waves, moving out into the sea.

"Reese!" Kay attempted to scream his name, and yet she was mute; no sound emerged.

There was not a flicker of movement from Reese. He stared steadily out toward the distant sea.

She raced down the beach, chasing after him, but by the time she entered the water he was a good ten lengths away, making distance. The boat bobbed up and down over the waves which grew in intensity as the dawn began to spread across the sky in earnest.

"Reese!"

Kay felt as if she were shouting at the top of her lungs, pleading, crying for him to turn, and a seagull overhead mocked at her lack of voice. She began swimming as strongly as she could, plowing through the waves, but the incoming tide buffeted her back. The oarsmen had already doubled the distance.

Reese was fading into the morning mist .. he was leaving her ...

"Reeeeese!"

* * *

The sound of her plaintive howl echoed in her ears. And then he was there, holding her, wrapping her in musk and warmth and shelter and tenderness. He held her tightly against him, soothing her.

"I am here, I am here," he murmured in her ear.

She clung to him, her face wet with tears, sitting up on the couch, slowly returning to awareness from her vivid dream. It was several long minutes before her breathing slowed and she felt willing to pull back slightly, to look up into his face.

"I dreamt you were leaving me," she explained weakly, dragging a sleeve across her cheeks. "I called and called, but you could not hear me."

He brought a hand up to gently stroke her hair, a tender

smile drawing on his lips. "I am here," he repeated again, his eyes full on hers. "I am right by your side. I am not leaving."

Em gave her sister a fond pat on the head. "No one is leaving," she reminded the pair, moving to take a seat by the window. "Not as long as we have our friendly invaders camped outside. Speaking of which, Kay," she added, motioning with her head toward the darkening sky, "it is about time for you to stop lollygagging around and get ready with those toasty arrows of yours. I think our friends might finally be coming within range."

A frisson of fear rippled through Kay as the situation swept back into her mind. "Let me up," she murmured to Reese, pressing him back.

He stood at once, putting out a hand to her, but she ignored it, springing to her feet. Or so she attempted - her leg immediately buckled beneath her, searing in pain. It was only Reese's arm sweeping around her waist which kept her from crashing hard to the floor.

"Easy there," he chided, hauling her back up to a standing position. "You only ripped that one open earlier today, remember?"

Leland, coming in through the main door, shook his head in amusement as Kay warily settled herself on her feet. "And the other leg is still healing up from - what was that, four days ago?"

Kay put her hands to her head to fight off the miasma of pain which swirled around her forehead. "Just give me a few minutes," she muttered in exasperation.

A hand offered a tankard of mead to her, and she downed it in relief. The aches faded and her vision settled into focus.

"So," she offered, turning carefully and moving to the window, "They are almost within range now?"

Em nodded from the bench alongside her position. "Take a look."

Kay settled herself on the cushion, giving her eyes time to adjust to the darkness beyond. The sun had just sunk below the horizon and tendrils of orange glow were fading into twinkling stars. There was no moon out; the landscape was barely distinguished by a series of darker blotches.

"Put out the candles," she asked softly.

There was movement behind her, and in a moment the room plunged into darkness. Only a soft glow flickered from the fireplace, the lowest of fires nibbling on a half-gone log.

Kay moved her gaze methodically along the ring of trees, starting from the far left. The carts had been near the ridge of Lover's Lane earlier in the day, and during the hours of light they would have stayed well clear of the castle's arrow distance. That would have meant traversing, at great effort and little gain, the marshy swamps and bogs of the outer area. She had every sense that, now that they had the cover of darkness, the enemies would attempt to move in closer, to take advantage of the far better terrain.

"There," she whispered, pointing toward the first tree on the left. "I think they are just passing it now."

Three other sets of eyes came to the windows, peering into the darkness, seeking to make out a hint of movement, a shadow against a shadow.

Reese's voice was low. "I do not see anything, but I trust in your judgment. Shall we begin?"

Kay nodded.

In a moment Leland had brought over the four unstrung bows. He set up banks of arrows against each window. Kay's pitch-soaked arrows waited, ready, in their pail by the fireplace.

Leland then stood by the mantle and picked up one of

Kay's arrows in his hand, waiting.

Kay reached down and lifted the bow. Reese made to come over, and she held up a hand. "If I cannot even string my own bow, I am truly done for."

She pressed herself to her feet, biting down on a grunt of pain. Her leg ached as if someone had dragged a red hot poker along its length. She pushed the feeling away with effort. Then she stepped through the string, pulled the bow's bottom hard against her foot, and threw her weight down on the top of the arc. The bow resisted, but she wrestled it down, in, and secured the loop of the bowstring on the top end of the bow. She turned to kneel on the bench with her better leg, took in a deep breath, and held out her hand.

"I am ready. When the arrow hits, hopefully the men there will scramble to put it out, and you will have your targets."

Reese and Em strung their bows, and Reese set up Leland's as well. Then all eyes went to Leland.

"Here we go," he called out in a low voice. He put the tip of the arrow down into the coals of the fire.

The pitch blazed into sparkling life, and in a moment he had run the arrow across to Kay, handing it over to her in a smooth pass. She nocked it, sighted it, and let the arrow fly.

In the onyx black of the night the missile arced like an earthbound meteor, leaving a trail of stardust behind it. It soared down and across and into the murk …

THUNK.

The blaze suddenly stopped, impaling itself into the tree. In the splash of the hit they could clearly see, for a long moment, a large wagon pulled by two black horses. At least four soldiers moved alongside it, helping to push and steer it in the inky blackness.

Three bows twanged into life. The whistling arrows rose high, then raced down with gravity and pent up energy. They slammed into a chest, an arm, and the rump of one of the horses.

The flaming arrow was yanked from the tree and thrown to the ground.

The night, again, went pitch black.

Kay found the experience to be almost surreal. There had been no noise at all beyond the singing of the strings and the clean sound the arrows made leaving the solar. No call of alarm from the soldiers had reached their high, distant location. No screams of pain nor cries of the wounded animal. It was as if the events below were part of a dream.

Another blazing arrow was handed to her, and again she sent her missile down. Again the three siblings followed in hot pursuit, seeking out their targets. The fresh light illuminated the men huddling on the other side of the wagon, dragging one of their fallen comrades to safety, and snapping the arrow's shaft from the horse's side.

Darkness.

A blaze of light by her side.

Kay fell into the routine; followed the wagons along as they moved from tree to tree. The archers' first few volleys caught the invaders off guard, but soon those below realized what was happening. They hung leather over the sides of the horses to protect their flanks, kept to the safe side of the wagons, and darted out only in-between shots to pull a flaming arrow free or to push the cart out of a rut.

The hours twisted through the night, the rhythm inexorably moving along, the wagons inching steadily forward.

Then the gentle fingers of dawn stretched out against the sky. The wagons had reached the front of the keep, pulling back into the field to join with the mounted troop there.

Kay fell against the window, exhausted.

Reese looked at Leland. "Perhaps fifteen slain, another twenty injured?"

Leland nodded in agreement. "I put the numbers in that range. With the odds being so close, we may have tipped the scales in our favor. As long as they do not attack before late afternoon, our reinforcements will arrive and the worst of the danger will have passed."

Em looked between the two men, her face serious. "What do you think the chances are that they will attack sometime today?"

Reese stared back out the window. The besieging soldiers were in busy motion, pulling long sheets of fabric out of the wagons and erecting a pair of large tents. "It looks like they are settling in. Perhaps they, too, are expecting fresh arrivals in the coming days. This might be a preparation for a long, drawn out siege, rather than anything immediate. I would guess that we have little to fear today."

Leland looked over the tents with a sharp eye. "Those are fairly large," he mused. "Maybe twenty feet on a side? Perhaps they are planning a substantial meeting between the two families, although for what purpose I cannot guess."

Kay gazed at the activity with growing curiosity. "I want a closer look," she murmured, drawing to her feet.

Immediately, stabbing pain lanced through her, causing her leg to crumple. She fell hard against the sill.

Reese was at her side, holding her up.

"You need to stay here and heal up," he insisted. "You are no good to anyone if that wound becomes infected."

Kay shook her head, willing the pain to subside. "I will

just stand on the curtain wall," she promised. "I can get a far better look from there than from this window." She turned to Em. "Just in case, you stay here, and I will send Anne and Jessica up to wait on you."

"You be safe," replied Em with a frown. "You are injured, you know."

Kay glared in frustration at her throbbing leg. "Maybe a stop by the infirmary would be a good idea first," she amended with a reluctant sigh. "I need these legs in working order."

Reese didn't hesitate. "I will give you a hand," he offered. "You must be in agonizing pain if you are agreeing to get some medical help."

Leland chuckled. "You are getting to know our favorite patient," he teased with a wry smile. "I will get everyone up and out on the walls who can hold a sword. We need every show of strength for today." He glanced back out the window. "Galeron might have documented every last member of our staff, but the people with him can still be impressed by a show of force. We need to take advantage of every opportunity we have." He nodded at the trio and headed down the stairs.

Kay allowed Reese to help her up, and then slowly made her way over to the stairs. The narrow, twisting spiral made it challenging for him to assist her down the flight, but at a slow, steady pace they made it down to the main hall. Anne was moving across the room with a pitcher of mead, and Kay flagged her down with a wave.

"Could you and Jessica spend the afternoon with M'Lady today?" she asked, making sure she used the title for Em. It still felt funny on her tongue to say that, and her cheeks pinkened, lying in front of Reese like that. Surely the deception had gone on long enough …

She shook her head, resolutely plowing forward. "I

need to go out and keep an eye on our new friends," she added.

Anne smiled with pleasure. "Yes of course. I will fetch Jessica immediately. She is down in the storeroom." She turned and headed off through the tables at a trot toward the back of the room, to the small spiral staircase there that the keep staff used during meal service.

Reese offered his arm. "One more flight," he smiled. Then they were in motion again, each step adding new pains to the previous one. By the time they had reached the infirmary Kay was exhausted. She fell back into the familiar bed with welcome relief.

Reese's eyes went to hers. "All right, then, we might as well take a look at both legs while we are here." He drew back the dress to her mid-thigh.

Kay shifted on the bed in discomfort, and Reese immediately looked up. "Oh, did you want a woman present as a chaperone? I had not thought to ask if -"

Kay stared at him as if he were daft. "After everything we have gone through this week? The thought had not even crossed my mind!" She winced, stretching her body to be more straight. "It is just that this leg of mine is not doing well."

Reese bent over it, slowly unwinding the bandage from the skin and pulling the cloth free of the wound. "Ah, here is the problem - it was wrapped too tightly," he commented, prodding gently at the flesh. He took a rag, dipped it in the nearby pail of water, and began wiping away at the medicine layer. "We can freshen this up as well."

Kay eased back against the pillow, closing her eyes against the pain caused by his movements. "The herbs are over there, in the -"

"Yes, in the third drawer," agreed Reese with a smile.

"I have become quite familiar with your infirmary over the past week."

Kay kept her eyes closed as Reese moved about the room, mixed up the paste, rebandaged the leg, and then moved to redo the salve and bandage of her other leg. It seemed that the entire week had been a long series of her injuries, of Reese getting her out of one jam after another.

Her chest tightened with angst. The thought came to her again, vividly, the image crystal clear in her mind.

He had been leaving her.

"I suppose I am not the image of a proper woman," she whispered, half to herself.

Reese's hands suddenly stopped moving.

She reluctantly opened her eyes. He was staring down at her in incredulous surprise.

"What do you mean? Because you are allowing me to help your legs to heal?"

Kay shook her head, suddenly trembling, a sense of vulnerability sweeping through her. "I mean, because ..." Her shoulders hunched, and she wrapped her arms around her torso for a long moment. Finally she waved a hand down at the injuries on her legs. "Just look at me."

Reese gazed down at the wounds, finished the wrap on the second bandage with a tug, and then pulled her dress back down over the pair. His eyes came up to meet hers, to hold them with steady regard.

"I see a woman who stands up for what she believes in. A woman who not only can talk about what is right, but is willing to back her words up with action."

Kay moved to sit up, and a sharp twinge wrenched her abdomen where the small hoof-mark still troubled her. She chuckled wryly. "Leland and Em would say my actions are sometimes foolish at best."

Reese tilted his head in confusion. "Em?"

Heat flushed through her face, and she looked down at her hands for a moment to cover her slip. Her mind raced to find a suitable lie. "I … I call M'Lady 'M' sometimes, as a nickname," she stumbled. "I guess we have been together so long -"

Reese knelt at her side, raising her chin with his hand. "Kay, you do not have to justify yourself to me," he soothed. "You are the most honest, the most trustworthy woman I have ever met. If anyone is above blame in their actions or words, you are she."

The bottom dropped out of Kay's world. Everything was a lie. Her entire relationship with Reese was built on lies. Even as he praised her for being honest, he was doing so as the result of a falsehood. It was simply too much to bear.

But she had sworn to Em that she would maintain this charade, at least until her father had arrived. It was tearing her apart …

Reese's eyes clouded with concern. "Kay?"

There were footsteps in the hall, and Stephen huffed into the room, his young, stout face flushed from the exertion. "Kay, there you are. Leland needs to see you up on the wall."

Kay pushed herself to her feet, wincing against the pain, but sturdy for the first time in a day. "We are on our way," she responded. Reese stayed at her side as she moved slowly but steadily out to the hallway and then through the main doors.

It seemed as if Leland was true to his word – every man and teenaged boy was lined up along the keep wall, spaced apart to present more of a show of force. Kay's frustration with her injuries mounted as she trudged in cautious deliberation across the empty courtyard. It seemed as if every eye were on her as she made her way step by step up the narrow stair to the top level. Leland waited there for her, and he smiled with approval.

"You are looking much better – your time spent with Reese was well worth it."

Reese came alongside them, looking out toward the pair of tents. "She is healing well; I am sure her legs will be as good as new in no time. Is there a change in the situation?"

Kay crossed her arms on top of the wall and settled into place, staring with careful attention first at one tent, then the second. They were apparently made of rough, brown hemp, and about twenty feet on a side. The wagons were on their back side, hidden from view, and there was an occasional bump or movement to indicate activity within.

"Any idea what is going on in there?" she asked, not taking her eyes from the tents.

Leland shook his head. "They have been very careful to conceal any hint of what they are up to from us," he observed, a trace of worry in his voice.

Kay settled into place, her eyes seeking, evaluating, watching for the slightest indication of what was going on.

Beside her, Reese was absolutely silent, and she almost held her breath, hoping he might use his own senses to add to the puzzle solving.

Reese turned his head. "I do not like it," he murmured. "I think I hear … woodworking noises?"

A twist of danger speared her heart. What in the world was Galeron up to? She turned to Stephen, who hovered nearby. "Stephen, please go through the castle and gather up all the remaining folk – the women and children. Get them all up into the solar. It is just a precaution, but I would feel better knowing they are all together and safe."

Stephen did not hesitate. "Right away, Kay," he agreed, and he was off running down the stairs, heading into the main doors.

Leland did not take his eyes off the tent. "Do you have an idea of what is going on in there, Kay?"

Kay shook her head in confusion. "I just have a sense of danger, and the knowledge that Galeron always had plans, backup plans, and tertiary plans. If any man had figured out a way to get into Serenor, it would be him. I do not want to leave anything to chance."

Leland's voice was quiet. "Lord Weston should be here by late afternoon. We only have to hold out until then."

Kay drew her eyes from the tent, scanning the landscape beyond. Would it be her father who first rode to the rescue – or would it be an unknown set of reinforcements for Galeron? Just what did the man have up his sleeve?

She was still staring in contemplation at the tents a half hour later when Stephen climbed the stairs again, his face red, but his smile speaking of satisfaction. "It is done, Kay," he reported with pleasure. "Everyone is safely up in the solar, as you requested. They are well stocked with food and wine; they will be fine until Lord Weston arrives."

"Good," replied Kay, her shoulders untensing, the tight bands around her heart easing. No matter what happened, Em would be protected and the innocents of the keep would be safe. Surely whatever fighting did ensue in the coming hours, they could hold on to their advantage until relief arrived.

"Kay ..." Reese's voice held a note of warning, and she turned her head with a snap, scanning out toward the tents. But now there was only one tent. The other one had collapsed, revealing its contents – an odd wooden frame, about five feet on a side, with a long tongue leaning back. She stared at it in confusion. Just what was that thing ...

Leland's voice came hard and sharp. "Get off the

drawbridge section!" he shouted. Immediately men scrambled left and right to move toward the further parts of the wall. Reese grabbed her arm, pulling her to the left, and she stumbled as he dragged her to an area further from the drawbridge and gate.

The catapult sprang into life. There was a sharp whistling noise, and a small, dark projectile flew through the air toward the drawbridge. The soldiers closer to the gates threw themselves at the walkway floor, shielding their heads, but Kay stood motionless, watching in abject horror as the missile seemed to focus its path, honing in, and then -

THWACK!

The rock slammed into the wall mere feet away from the corner of the drawbridge. The walkway shuddered violently beneath their feet, and she fell hard against Reese.

Leland's voice rose up over the chaos. "His calculations were barely off," he yelled, looking out over the troops. "Everyone, down to the courtyard! Immediately! Prepare for incoming attack!"

The men scrambled for the stairs, and Stephen looked between Reese and Leland in confusion. "But if Galeron destroys the drawbridge, he cannot get in," the lad objected. "The moat will become impassable, and we will be safe!"

Reese glared out at the tents, his jaw tensing. "He is not trying to destroy the drawbridge," he corrected with an angry snap. "He is going to pop the support chain that he knew was weak. The support chain that he refused to allow me to fix."

Leland's shout carried across the keep. "Incoming!" There was another high whistle; another dark blob growing closer. This one crashed into its target with a slam which undulated the floor beneath them. Kay's ears filled with a cacophony of wood and stone. Then half the drawbridge was listing, hanging all its weight on the one remaining chain.

For a long minute it teetered, swinging, almost balancing.

A long groan - the other chain's anchor ruptured under the weight. The entire drawbridge gave a low moan as it plummeted, slammed into the earth, bounced heavily once, and lay open.

Leland sprinted for the stairs. "Get her into the keep!" he shouted to Reese, drawing his sword. "You, men, with me!"

Kay had not even drawn in a breath when Reese swept her up in his arms. He took two steps away from the stairs, turned - and leapt.

They hung in the air. They soared. They floated. She was pressed close against his chest. For a moment it was as if the earth stood still, as if she and he were the only two people.

She closed her eyes, wishing that time would stop, that the horror of events could be rewound and undone.

They landed with a cascade of color in the dense pile of leaves. Reese rolled to his feet, hugging her close to him. He sprinted across the courtyard filled with men and shouts and activity, heading toward the large, open doors which fronted the keep.

There was a thunderous crash from behind her. A large boulder skittered past, followed by stray bits of the main curtain wall doors.

Leland's cry was sharp with panic. "Reese! Watch out!"

Reese turned mid-stride to look behind him – his breath blew out of him. He twisted and leapt sideways toward the stable, rotating so his back took the brunt of the fall, cradling Kay in his arms. Then a blur of black horses pulling a sturdy wagon blazed past them, heading on a direct collision course with the keep's main stairs.

Kay cried out in shock; it appeared the horses would run headlong into the entryway. They veered off at the last minute, suddenly free of their burden. The wagon, its nose shaped into a sharp point, plowed through its momentum into the still open doors, embedding itself there with a splintering crash.

With a roar the men within leapt out through the timbers and raced into the keep proper.

Kay could not breathe. Panic and hysteria warred within her, and she screamed, "Em!"

Reese rolled to his feet beside her and raced toward the doors, Leland close on his heels. Kay spun to look back toward the shattered drawbridge, but to her surprise there were no waves of attackers following in after the wagon; no flood of troops seeking to challenge their foot soldiers. The sole tumult in the courtyard was her own troops running to the wagon, flinging away the wheels and wood supports in order to get back inside the keep.

Leland scrambled on top of the wagon's debris and turned to the men. "All of you, stay here and protect those gates!" He looked to Reese, and in a moment the two had leapt through the opening, disappearing into the darkness within.

Kay drove herself to her feet, nearly falling back as her leg screamed in pain. She stumbled forward as quickly as she could, as the men around her sped in the opposite direction, racing to form a wall of bodies across the open gate. As she reached the keep's doorway, the building's foundation shuddered. The source of the tremor seemed high within the keep.

Her heart thudded in wild panic. The solar door. The attacking soldiers were trying to breach her sister's protective sanctuary! She clambered over the pile of timber and debris, pushing her way into the entry hall of Serenor.

Shouts echoed from above, the sharp clash of swords rang out, and the floor shook with another heavy, resounding thud. She pressed herself harder, taking the stairs as quickly as her legs would allow. There was an ear-shattering CRACK, and then desperate screams. She wove for a moment, almost tumbling back down the stairs.

It was all lost. Her sister, Anne, Jessica, young Molly, all was lost.

She gripped on the handrail and put one foot in front of the other, pulling herself up more than walking, the pain nearly unbearable. It seemed an eternity before she had made it to the top floor landing. Her heart felt as if it would tear into pieces. The door lay in shattered remnants across the floor. A pair of heavy, metal maces were left to one side, undoubtedly the instruments of destruction. And within …

An agonized moan escaped from Kay's lip. A wall of soldiers stood, swords drawn, facing the door. Galeron held at their center, a satisfied smirk on his face. Beyond them the women and children of the keep huddled in fear. To the back was a couch, and on it lay …

"Em!" Kay cried out, diving forward, all pain forgotten. A hand at the side of the door swiped to hold her back and missed. The enemy soldiers parted like a river to let her through, and she was falling to her knees by the sofa, her heart pounding in panic. Her hand moved to gently draw the blonde curls away from Em's face.

"Oh, Em … are you all right? Is the baby …?"

"The baby is fine," soothed Em, her voice steady, her

hand patting Kay's in reassurance. "It was a fright, to be sure, when the men came in. But this baby is born to be a fighter, be it male or female. Here, feel."

Em moved Kay's hand to her distended abdomen, and indeed, Kay could feel a solid kick come through the skin. She smiled hesitantly.

"I hope it is a girl, although I imagine Eric is dreaming of a son," she offered with a smile.

Em smiled fondly. "Eric simply wants us to both be happy and healthy," she murmured.

Kay leant forward to press her forehead against her sister's. "He will be here soon for you," she vowed, her voice soft but sure. "Then everything will be all right."

Reese's cry echoed across the room, rough with concern. "Kay?"

Kay turned, drawing back into the reality of the situation around her, of the muffled whimpers of the children, the steady line of men facing off against Reese and Leland. She stood carefully, the pain in her legs throbbing into fresh life. Her gaze moved down the row until she found Galeron. He smiled at her with rich satisfaction.

Kay pitched her voice low and steady, her eyes flashing. "So, Galeron, you always have a plan in that codex of yours. What do you have arranged for us today?"

Galeron's grin grew wider. "I am glad to see you appreciate my talents, Kay! I must admit, while I was planning to take hostages, to discover this blonde, pregnant beauty in the solar was even more than I could even have hoped to imagine. It puts a whole new light on my possibilities."

Kay's blood ran cold. "Lord Weston will ransom Keren-happuch, whatever price you set. But she must not be harmed."

Galeron spread his hands in innocence. "Of course, my dear. Harming Keren is the furthest thing from my mind. The core of my plan is to talk with her father, Lord Weston, and arrange for the truce conditions once he arrives."

Kay's heart began to beat again. This was simply a business transaction for him. Everything could work out. "Keren needs quiet – we cannot risk the child," she pressed.

Galeron put a hand to his heart. "I concur exactly, my darling Kay. We must protect Keren from all excitement and noise. That is why I request that all troops leave the keep immediately, so that we can resume normal operations under my watchful eye. Solely until Lord Weston arrives for the truce talks, of course."

Leland snorted in anger. "Never, Galeron. I would never leave them in your hands, not even for one minute."

"Ahem," came a voice from the left. Kay looked to follow the sound - and found her mouth hanging open. It was Jack, his blond hair almost white in the morning light, a smirk spreading across his face.

"You," she gasped, almost mute in shock.

He took a step forward and drew Molly up in his arms. The girl's red curls bobbed at the motion. With one arm wrapped around her tiny waist, he used his other hand to hold out her thumb, examining it carefully.

"This little piggy went to market …"

Kay's throat constricted, and she staggered back against Em's couch. "You would not hurt a child," she choked.

Jack raised an eyebrow, and the vision of Jack's whip smashing down on the young boy's arm enveloped her mind. With a slow motion, he drew out Molly's index finger, twisting it slightly.

"This little piggy went home …"

Kay heard her sister moan behind her. "Oh, Kay ..."

Molly wriggled, and Jack snugged her up even more tightly. "This little piggy had roast beef ..."

"Enough!" cried Kay, her heart thundering against her chest. She turned her face away from Molly's innocent eyes, staring hard at Galeron. "If we agree to your terms, I want you to swear that your men will withdraw from the solar and leave us completely alone in here until the conference begins."

Galeron tapped a finger against his chin. "We do have to set up a table in here for the meeting itself. As long as you allow for a half hour of preparation for the truce talks, then your terms are perfect."

Kay sighed in relief. There would be calm, and then her father would find a solution. She turned to Leland and Reese. "Then we are agreed. Move the men to the ring outside the keep; Lord Weston will be here soon enough to treat for our safe release."

Reese shook his head, taking a step forward. "Kay, we cannot leave you in here like this!"

Jack calmly pulled on Molly's ring finger, giving it an extra twist as he recited, "This little piggy had none ..."

Kay met Reese's eyes and held them with her own. "Reese, do not send them down this path. I could not live with the consequences, and Em ..."

She turned to look at her sister, seeing the pain glowing in her eyes.

Galeron's eyes twinkled. "Em, is it?" he asked with a chuckle. His brought his gaze around to meet Reese's. "Well, then, gentlemen, the choice is yours. What shall it be?"

Reese hesitated, looked over at Leland, and then as one the two men lowered their swords. Reese's voice was low and guttural. "If you harm one hair on these hostages' heads, I swear to you, I will find you and kill you."

"Ah, threats, threats," sighed Galeron with a smile. "Believe me, my plan does not call for any unnecessary harm to come to these most valuable possessions of mine. For now, see that you get the castle cleared out in record time. The presence of strife is upsetting the pregnant one. The sooner you get the courtyard cleared, the sooner we can remove these soldiers from her solar."

Reese brought his gaze back to meet Kay's. She was warmed; strength flowed from him, filling her soul.

Then he and Leland turned, heading down the stairs at a fast pace. She moved to the window. In only a few moments they were drawing in the men in the courtyard, talking in a huddle with them. In short order the group made their way across the drawbridge to the outer tree ring.

Kay found herself astounded at how quickly the exchange took place. It seemed a mere swallow's swoop before the keep's troops were hunkered down by the now-empty tents, before Galeron's forces were circling their wagons and supplies in the courtyard area, setting up workshop locations to the right side.

Kay's heart dropped as the keep became even more under the control of the black-curled enemy, but she kept her voice tight as she addressed him. "You have your wish, Galeron. The keep is yours for now. Hold up your side of the bargain and clear out this solar."

Galeron smiled with bright acceptance. "Of course, my dear! All of you now have full run of the keep. You may go anywhere you wish, do anything besides, of course, interfere with our activities. Make yourselves at home!"

With a wink, he turned, and Jack followed him down the stairs. In a moment the soldiers had followed suit. To Kay's surprise and pleasure the women and children were left completely alone in the solar.

Kay and Em stared at each other in exhausted relief. A hesitant smile grew on Em's face. "See," she offered, "it will all work out. This is a money making scheme for him. Father will pay up, and Galeron is not the type to risk his own skin. Father's troops will vastly outnumber him. So we just need to settle in until evening."

Kay looked around the nervous crowd in the room and nodded. "Everyone – I know this was nerve-racking, but the worst should now be over. Lord Weston will arrive soon and sort this out. He is only a few hours away. In the meantime, we apparently have the run of the castle."

She glanced at her sister for a moment, then continued. "Feel free to stay here if you want, but I trust in Galeron's logical side. I do believe that you should be safe to venture out into the keep proper. Let me know if anything seems dangerous to you, and we will address it."

She smiled slightly. "Of course, if you learn anything which seems like it might help our cause, I would be eager to hear that as well."

Anne and Jessica glanced at each other, then both headed for the stairs in a flash, their eyes bright with nervous curiosity. Slowly the rest of the group followed suit, and soon only a trio of young children, including the now-sleepy Molly, were left behind, tucked into Kay's room for safety.

Em's voice took on a nervous edge. "What do we do now?"

Kay took in a deep breath. She had to keep her sister's mind off the coming discussion - to help her relax and avoid stress. "Why, my dear, your husband is coming to see you, and you have not freshened up!" she replied, forcing a smile onto her face. "Let us head into your room and see how more beautiful we can make you in the time we have available."

A hint of a twinkle shimmered in Em's gaze. Together they moved their way into Em's bedroom.

From below, in the courtyard, came the sounds of carpenters carefully doing their craft.

Chapter 16

Kay and Em kept attentive watch at the central window in the late afternoon sunlight, sitting on a low bench which had been dragged up against it. They strained for the slightest movement, the merest hint of approaching riders coming from the east road. They had not moved from their location for the past hour.

Kay glanced at her sister for what must have been the fiftieth time. "Em, really, please lie down on the couch. There is no need for both of us to be on lookout. I will let you know the moment I see anything."

Em resolutely shook her head, her eyes pinned to the narrow ribbon of dusty brown. "Eric is coming for me," she repeated quietly, a mantra almost, a fervent hope and wish. "He will be crazed with worry when he reaches those gates and hears what has happened. I will be here, in the window, to at least reassure him with my presence that things will be all right."

Kay patted her hand and looked back out toward the rolling hills, toward the swells of moss green, doe brown, and twisting scrub. The sunlight's strength created sharp shadows for every tree and hillock. Their shadows slowly migrated across the earth, drifting like clouds, reminding her that time did indeed progress outside their room. For some reason she almost felt as if the world were holding its breath …

"There -" she whispered, almost afraid to shatter the moment. She had seen a kick of dust, a drifting of something at the far edge of her vision. Em leant forward, and Kay could almost feel her sister's heart thundering as the two strained, searched ...

Yes, it was a lone horseman. The steed was black, large, and it was only a few seconds before Em relaxed against her sister, breathing out the name in shaky relief.

"Eric."

A cheer went up from the soldiers gathered along the tree ring as he thundered toward the keep. Over the rise the rest of the force slowly came into view. Kay estimated that her father had brought perhaps fifty men – a healthy contingent to witness his daughter's marriage and to restock the keep under its new master.

Kay's heart skipped a beat. It was all upside down now. The new master could very well be a traitor, a man who had deceived them all.

The horse faltered for a moment, as if reined in, and then it reset to gallop at top speed toward the group of men waiting in the clearing. Kay watched as Eric pulled to a hard stop, looking around in confusion at the collection of men camped out there. Leland ran over to him at once, talking with him urgently, while Reese paced the sidelines.

Kay shook her head in frustration, her eyes scanning the scene. "They haven't told Reese yet," she muttered under her breath. "Leland is keeping him in the dark. Surely by now he can be trusted?"

Em squeezed Kay's hand gently in sympathy, her eyes not leaving her husband's form. "Trust in what they are doing," she whispered. "They are going to get us out of this. We have to trust them."

Suddenly Eric was standing in his stirrups, turning in shock and staring up at them. Em stood at once, leaning her head out the window, and even though clearly her voice would not carry at this distance, she called out with all her might, "Eric!"

Her husband's anguish was clear. He spun his mount in a frustrated circle, his eyes going to the main keep gates and then back up to his captured wife. Then, with one more glance at Leland, he turned his steed again and rode back down the road, at a hard gallop, moving to rejoin the main party.

Kay gave her sister a gentle hug. "He has gone to tell father," she reassured Em. "Soon they will all be gathered, and then the negotiations will begin. You and I must prepare."

"Prepare?" asked Em distractedly. Her eyes followed her husband with single minded focus, her hands still pressed against the windowsill.

Kay leant her head against her sister for a moment. "Em, we must be strong. The men will have a plan of some sort. They will do everything they can to get us out safely. We must be fully ready to react to whatever they say, to follow their lead, and to assist them in their quest." She took her sister's hands in her own. "Also, we must reassure them that we are fine. That way they can concentrate on rescuing us and not be distracted by our current situation."

"Yes, yes, you are right," murmured Em, slowly shaking herself into awareness. "If Eric feels I have been mistreated, it might cloud everything else he is doing."

Kay smiled fondly at her sister. "Of course it would," she agreed. "Come, let us go into your room and sit quietly until we are called."

Kay did her best for the next hour to keep her sister relaxed and distracted. She could hear noises in the outer room while Galeron's men set up the pair of tables which would serve as their negotiation area, and she peered out occasionally to keep an eye on their progress. Most of her time, though, was spent in brushing out Em's long, blonde hair, then plaiting it in an intricate braid. It was almost as if they were back to the days before Em had gotten married, to the afternoons of relaxation, courting, and fun. Kay kept the conversation light, doing her best to draw Em's mind away from the situation that was swirling around them.

Finally a knock came on the door. Kay went to the door and cracked it open. Galeron was standing there, a smile on his lips.

"Women, we are ready for the main event," he offered, sweeping his hand out in invitation.

Kay moved back into the bedroom, twined her fingers into her sister's, and gave her a smile of support. Then together they walked out into the solar. The two tables had been set up across the waist of the room, splitting it into two parts. Four chairs were on either side of the length, and a guard stood at each end, preventing anyone from easily moving to the other side. There was already a man sitting on their side of the table in one of the end chairs. He turned as they approached ...

"Jack," snapped Kay, visions of him holding Molly still fresh in her head.

The blond man gave a twisted version of the smile Galeron had offered a few minutes earlier. "Surprised to see me out of custody, I might imagine?" he queried with a wolfish grin.

"I am surprised to see you included at a negotiation table," growled Kay.

"Galeron and my aims align for the moment," mused Jack, his eyes sharp. "He needs an extra sword arm and I found myself available for employ. We will see what the future holds."

Galeron came around her other side, gently guiding her. "You sit here, next to me," he instructed with a calm smile. "Your Lady will be right at your side. We will keep the two of you at the center of the table, since you are indeed the focus of this little meeting."

"You mean to keep us further from any chance of moving around the edge of the table," corrected Kay, her mouth tight.

"Oh, Kay, do not be like that," soothed Galeron, his eyes twinkling. "This is simply a business transaction. In a short while it will all be over and we can each go on with our lives."

Kay helped her sister settle into her seat, and then took her own. Her eyes scanned the four seats facing them.

"Why four?" she asked, looking down the row. "Why not just a chair for Lord Weston and perhaps one guard?"

"A man of his stature?" responded Galeron with a raised eyebrow. "I thought it more fitting to allow him some dignity and to reassure him that this negotiation was safe to attend. He can bring up three men – unarmed, of course."

Kay pursed her lips. Galeron did everything with a purpose. Perhaps her father's comfort was part of it – Lord Weston might be more willing to negotiate at length, and meet concessions, if he felt secure.

"You plan everything," she bit out. "You know exactly who he will bring with him. You want to watch them and see their reactions to what you say."

Galeron's smile grew, his eyes meeting hers with sharp admiration. "I knew you and I were well matched," he praised with a chuckle. He turned to her sister. "Ah, Keren-happuch, if only you had chosen me on your own before Reese's little discovery and not made me resort to my back-up plan. How much smoother things would have gone."

Kay turned to her sister, meeting her eyes with steady seriousness. "We must be strong," she emphasized again, her voice low.

Galeron was setting a scene and would look for every advantage. They could not give away their true natures with a word or a glance.

Em nodded her head.

Kay prayed that they could get through this without incident.

There was a noise from the stairs, and all eyes turned toward the door.

Galeron smiled. "And the party begins." He settled himself into the seat at the far right. He leant back slightly in it, his eyes focused on the doorway, attentive and calculating.

Footsteps worked their way up the spiral, and then a man stepped into view.

Reese.

His eyes locked with hers.

Kay staggered beneath a crazed desire to leap from her chair, to vault the table, to run into his arms, to be held by him, comforted … she held herself still with an effort. She saw the same tightness in his muscles, the tension in his neck as he remained where he stood and took in a long breath.

Then, without turning, he called back over his shoulder. "Come on up."

He moved forward into the room and stepped to one side. His eyes held steadily on Kay's for a long moment before he scanned the rest of the room. His hand dropped to his hip and swept the open air where his sword hilt usually lay ready. Tension rippled through his shoulders and was forcibly relaxed.

A blond man moved into view – graceful, sturdy, his face handsome and weathered. Em squeezed her sister's hand hard, drawing in a long breath, but she was true to her word and her face stayed steady. Eric's stride hitched as his eyes came to those of his wife. He moved to the other side of the door across from Reese, his gaze carefully neutral.

A slower shuffling came from the stairs and in a moment Lord Weston entered the room, accompanied by Leland. The two moved to the center chairs and Leland carefully helped Lord Weston sit.

Galeron stretched out a hand, waving to Reese and Eric. "Please, gentlemen, come sit with us," he offered. "I swear no harm will come to anyone during these talks."

Reese glanced at Eric, and then the two men moved forward and took their seats opposite Jack and Galeron. They were so close, they were almost within the reach of a hand.

Temptation flooded through Kay. It would be so easy to reach across to Reese, to wrap herself in the reassurance of his steady grip. She felt Em twine her fingers even more tightly into her own, and wondered if her sister was under the same strong spell.

Lord Weston began without preamble. "I would like to protest the unchivalrous and uncalled for action of kidnapping a pregnant woman," he ground out in a hoarse voice. "If she were to lose the child, I will make it my mission to grind you into dust. She is a complete innocent in all of this!"

Galeron leant back, his face carefree and relaxed as he chuckled at the lecture. "As I seem to recall," he pointed out, "you offered this woman as a potential wife and stated she was indeed *innocent*." He moved his eyes to look pointedly at her round stomach, protruding slightly over the edge of the table. "Instead, we have proof here that she is a harlot who cannot keep her legs together and who carries a bastard child. Just what coward of a man abandoned her in this state, that you had to foist her off with this deception?"

Eric's face flared crimson, and a thick vein in his neck began pulsating. Kay felt as if her fingers would be crushed by Em's grip. She prayed with every ounce of her being that the men would not give into this blatant goading. Galeron was trolling for information. It was the reason he had allowed her father to bring the men with him.

Already it was working.

She leant forward. "What are your demands," she interjected with a snap, attempting to move the discussion onto more concrete grounds. "You said this was a business transaction. Let us get to it."

"My, my," grinned Galeron, turning his eyes from Eric's face to hers. "No appreciation for the niceties of negotiation, I see. Well, then, I will accede to your wishes, my dear."

He pulled the codex from a leather bag on the floor and flipped it open a few pages. "Ah, yes, here we go."

He looked up at Lord Weston. "First, I am, of course, technically the winner of your little game. Keren-happuch convinced both Uther and Alistair that they should move on to new opportunities. Both men went willingly away. We have witnesses to that."

He turned to nod toward Jack. "Our third contestant has an issue with how he was treated, but for now he is willing to state that he was put out of the running by your daughter."

Kay glanced down the table at Jack. His face held a deep frown, but he said nothing to contradict the statement.

Galeron's smile grew. "Which only left us with Reese here. Just two days ago, Reese voluntarily, and quite deliberately, removed himself from the game."

Kay's heart dropped. Everything had moved so quickly – the enormity of what he had done still had not registered with her. He had chosen to leave. He had been actively abandoning her when the fighting had begun. Why?

Her eyes seeked to his, and his face was a mask of control, covering – what emotions? Was there pain in there? Regret? The frustration of the situation almost overwhelmed her. If only she had five minutes to talk with him alone …

Galeron looked up from his codex. "So that just leaves me as the winner," he continued, apparently oblivious to the sea of emotions roiling around him. "I should therefore get the prize."

Kay could almost see the force of effort holding Eric in his chair; the tight press of his lips holding in any words. It was her father who, after a long moment, spoke in a wheeze.

"So your intent is to force my daughter into marriage, even seeing her state?"

Galeron let the silence drag on for a long moment, then he sat back, rolling his shoulders, his twinkling eyes moving down each man's face in turn. "Ah, Lord Weston, I find that there is often no need to resort to force to get what you want. If you plan things out properly, what you desire in life comes willingly to your doorstep."

Kay was stretched taut with this game of cat and mouse. "Spit it out," she snapped. "What is on that damned list of yours?"

Galeron turned to gaze at her, grinning, slowly shaking his head. "I could watch you all day," he responded with a contented sigh. "You wear your emotions on your sleeve, my dear. Again, I will acquiesce to your wishes." He glanced down at the parchment.

"Hmmmm. Item one. With my dowry, I was promised a payment of ... let us see ... eight thousand pounds. I believe that money is in the cart outside?"

Lord Weston nodded, his wrinkled face somber. "The money is here," he confirmed.

"Check," noted Galeron. "Second, with Keren-happuch's hand I was promised the Keep of Serenor, with all the property, servants, and associated materials. I already have possession of it, as you can well see, and I do not intend to relinquish it."

"A master of a keep is one who can hold it against attack," growled Lord Weston, his eyes sharp.

"Right you are," agreed Galeron without malice. "When we settle our negotiations here, I will give you and your men time to get out of my courtyard and out of range of my walls." He spread his arms wide. "Then, by all means, give it your best shot to take Serenor back. I think you will find that I am quite capable of defending what is mine."

Lord Weston's eyes moved to Em's face. "And my daughter?" he asked, his brows coming together.

"Do you mean the pregnant lady here?" replied Galeron in innocence, looking across Kay toward Em. "Clearly she is already tainted, and I would have no use for her here. You can have the wench back."

Relief washed through Kay's body, and she saw the relaxing of tension in the four men across from her. It seemed almost too good to be true. Yes, Galeron would get the money – but her father's forces sat right outside the keep. The drawbridge was still broken and both sets of doors were caved in. Galeron's forces had caught them off guard, but their small numbers should be no match for the combination of the keep's own units and her father's. They could retake Serenor. She knew it.

By the look in her father's eyes, she sensed he felt the same way. His voice was firm. "Agreed."

Galeron put his hand across the table. "You will shake on it, on your honor?"

Weston did not hesitate. He put his hand into Galeron's, and gripped it tightly. "I agree to your terms."

Galeron smiled with bright approval. "Well then, send up the money and let us get this process on the way," he encouraged the men before him. "When I have the money, you can have the lady."

Weston nodded to Leland, and in a minute the captain was jogging down the spiral stairs. Kay wondered if they had planned for this condition, because he was barely gone from the room before a group of Galeron's men were lumbering back into the area burdened by heavy sacks of coins. The men lined the side wall with the burlap bags before moving back out of the room.

Galeron nodded to the guard at the far edge of the table. The heavyset man moved over to the sacks, untying each one in turn. He dug into each one with thick fingers, stirring the coins around, peering within. When he was done with the last bag, he turned back to Galeron and nodded.

"Good, good," agreed Galeron, turning to the four men with a grin. "This should do quite nicely to pay for the Grey Wolves' services."

Reese and Eric both snapped into focus, staring at Galeron with dawning awareness. Lord Weston was slower, shaking his head in confusion. "What is this?"

Galeron smiled, turning his head to look at Kay. "I am sure Kay can tell you the hold this place can have on a person. I am master now of Serenor, and I intend to keep it. The Grey Wolves will be arriving first thing tomorrow morning with a force of two hundred men. They have agreed – for a small fee, of course – to help ensure that what is mine stays mine."

Kay sagged as life drained out of her. This would not be a small rag-tag group of men that they could easily overcome. The Grey Wolves were famous throughout the land for their fighting skills. If Galeron truly had them on his side, her father's forces might never wrest control away from him.

The soldier by the window made a hand motion to Galeron, and his smile deepened. "Ah good, apparently my supplies have just arrived as well."

Lord Weston's brow furrowed. "Supplies?"

"Yes, for the repairs," explained Galeron. "We should have that drawbridge and both doors fixed up in a few hours. I had of course planned for both to be damaged in the attack. The replacement boards are all precut and shaped. So, rest assured, *my* keep will be snug and secure, in case of any unwarranted attack."

Kay's sense of hopelessness grew. He had planned for every contingency, every last detail. The moment the soldiers left the keep, the doors would seal behind them and it would be lost forever. Everything she had dreamed of her entire life would be gone. And the people within – what would happen to them?

If was as if Galeron had read her mind. He turned to smile at her. "Jack and I will be able to run this keep in any way we choose, for years to come."

Kay looked away from him and gazed toward the solar door in hopeless frustration. Anne, Jessica, all of them would be trapped at the keep, held without anyone to speak up for them, and subjected to a life of voiceless isolation. There was nobody to keep them safe.

She gave herself a shake. She had to think. Nothing Galeron was saying was unplanned for. He was laying out a path, just as he had deliberately toyed with the men earlier. What was his purpose now?

Lord Weston's voice growled out from across the table, stirring her from her thoughts. "You have your cash. Give me my daughter."

Galeron spread his hands wide. "Of course!" He looked over to Em. "My dear, feel free to go around the table now."

Em stood up onto shaking legs, pushing her chair back, and the guard moved aside to let her make her way around the table's edge. The four men stood as she approached, and Kay saw her hesitate a second, almost moving toward Eric before taking another step and gently embracing her father.

Lord Weston patted his daughter on the head, his voice rough. "There there, dear, we have you now," he soothed her. "You go stand with my knight, Eric - he will keep you safe."

Em did not need a second prodding. She moved to stand behind Eric, almost pressing up against him. To Kay's eyes it seemed that Eric became a human shield.

Reese glanced over at Kay, then toward Lord Weston, his face tight. Lord Weston saw the look, then seemed confused.

"Kay, you too," he prodded.

Galeron arched his eyebrows. "Lord Weston, you agreed to the terms of our arrangement. Serenor, and all servants within, belong to me now."

Lord Weston's face flushed beet red. "Kay is no servant!"

Galeron's face was a picture of innocence. "Oh? She is not? What could you mean?"

The room went dead quiet. Kay's heart thundered against her chest. Would her father reveal her true identity or hold onto the ruse that she was merely a maid? Which would give the advantage at this stage of the negotiations?

Finally, he wet his lips and spoke. "I mean that Kay is a lady's maid to my daughter. They have been together since Keren-happuch was a child. They cannot possibly be separated now, not when Keren-happuch is about to bear her first child."

Galeron shrugged his shoulders. "I am sure someone else could help the bastard child be born," he pointed out. "As for Kay, as a servant, she is part of the deal. Besides, she belongs here at Serenor. Her heart is here; her very soul."

Suddenly it clicked for Kay. The phrasing of the comments, the sequence of events, even Jack's presence at the table. Galeron was working to sway her into staying on her own. He wanted to convince her that she *must* stay, to protect the servants and to look over her beloved keep. And she had responded that lure. She had been caught by the almost overwhelming desire to remain here, to be a buffer for Anne and Jessica and the others. To protect her beloved home.

Perhaps to find a way to regain control …

She looked up at Reese, and her chest constricted in agony. She could see the tension in his face; the pleading look in his eyes. He wanted for her to fight for her position at Em's side, to insist that she should be allowed to leave as well.

Her gaze moved to her father. His eyes were calculating, considering. She knew what was going through his head. If he admitted that Kay was his daughter, then she would not be bound by the servant clause of their agreement – but it could create an entirely new ransom situation. One which might be much more challenging to negotiate. Could he lose control of his main keep as well?

And, perhaps, was Galeron right after all? Could she really walk out through those gates? Could she turn her back on the keep she adored, knowing it was being destroyed from within by these two men? Could she sleep at night knowing the people she cared for were trapped within, with no salvation and no escape?

He had spoken the truth – her soul was deep within this keep. Her heart was at its very base.

A glimmer of hope sparked within her, and she lowered her eyes, holding herself very still. Her heart. Her carven heart, on the hollow wall. Perhaps a tunnel lay behind it, providing a secret path in – perhaps even a path which could be used in time to retake the keep before the mercenaries arrived.

She raced through the possibilities. It was only late afternoon now. Her father's troops would have to wait until nightfall so Galeron did not guess what they were up to. They could then sneak to the ocean cliffs, unseal the tunnels, and make their way into the castle. If they were able to make it to the cellar wall and break it down before morning, they could take the keep from within. And once they had the keep and the money, the mercenaries would have no reason to fight.

The keep could be saved.

She trembled with nervousness. There was so much riding on such a short period of time. She knew one thing for certain. She had to remain within the keep to help coordinate the attack. Someone had to ensure the cellar was kept clear of prying eyes during the long night so the soldiers were not alerted until it was too late.

She almost smiled. Galeron's plan had worked in her favor. He had constructed everything to lure her into staying in the keep. All she had to do was convince him that his scheme had been successful. She had to trick him into believing that she was staying for the reasons he had laid out, not in order to launch a counter-assault.

She closed her eyes for a long moment. She could not do or say anything to give even the slightest impression of her plans. Galeron was exceptionally observant. If he sensed the merest whiff of trouble, all of her hopes could come to nothing.

Taking a deep breath, she marshaled every last drop of reserve she possessed. Then she slowly stood. She focused her gaze on her father, on the weary lines in his face. She knew if she looked at Reese that she might falter, might give away her emotions with a look, a movement.

"I am staying here at Serenor," she informed her father in a low voice.

All four men's eyes turned to her in shock. Reese's cry ripped out of him. "Kay? Why?"

She forced herself not to turn, not to look into those eyes she knew so well.

Lord Weston shook his head in confusion, staring at her. "Kay, what is the meaning of this? Are you under duress?"

Kay spoke deliberately, tingeing her voice with reluctant resolve. Galeron had to believe in her performance without a shadow of a doubt. It made it easier that she believed in each word she spoke as an absolute truth.

"All my life I have vowed to look out for Serenor and the people here. I promised to do that to the best of my ability regardless of who the master was. I will not turn back on that vow now simply because it has become difficult."

Kay's mind raced. What else would a woman in this position do? Ah, yes. She turned, adding a nervous hitch to her voice, and looked at Galeron almost meekly. "Galeron, do you swear, if I stay, that I will not be harmed or touched in any manner?"

Galeron's eyes lit up with delight, and he gave a sweeping bow. "Of course," he agreed without hesitation. "I swear that on my life. You will not come to any harm, through any person." He glanced over at Jack. "That includes my friend here."

Jack's face flared with color, but he nodded with a sharp movement.

Kay fought to keep even the smallest glimmer of hope from showing on her face. She modeled a portrayal of abject misery and resignation as she turned her gaze back to her father. "Then this is where I must stay. I owe it to the household of Serenor."

Reese's voice was rich with anguish. "Kay ..."

"Ah, yes," commented Galeron, looking at Reese with a smile. "You remind me that there remains just one minor loose end to tie up on my plan which, so far, has played out quite nicely." He glanced over to Kay, his eyes twinkling. "My dear, now that you have so graciously volunteered to remain, you are free to go around the table to say your goodbyes." He nodded with his head for the two soldiers to take a position by the door.

The men moved to stand blocking the exit.

A shiver of nervousness ran through Kay. What new scheme was Galeron up to? Every step he had taken had seemed to propel her along a specific path. She took a deep breath and moved around the edge of the table, standing before the four men.

Her sister came around Eric's protective stance to stare at her, open mouthed. "Kay what are you doing?" she asked incredulously, coming forward to give her a long hug. "Come home with us. The keep is not worth it."

Kay gently put a hand on her sister's face. "Do not worry about me," she soothed, "I will be fine. You get to safety, and take care of that infant you are carrying."

Lord Weston shook his head as he gave her a rough hug. "You were always a stubborn, headstrong girl," he snapped. "I can understand loyalty, but this time you have gone too far."

From behind her, Galeron chuckled. "It did seem as if following orders was a challenge to her," he commented dryly.

Kay dropped her eyes. Apparently Galeron had sent her to give her farewells in order to test her purpose. He was certainly watching her every move, her every word. She could not in any way stir up suspicions in his mind. She nodded meekly in agreement, as if chastised.

The room went silent, and a single thought began drumming in her head. She could not look at Reese. One touch of his hand, one look into those deep eyes, and she might lose herself. She might lose all resolve and leave with him now, abandoning any chance to retake the keep and save those within. She would destroy their only opportunity. She knew she could never live with herself if she made that choice.

Galeron's voice came lightly from across the table. "Oh, Kay," he murmured, "I think it time that you tell Reese the truth."

Kay's eyes snapped up in shock, and she saw the same surprise echoed in Reese's face.

Reese looked at her in confusion. "What truth?"

Kay's throat went dry. Suddenly everything became crystal clear. Galeron had known all along who she was, and had held back the knowledge for this very moment. He would use the week of lies to drive a wedge between her and Reese, to convince him she was unworthy of being rescued.

She shook her head, almost taking a step backwards. She could not do it. It was too much to ask of her, after everything else she had gone through. She could not tell Reese like this. Not with everyone watching, not in the middle of this crowd -

Galeron chuckled. "Ah, Kay," he prodded, "Come now, is it that hard to be truthful with Reese? He is a man of honor, after all. Surely now that you have chosen to leave him you can stop lying to him."

Kay winced at Galeron's choice of words. She saw a furrow of doubt ripple through Reese's face. She could not do it. Not here. Not like this.

Galeron cheerfully sighed. "Or would you rather I phrase it? Let's see -"

Kay rushed through the words to get them out before Galeron could further twist the situation and drive Reese away from her forever. "This whole week has been a lie," she burst out, her face flushing crimson with shame. "I am not who I said I was." Her throat constricted, and she could barely continue, her heart pounding in near panic. Her voice dropped to a whisper. "My full name is not Kay. I am ... I am Keren-happuch."

The silence hung in the room for a long moment, and Kay's heart thundered to near bursting. He had already left her once. Would this cause him to turn away completely?

Reese's face held disbelief and shock. Finally he gave himself a small shake, turning. "But then who ...?" He brought his eyes around to gaze at Em, and his focus went from her round belly to the man who stood protectively by her side.

Galeron chimed in gleefully. "Yes, indeed, that blonde sphere is her elder sister, Mary Magdalene. With her lawfully wedded husband, I would assume, judging by the jealous streak so easily prodded at."

He stood and nodded to Jack, who also got to his feet. "So there you have it, oh honorable Reese. Everything our little Kay here has told you is a lie. She has been merely playing out her silly little game. We all witnessed her seductive manipulations with Uther, how she toyed with him to learn his secrets. Now you realize you were simply another pawn she moved at her pleasure."

He spread his arms wide, and the men began moving around the table, herding the people toward the door. "I am afraid I will now have to ask you all to leave. The mercenaries are coming, after all, and I would hate to have to mow you down for not being the agreed on distance from the castle before then." He casually dropped his hand to his sword hilt. Jack matched his movement, an eager gleam in his eye.

Eric dropped his hand to his hip in response and swore as it swept empty air. He instantly moved in front of Em, shielding her with his body.

Reese's voice was tight and low. He brought his gaze to return to her face.

"Kay?"

Kay turned her head away, hearing the pain saturated in that one word, unwilling to look in the grey-green eyes which reminded her of the rolling ocean waves. She knew she would see the hurt and shock at the revelation that every moment of their time together had been based on lies.

Would he believe in Galeron's insinuations, and assume that her actions were part of the game and not based on her real feelings? As Galeron had so pointedly stated, Reese had seen her playing a part with Uther, that night in the chapel. Would he assume that her times with him were part of that same play-acting? The thought wrenched at her heart, twisting her in agony.

But she could not say anything further now, not when it was critical that the castle clear out quickly. She needed for the enemy soldiers to settle down into quiet so that she could set her plan into motion. She had to trust that things would work out, that Reese would forgive her ...

Galeron made a waving motion with his hands. "Shoo, shoo."

Kay leant back against the table, her heart racing, her eyes at the floor. In a moment the group was pushed through the door, with Galeron, Jack, and the soldiers following them. The heavy wood door was pulled shut behind them, leaving the solar empty.

Kay slid slowly to the floor, crumpled, utterly exhausted, her thoughts racing in a million directions.

She had done it. She had fooled Galeron; had remained behind in the keep. She had kept alive their one chance to retake it before morning, before the mercenaries arrived to make the conquest complete. Her sister was safely out, and Kay breathed in overwhelming relief at that. Her sister would be safe.

And Reese ...

A cry of anguish spilled out of her. She rolled on her side, curled up, and lett the tears flow unabated. No matter how her sister and father might try to spin the events, no matter how they justified it to him, he might never forgive her for the things she had said and done. She might have just lost him forever.

She closed her eyes and took in a deep breath, steadying herself. She would have the rest of her life to mourn Reese, if he had lost faith in her. But right now she had less than twenty-four hours to regain control of her keep. The first challenge was making sure someone knew what she was up to without Galeron finding out.

She wiped the tears from her face and made her way over to the window. Eric was supporting Em as they walked through the main gates together, and her father was just behind them. Ahead by the ring of trees her father's troops were already setting up camp. She had no doubt they wanted to see for themselves if the mercenaries were going to show up tomorrow.

But how could she be sure that Reese would remember about the tunnels? She had been afraid to utter even a word when Galeron was in the room. Galeron's insightful mind would have picked up on even the slightest of hints that she was conspiring against him. Had she lost her only chance?

Her eyes dropped down to the wall – and her heart stopped. Reese was standing there, looking up at her, motionless. She leant forward out the window, holding her breath. She felt as if she were balanced on a knife's edge.

He brought his hand to his chest, and after a moment, gave a low bow, holding it in respect. When he stood again, she could see the tenderness, the understanding glowing from his eyes. She staggered back against the edge of the window frame. He understood that she truly cared for him; that her feelings for him had been honest. A fresh wind of hope swept through her. Perhaps he could forgive her for the lies she had been forced to tell.

Reese glanced toward the gate, and Kay saw Leland waving him down, to head out to meet with the rest. She realized that she was running out of time. If she was going to get a message to him, now was her only chance.

She looked around quickly. She needed something to write with … the red clock candle! She ran to the end table and grabbed the candle, racing back to the window. Reese was still standing there, looking up at her. Her eyes scanned the wall … a few of Galeron's soldiers were up there as well, and now some had turned to look at her.

She had to write something that Reese would understand – but that the soldiers would find harmless. There had to be no hint that any danger lay in the next twenty four hours. Her mind raced for a solution.

She looked down at Reese and it came to her with a simple clarity. She carefully settled herself astride the window's ledge, holding onto the edge of the window firmly with her left hand, then leant out with her right to face the outer stone wall of the keep. She pressed the candle against the weathered grey stone, and slowly, carefully, drew a giant, red heart.

Reese gazed up at her for a long moment, then slowly lowered himself down on one knee.

Tears sprang to her eyes, and for a moment a flood of emotions overwhelmed her. Here she had been worried about Reese abandoning her for the lies, and instead he loved her, he truly loved her. She rested her head against the warm stone, the tears flowing down her face. She knew he could not hear her, but the words came to her lips just the same.

"I love you, Reese."

He looked down sharply again, as if he'd been called, and panic swelled within her. He could not leave, not before she knew he understood. She waved her hand over her head, catching Reese's attention again; drawing his eyes back to hers. Then quickly she wrote out, in the heart, "KAY +". She turned her head to hold his gaze, every fiber of her being pleading with him to see the connection, to understand her message.

He stood slowly, staring at the heart, and then suddenly it was as if his body snapped to attention. He looked over the wall at the gathered troops, then back up to her, his movements quick and full of resolve. Then he was in motion, taking the stairs two at a time, sprinting across the courtyard and then running full tilt through the main gates. A pair of soldiers began clearing away the remnants of the large doors, and the drawbridge – sporting a fresh, solidly made hinge, slowly began to raise.

Kay climbed back into the room and sat down wearily on the bench. The plan had been put into motion. Now she had less than twenty-four hours to see it through.

Chapter 17

A wave of exhaustion tumbled over Kay, and she let her head fall into her hands for a long moment, desperately marshaling her strength. Her legs throbbed in pain, her shoulders ached, and her eyes were having trouble staying focused. She could not remember the last night she had slept soundly. Maybe if she spared a few hours to rest, she would be primed to assist when night fell and the outside forces were able to move into action.

She shook her head, pushing aside the thought with force. She could not let her men come into the situation blind. It was her duty to scout out the situation, to know where the guards had been stationed, and to do all she could to help the invasion succeed.

She chuckled wryly as she pushed herself back to a standing position. Of all things, for her to be planning an attack on Serenor! Only a few days ago it would have seemed the most unlikely scenario she could possibly imagine.

She moved slowly over to the door, cautious of her injured legs, and pulled it open. There were no guards stationed on the other side, and the staircase seemed quiet. She took the steps with care, making her way down the long spiral to the first floor. Several men lounged at the various tables, sipping at ale or playing dice. One or two looked up at her approach, then dismissed her without a second glance.

Good. She would not be watched as she went about her explorations.

She moved back into the stairwell, continuing down to the lower floor. Her first order of business was to examine the cellar again, to clear out any boxes or bags which might block the tunnel wall. She wanted the incursion to be as risk-free as possible for Reese and the others.

She reached the barracks floor, and again the few men present paid her little heed as she moved back toward the storeroom and cellar door area. She just had to round the corner and …

Kay froze in unbelieving shock. An iron frame had been bolted to the stonework around the door, holding a thickly grilled portcullis in place. A pair of hinges on one side would let the gate swing free, but a sturdy lock hung from the other edge, securely keeping the metal grid closed.

Kay fought to keep from sinking to her knees in abject horror. There was no way the men could get through that metal in one evening, never mind without attracting the attention of every soldier within the keep complex. The plan was lost. She was lost. She was trapped in Serenor, of her own volition, and tomorrow her family would abandon her to her fates. Reese would leave her …

Her world closed in on her, drowning her …

"It is a bit of a shock, I know," came a calm voice over her shoulder.

She drew in a long breath, not turning to face Galeron, not wanting him to see how much the grill had affected her. She fought to keep her voice as steady as she could. "Yes, I had not expected changes so soon."

Galeron came quickly around to her side, his eyes sharp. "You sound awful," he commented, looking down at her. "What is it?"

Kay looked down, her mind racing. She could not allow him to be suspicious. There had to be a way to salvage the situation, if only she could think. But her mind was fuzzy, exhausted ...

"I think I need some food," she admitted truthfully. "Between my leg wound, and the events -"

"Of course!" agreed Galeron, his gaze gentling. "I should have realized that myself. I apologize. Here, come to the pantry. A meal is exactly what you need."

He took her arm and escorted her around the corner through the workroom. Kay's heart dropped even further. A similar metal grill was now on the pantry door as well, sealed with a solid lock.

Galeron followed her gaze and smiled. "My dear, while you might be trusting of your staff, you will find I take a much more pragmatic view on things." He pulled a heavy key from a pouch on his belt, fitting it into the keyhole. "This key unlocks both gates. If ever you need access to either room, feel free to ask me. I will be glad to come escort you in and out of the pantry or cellar."

He undid the lock, pulling open the grill and then the wooden door behind it. Together they moved into the pantry. The small room was lined with wall to ceiling shelves, filled with a variety of breads, cheeses, dried meats, and fruits.

Kay's mind was a whirl of confusion. The cellar door was locked. She could hardly ask Galeron to open it for her, to wait patiently while Reese and the others bludgeoned their way through the wall to free the keep from the hostile invaders.

Everything hinged on that key.

"Could I see the key?" she asked, her voice fragrant with curiosity. Just what was this nemesis which now confronted her?

Galeron shrugged, handing over the metal object. It was perhaps four inches in length, constructed of a solid shaft with a fairly basic pattern at one end. She stared at it in fascination. Such a simple thing to thwart the saviors from entering. Why, it was something a child could carve.

A flash of hope shot through her. Stephen could certainly carve a key like this, if only he had a model to work from. It only had to work once, after all. If he made it with the hardest wood he had available, and she greased it to turn carefully, it might just succeed.

It was the only chance she had.

But how could she make a mold of it?

She glanced around the room again, and her eyes lit on the blocks of cheese. Not the goat's cheese – that would crumble and lose the impression. The newer sheep's cheese would be gooey, unable to hold a form. But ... there! She moved over to a rich yellow form and sunk a finger into it. The hole she made stayed perfectly in shape, conforming to her finger's size.

She turned with a quick movement, putting her back to the cheese, her mind seeking for something to distract Galeron with. He would sense if she began babbling idle chatter; it had to be authentic.

A thought blazed in her mind, and she looked up with curiosity.

"Galeron, now that you have won the game, I am intrigued – just how did you manage to get the other men eliminated? It seemed in each case that you had a hand in the results."

Galeron's face lit up in delight, and he leant against one of the side walls. "My dear, you almost match me in your powers of observation," he praised her. "Yes, of course I developed a detailed plan for each man the moment the game began. I carefully charted a path to ensure that they would fall one by one."

Kay slid the key around behind her with one hand, seeking with her fingers for the cheese. There, it was just behind her now. She pressed the key with careful attention down into its firm top, giving even pressure to make a good impression.

Kay gave him a smile. "So, Uther, the flamboyant peacock. I recall that you encouraged me to sit next to him. Was that so I could see his true nature?"

Galeron chuckled, his eyes sparkling. "Oh, my darling, I did more than that," he admitted with glee. "I scoffed at his stories of conquests in London. I stated in no uncertain terms that I did not believe him. On the ride here I challenged him to bed even three women in the keep within three days, to prove he was the great lover he claimed to be. I knew his pride would not allow him to refuse."

Kay's eyes widened. So it was Galeron's doings that Uther was so aggressive in those opening days!

She was becoming fascinated with Galeron's machinations. "And Alistair? Was he even a threat, with his tenuous nature?"

Galeron smiled with delight. "Alistair was not tenuous at all when we met at Lord Weston's keep. I found him intelligent and immensely well read. However, he quickly became almost paralyzed with horror when I regaled him with countless tales of the sickness which infected Serenor. He was soon convinced that, if he got even the slightest scratch, that the disease here would kill him off – after a horribly slow, lingering illness, of course. He became petrified that even the slightest nick could be his last."

Kay shook her head. Galeron's work had certainly been thorough. She wondered what impressions she might have had of the men if she had met them untainted, before Galeron's lies had done their work.

She tested the cheese mold with her fingers. The edges of the first impression seemed well defined and firm. Carefully she rolled the key over and pressed the opposite side into the unmarked area of the cheese block.

"Jack had almost been in the running," she commented with interest. "Until that day at the village."

Galeron nodded. "He might have remained, had I not warned him about Keren-happuch's hatred of weak men," he agreed. "I told Jack that Keren despised her father's mamby-pamby ways with the servants, reviled how cosseted the villagers were. I explained to Jack that she was seeking a real man, a man of firm action and determination."

"Of course you did," responded Kay, seeing the events of the past days in a new light. "Although, to be fair, it seems in each case you simply emphasized a defect which already existed. The men went along with your suggestions, considering them natural."

A band constricted her heart, and she had to take in a breath before she asked her next question. "And Reese?"

Galeron rolled off the wall and took a step toward her with a smile. She froze, immediately withdrawing the key from the cheese. She wrapped it in the fabric of the back of her dress, trying with only minimal movements to wipe any cheese remnants off the key.

"Ah, my dear," grinned Galeron, running a hand down her cheek. "It seemed clear to me, from the very first day, that Reese was drawn to you, the maid. He was the most straightforward of all, but also the man to be played most delicately. I simply had to encourage his affections and the main prize would remain mine." His smile grew. "Of course, I did not realize at the time that I was undoing my own game, but in the end things have worked out just the way I had planned."

Kay's heart thundered in her chest. Reese had cared for her from the start? It was his love for her that had caused him the indecision about marrying the woman behind the curtain? She had not had time to process any of this, to put thoughts to actions and to sort out what had happened.

The pieces all fell into place. A warm glow suffused her, filling every nook and cranny of her being.

Reese loved her.

Suddenly Galeron's presence felt stifling; she needed to get out, to get free. She smiled apologetically, handing him back the key, then reaching behind her to take the cheese.

"I apologize, Galeron, I still am feeling unwell. Maybe if I go eat this in the courtyard, it will help to refresh me." She drew the cheese close to her chest, holding the impression side inward. "I appreciate you opening the pantry for me. I am sure you have far more important tasks to take up your time right now."

He smiled down at her, escorting her from the room. Once they were both out, he securely closed the wooden door, then drew shut the heavy metal grill, locking it back into place.

"I do have a number of tasks to look over," he agreed, reaching down to tap on the bag which held his codex. "A plethora of items need to be checked off my list before tomorrow. Will you be all right?"

Kay nodded. "It is just a short walk to the courtyard, I will be fine. Thank you again."

Galeron bowed, then headed off into the barracks.

Kay took a long breath, pressing the cheese to her chest, her heart thudding. There was still hope. She had to cling to the faintest of chances that this might somehow work.

She waited another moment, then moved with steady steps across the ground floor, through the nearly empty barracks, and out into the open courtyard.

Her heart sank. A line of soldiers manned the top of the wall, ready with bows and crossbows. The drawbridge was up, and the new boards of the replacement gate were nearly in place. Men scurried around the area, dragging supplies and lining up weapons. If her forces had to come in this way, they would face quite a challenge. It would be a hard fought battle if they tried today. Come tomorrow, with the mercenaries added to the defenses, it would be nigh impossible.

She moved with determination toward the stables. She would see that it did not come to that end.

Stephen met her almost immediately as she moved into the quiet building. "I am sorry, Kay," he apologized, "but I am under strict orders not to let any horses out for the next few days."

She nodded in agreement, drawing him to the very back of the wooden building. There was nobody else in the stables, but even so she crouched down with him against the rear wall.

"Stephen, can you carve me this key?" She held out the block of cheese, showing him the shapes.

Stephen tilted his head in curiosity, then took the block, examining the mold with careful attention. He ran his finger down one of the indentations, testing the firmness of the side.

"What type of a lock is it?" he asked, his attention focused on the cheese.

"A metal one, about four inches in diameter."

"So it would be a metal key," he nodded to himself. "The replica would need to be a hard wood, then, to move the tumblers." He glanced up at the shelf behind him, reaching up with one hand and sorting through a few pieces of wood before bringing down a small bar shape. "Here, rock maple," he mused. "I think I could carve a key from this block that might work. It would only be good for one or two uses, though," he added. "The twisting strain on the key would do it in after that."

Relief washed through her. There was hope. "Thank God," she breathed out.

"When do you need it by?" asked Stephen, holding the wood block against the cheese, examining how the shapes overlay.

"Tonight, after dark."

Stephen's head jerked up, his eyes round with shock. "You must be joking," he coughed out.

Kay's heart stopped. The blood drained from her face. "It has to be," she insisted, not willing to believe that she had come so far, only to hit another wall. "There is no other way. The mercenaries will be here tomorrow morning."

Stephen stared again at the block of wood. "If I do it with softer wood, the key will never turn," he insisted. "But to carve through this stuff in only one afternoon, and to get the shape you need to fit into the lock?"

Kay lay both of her hands on his. "It has got to work, Stephen," she pressed. "How can I help? Is there anything I can do?"

Stephen glanced around him. "Perhaps if the stable chores could somehow be done for me, so that the soldiers did not realize I was up to something suspicious -"

"Done!" vowed Kay with relief. "I can do every chore in here and anything else you need as well. It will keep me occupied and give you every spare moment to get that key carved."

Stephen did not waste another moment. He took a final glance at the key mold, scratched a length indicator on the block of wood, then sat down against the back wall. Pulling out his knife, he began whittling with furious intensity.

Kay strode toward the first stall and grabbed the pitchfork. This stable would shine when she was done. The soldiers would have no cause to question Stephen or to intrude on their activities of the afternoon.

* * *

The sun was beginning to set when Kay heard footsteps approaching the stables. She waved desperately for Stephen to hide his supplies. He had just tucked them beneath a feed bag when Galeron pushed open the main doors, his head swiveling around the interior.

"There you are," he called out to Kay. "I did not think to look for you in here."

"I do love my horses, after all," replied Kay, infusing her voice with calm contentment. "I wanted to make sure they were taking their temporary confinement well."

"You are a good mistress," praised Galeron with a smile. "In any case, dinner is being served."

"Of course, thank you," she responded, glancing at Stephen, her shoulders tight. She knew the key was in a roughly appropriate shape, but it still needed carving and finishing to reach the exact right dimensions. Could she sneak out to the stables in the evening without being detected, in order to retrieve the final result? She would have to risk it.

She nodded at the young lad, then moved with Galeron across the courtyard and into the main hall. The room felt so different to her now. The tables filled with strange MacDougal soldiers. The staff was tense and on edge. She moved along to the head table, holding back a shudder as Galeron settled himself with contentment into the main chair at its center.

Then Anne was at her side, helping her to sit and pouring her out a large tankard of ale. "I heard you stayed for us, Kay," she whispered, her eyes wide. "You are the most noble mistress we could ever hope to have."

Kay put her hand on Anne's arm, giving the woman a gentle squeeze. "You all deserve the very best," she vowed. "I will see that you are taken care of and treated fairly."

"And we will look out for you," returned Anne, blushing, then moving on to continue serving the rest of the table.

The food was brought out – a plain stew with only a few chunks of meat in it. Kay's mouth quirked into a smile. The staff was showing their disapproval of the new masters.

She heard a snarl from Galeron's other side, and looked up sharply. Jack was staring down at his food, a frown growing.

"They call this a meal?"

Kay winced. While she understood completely the feelings of the staff, she also had to keep them safe for the next day, free from the ire of the current occupiers.

She leant forward. "Galeron, Jack, where do you plan on sleeping tonight?"

Two pairs of eyes swiveled to her with bright interest. Galeron spoke first, his voice rich with curiosity.

"We had planned to stay in the barracks. We would give you some time to settle in to this new situation and grow accustomed to how things will now run."

Kay shook her head. The last thing she wanted was for the two best fighters in the keep to be immediately adjacent to the invasion point. "I think I see the issue here, with the servants," she explained, as if it was the most logical thing in the world. "By tradition, the master always sleeps in the master's room. It is what they expect. Because you are staying in the barracks, they are treating you as soldiers. Once you start living as the master, they will start behaving as if you were."

Jack glanced down at the food again, and then back at her. "Is it really that simple?" he asked, askance.

Kay innocently shrugged. "They are simple servants, after all," she pointed out.

Jack nodded. "That does make sense," he stated, his shoulders relaxing. "Dogs in a pack fall into line once they know who the leader is." He grunted as Jessica moved past him, stopping to fill his ale mug up to the brim again. "The minions are well trained in general," he conceded. "All right, then, we will try it your way."

"You will not be disappointed," promised Kay, hoping against hope that she would not have to find out.

* * *

The courses of the meal came and went. Soon Jack and Galeron were off to see to the final updates to the keep's defenses. Kay moved to sit in front of the fireplace, a mending project for Molly lying neglected in her lap. Bands of iron slowly tightened around her entire body.

Darkness had settled across the room, and the flickering fire cast dancing shadows across her body. Reese and the others would be moving down into the cave complex, working by torchlight to seek out whatever series of tunnels led to end at the stone wall of the cellar. Tension ratcheted even tighter around her chest. There were hundreds of tunnels! What were the chances of them finding the right one?

She drew in a long, shuddering breath, closing her eyes for a moment. She had to be strong. Somehow they would find the right tunnel. When they did, she would be ready for them.

She worked with half-hearted interest on the mending, watching the minutes tick by. The room had only three soldiers in it, then two, then it was only her and the softly licking flames of the ebbing fire. The men were either manning the walls or sound asleep below, preparing for the morning.

She looked again into the glowing embers. What time was it now? Nine? Ten? Was it safe to try to sneak out to the stables?

There was a movement in the entryway, and Stephen was there, smiling at her. Relief washed over her, releasing away her tension. He nodded, then came over to stand beside her.

"I thought you might like to know, Kay, that the horses are all bedded down for the night," he offered quietly, his hand hanging loosely at his side. "You have no need to worry about tonight. Everything is prepared."

"That is very sweet of you, Stephen, to let me know," she responded, her eyes glowing in heartfelt thanks. "You have set my mind at ease."

He gave a small movement of his hand, and a dark object slipped from his grasp into the folds of her dress. She drew her legs together, catching the item in the fabric.

"I will be heading to bed then, M'Lady. Good night."

"Good night, and thank you," she returned, imbuing the words with every ounce of meaning that she could.

He bowed, and headed back toward the stairs, down toward his quarters.

Kay took in a long, deep breath, waiting long moments to ensure nobody else was around. Then she surreptitiously slipped her hand into the folds of fabric, to wrap them around the wooden key. It felt firm, defined, and durable.

She carefully tucked the mending into a corner of the chair. If she was caught prowling around later, she could simply say she was looking to find it. It would provide the perfect excuse.

In a moment she was in motion. She had just reached the entryway when Galeron came up from the courtyard. He smiled when he saw her, offering a short bow.

"Heading up to bed, my dear?" he asked with a gentle smile. "Let me accompany you, since we are now sharing a suite."

"Of course," agreed Kay, her throat tight. She wrapped her fingers around the key, hiding it from view, and allowed him to guide her up the stairs to the solar.

Jack was already there, sprawled on the sofa, finishing off a tankard of ale. He rolled to his feet when Galeron and Kay entered the room.

Jack's voice was a sour grumble. "So, I am to get the smaller, middle bedroom, I assume."

Kay nodded. "These are the nicest rooms in the keep," she pointed out, keeping her voice even. "Far better than the barracks below. I am sure they will do for now."

Galeron frowned at Jack for a moment, then looked back to Kay. "They will do just fine," he assured her. "I am sure we could not ask for anything better."

Jack looked as if he might disagree with that statement, but he held his tongue.

Kay dropped a curtsy. "Good night, then," she murmured, then retreated to the safety of her room. She closed the solid door behind her, dropping the bar. Once safely locked within, she hurried to the fireplace to drop down beside it, to draw out the key and examine it closely.

Stephen had done an excellent job in the time he had available. It looked exactly as she had remembered the metal key. He had polished it to a smooth finish to give it the best chance of sliding the tumblers without a catch. It felt firm in her hand.

It had to work.

She went to the window, staring out at the rolling ocean waves. From her room she could not see the front of the keep. She could not see her father's forces encamped there. The cliffs blocked her view of the beach, so she could not tell if soldiers were in motion there either, making any progress on the maze of caves.

She wrapped her fingers around the key. She had to hope that the plan was a success.

The world outside wavered for a moment, the ocean waves melding into a long ripple of grey. She shook her head, moving away from the window and sitting down on the bed. She was simply exhausted. If only she could but sleep, even for a few hours.

She knew she could not. What if she closed her eyes and awoke only in the full brightness of sun, the mercenaries already safely within the castle walls and all hope lost? No, she had to make it through the night. She had to do her part in ensuring the attack succeeded.

A loud snoring noise suddenly boomed from her sister's bedroom. She started in surprise, then relaxed, almost laughing. It always astounded her how quickly soldiers could fall asleep when they needed to. They knew how to conserve their strength - how to grab a hold of any moment available to be fresh for a fight. Apparently Jack had learned that trick. Which only left …

She listened closely to the sounds around her. Were there snoring sounds coming from her father's room as well? She had to take the chance. It was perhaps almost eleven by now, and she had to get to the cellars. She had to hope that neither man would risk her ire by intruding on her bedroom before dawn.

Just to be safe, she placed several pillows beneath her blankets and arranged them in the shape of a sleeping person. Then, slowly, carefully, she drew out the bar from the door, laying it to one side. She gently pulled the wooden door open, peering around the edge. If one of the men were still awake, she could simply say she was looking for the mending items to keep her occupied.

The room was empty. Both other bedroom doors were solidly closed. There was no sound other than the snoring which seemed to grow louder as she waited.

She slipped through her doorway, drawing the door gently closed behind her. She worked her way across the room, the precious key clutched in her hand, and reached the main door. She drew in a deep breath.

She carefully eased the door open and smiled. The hallway was empty. Apparently Galeron and Jack were conserving all of their troops' strength for the morning, the most likely time of an attack, if there were to be one. They were not wasting one man on unnecessary duties.

To her benefit.

She moved into the hall, closing the door behind her, and slowly descended down the stairs. The main hall was deserted. She barely stopped before continuing down toward the barracks level.

She drew herself up as she reached the ground floor. It seemed that the vast majority of Galeron's forces were sprawled on a bed or mat in various stages of sleep. One or two sat hunched over a blade, sharpening an edge. They glanced up in idle curiosity as she stepped into the room, but dismissed her and went back to their work. She was not stopped or questioned as she moved across the room toward the workroom.

She turned the corner and took in a deep breath. She had made it through the barracks without incident – but now the final test stood before her. If she could not get this lock open, all else would be lost. The gate loomed before her, solid, black, and sturdily sealed. Would the wooden key turn the tumblers?

She glanced into the workroom and spotted a block of soap standing by the wash basin on a counter. She moved over to it, glancing again around the empty room, then drew the key from her hand. She rubbed it carefully along the bar, first one side, then the other.

When she was satisfied with the task, she moved again to the lock, giving a final look around to be sure no guards were moving in her direction. Carefully she inserted the key into the keyhole, and slowly, oh so slowly, she turned it.

She felt the resistance of the tumblers, and her heart thudded in her chest. She applied more pressure, praying that Stephen had chosen a solid piece of wood, that he had followed the mold accurately, and that she had pressed the key into the cheese in an even fashion. A thousand little things could go wrong, to cause the parts of the key not to exactly match the inside of the iron lock. She pressed … pressed … the key slowly rotated within the housing.

Click.

The lock came open.

Kay let out her breath in a long gasp; she had not realized she was holding it in. She quickly withdrew the key, tucking it into the pouch at her belt, then slipped the lock free, pulling open the grate. The cellar door opened inward, and she gave it a push, reaching past it for the torch that hung on the wall. She moved quickly now, going to light the torch from the fire in the workroom, returning to slip within the gate, pulling it closed. She put her hand through the grate, re-seating the lock in its place, closing it so it was almost fully shut. That would pass all but the most close examination, should anyone walk past it. Then she stepped back and closed the wooden cellar door.

Her heart soared. She had done it. She was in the cellar, the grate was unlocked, and now she simply had to wait for Reese to come for her!

She moved carefully down the stairs, settling the torch on the far wall, not lighting the others. Not tonight. She would only have this one light so the glow did not shine beneath the door at the top of the stairs.

She began lifting each box, one by one, and moving them from the hollow wall to other parts of the cellar. It seemed a long while before she had cleared the area. She sat, exhausted, on one of the boxes to stare at the blank stone wall.

What time was it now? Midnight? Maybe the soldiers had been unable to get to the caves at all. Perhaps they had been stymied by the men on the wall or another force beyond their control. Were they even coming for her? Was this all a hopeless gesture?

She moved over to the wall and put her ear against it. She could hear nothing. Was anyone beyond that solid barrier?

She glanced around the room and spotted an old iron bar which was used to pry open boxes. She picked it up and went back to the wall. Holding the bar by one end, she rapped solidly against the wall.

Thunk. Thunk. Thunk.

She put her ear against the wall. There was no response.

She slumped, her hope fading. She sat down against the wall, her fingers finding the carven heart in the stone, and she laid her head against the wall. With the other hand she continued her message.

Thunk. Thunk. Thunk.

Silence.

Thunk. Thunk. Thunk.

Silence.

Thunk. Thunk. Thunk.

The faintest echo came to her, as if the most far off mountain had rebounded her call to her …

thunk … thunk … thunk …

Kay almost cried out in relief. They were coming for her! Reese was coming!

She renewed her tattoo, and with each round the answering call got louder, more steady. It seemed like no time at all before the response was immediately on the other side of the wall, vibrating her hand with the force of the message.

She stood, backing away, and now she could see the wall shiver, shake, as the blows began to push the individual blocks out from the flat surface. Dust cascaded loose, and she glanced nervously up the stairs. She knew that she and her sister had played loudly in the cellars many times without the servants knowing their location, but attentive soldiers were not absent-minded maids. Would the men in the barracks feel the vibrations?

There was a grinding noise and the center block slid toward her. She rushed forward, putting her arms out, catching the heavy stone with a grunt and carefully lowering it down to the ground.

There was a low call, soft and urgent. "Kay?"

Kay ran to the dark hollow, putting her face against it, desperately trying to see a face within. "Reese?"

A hand came through the opening. Strong. Sturdy. She clung to it, almost crying. She clasped it with both of her own, bringing it to her face and kissing it.

"Kay, it is all right," came Reese's voice, comforting from the darkness. "I am here for you."

Kay's throat closed up; she could barely speak for the emotion that overwhelmed her. "Reese ..." she cried, pressing his hand tightly to her face, to her lips, wishing she could climb through the narrow opening to wrap herself in his arms.

Reese's hand held her cheek for a moment, then it gently began to draw away. "Kay, you have to let go."

Kay knew this was true, and yet she found it almost impossibly hard to relinquish her hold, to draw her fingers back. The hand vanished again into the darkness, leaving her alone ... alone ...

The work began in earnest, and soon the blocks were sliding free in quicker succession. Some were drawn back into the darkness, while the others coming toward her she took with effort and lowered them down. Then the hole was large enough for a man, and Reese was climbing his way through. She was in his arms, was being spun around by him, was being kissed ... kissed ... She wrapped her arms up his back, pulling him close, melding her body against his with every ounce of her strength.

Finally he drew back, looking down at her with shining eyes. "Keren-happuch, I am so proud of you."

Kay nearly laughed out loud, and her body shone with her joy. "Only my father calls me that," she admonished

Reese, running her hand through his thick hair, relishing the feeling of his arms strong around her body. "Kay is how you have known me, and Kay I shall be."

The hole had widened as if by magic, and in a moment Eric was stepping through, sword out, looking around the cellar with a quick eye. His gaze stopped on Kay. "I suppose we cannot convince you to head back down the tunnels, to go to the safety of the camp with your sister?"

Kay's eyes grew fierce. "What, abandon Serenor when it needs me the most?"

Eric chuckled, glancing at Reese. "I practically had to tie Em to her bed to get her to stay behind," he admitted.

Reese nodded. "That is why I had Leland come prepared," he responded.

Leland moved through the opening, carrying a leather tunic and sword. "Did I hear my name being mentioned?"

Kay put her hands above her head, and in a moment she was suited up. When Reese handed her her sword, she stared at it for a long moment.

Her voice was a whisper. "For honor."

The sword seemed to shine in the torchlight.

Reese gently turned her to face him. "The only reason I am agreeing to this is, if you are out of my sight, I will be obsessed about your safety," he cautioned, his eyes serious. "I need you to stay right behind me. If I get distracted because I am worried about you -"

Kay nodded. "I will shadow you and stay quiet," she promised without hesitation.

The room filled with soldiers, and Eric came over to join them. "What is the situation?" he asked Kay, rolling his broad shoulders in preparation.

"They added a grate before the cellar door," explained Kay, looking between the two men. "However, with Stephen's skilled help, the lock is now open. The servants are all abed. The barracks are stuffed to the gills with soldiers, most of them asleep, but a few are awake. Only a few can be on the walls, I imagine, as lookouts. It seems they expect the main attack would be in the morning if the mercenaries did not show up."

"That makes sense," agreed Eric. "It is what I would have done."

Reese settled his hand on the hilt of his sword. "Where might we find Jack and Galeron?"

Kay smiled. "They are up on the top floor, isolated and alone."

Reese's face drained to white. When he spoke, he voice was wound tight. "They slept in your suite?"

Kay placed a hand against his cheek, reassuring him. "I told them to take the two empty rooms – my father's and my sister's – to keep them as far away from the initial attack as possible. I thought it would help you make progress through the soldiers, to have those two distant and unable to coordinate a defense."

The color eased back into Reese's face. "Yes, that will help immensely. Thank you."

Leland moved up to the group. "We are ready," he informed the others. "We should get this started."

Reese turned to Kay again. "I need you by my side," he stated again, his face tense with concern. "Stay with me."

"I swear," she vowed, stretching up to give him a long kiss.

His arm slid up her side, almost drawing her in again, but then he was stepping back, smiling ruefully. "I would lose the night in your embrace," he groaned, his gaze held on hers. Finally he turned, bringing his attention to Eric and Leland.

"Let us start."

Kay resettled her grip on her sword, and her heart firmed with determination.

Whatever it took, she would see Serenor freed.

Chapter 18

Kay pressed herself to the front of the group, her voice the barest of whispers. "Let me take the lead, at least for now," she suggested, her hand on the door. "If I am spotted, no alarm will be raised. I can act as a scout for as long as we can remain unseen."

Reese's brow furrowed, but he nodded. "You stay nearby," he instructed, his tone brooking no argument.

"Of course," agreed Kay. In a moment she had cautiously pulled back the basement door, then peered through the metal grate toward the quiet barracks. The room was completely still now; only the sound of a chorus of snores emanating from the dark room. All soldiers were taking every opportunity for rest before the battle to come.

She nodded. One by one the crew slid off to the left, staying in the shadows. They moved their way along the back edge of the work room and toward the narrow servant's stair which led between here and the floor above. This smaller path allowed food and supplies to be brought up to the main dining hall without disturbing any sleeping soldiers.

Reese motioned his hand toward the wall nearer to the barracks. Half the men crept to press their bodies against it. One soldier acted as a lookout, peering carefully around the corner at the slumbering soldiers.

Kay took the lead again, moving cautiously to the narrow stairs. She worked her way up them one at a time, the pain in her legs reminding her that she was far from healed. At the top of the stair she peered out into the main hall. She was in an alcove behind the head table. The embers glowed softly from the fireplace, but otherwise the large room was deserted. Everyone was either sound asleep or manning the walls, watching for any sign of danger.

She breathed a sigh of relief.

Slowly, carefully, the remaining crew made their way across the expanse. They wove around tables and stools, and, after long minutes of tense care, they reached the other side.

Another motion from Reese, and the other half of the men moved their way silently down the front stairs, cutting off the second egress from the barracks. Only Reese, Leland, Jevan, and Eric remained with Kay.

Reese started up the stairs first, ensuring Kay was safely nestled between him and Leland. They took the stairs slowly, cautiously, alert at every step for the sound of metal on metal, the sign that the battle had been raised below.

The keep echoed in its silence.

They reached the top landing. Reese carefully pressed the door open, peered inside, and then waved the group in. The room was stark in the deep night. Shafts of moonlight streamed in the row of windows, creating a patchwork of light and dark that patterned the floor. The three doors on the far wall were closed.

Kay tapped Reese on his shoulder. "Let me lure Galeron out," she whispered. "If you can take him unawares, that only leaves Jack to deal with."

Reese's eyes held hers for a long moment, then he nodded in agreement. The four men moved to stand in the deep shadows on either side of the master bedroom doorway. When they were set, Kay took in a deep breath, then approached the sturdy wooden door.

She gave a gentle knock on it, calling out, "Galeron, I need to talk with you."

Almost immediately there was an answering creak of motion, then the thud of feet on floor. Kay took several steps backwards, moving clear of the door area and standing in a dark strip between shafts of moonlight so her form would be shadowed. She did not want Galeron to spot her sword or armor until it was too late.

The door creaked open and Galeron emerged from his room, running his hand through his curls as he shook the sleep from his eyes. "To be called by your voice in the middle of the night," he mused, his lips curling in a smile. "Few things could be higher on my list. Just what would your pleasure be? Feeling lonely already, are we?"

Reese's dagger was at his throat in an instant, and Galeron's eyes flashed with surprise. "You? How in the world?" He glanced out the window, his confusion becoming even thicker as he saw his men quietly walking the ramparts. "What could I possibly have overlooked?"

Reese pressed the blade tighter in against his skin. "Hush," he snapped in a low whisper.

All eyes turned toward the remaining closed door. Reese backed up with his hostage while Jevan, Eric, and Leland moved cautiously toward the room.

The door flew open. Jack strode out, his head held high, a sword in one hand, a dagger in the other. He ran his gaze scornfully over each person present, shaking his head when he saw Galeron's state.

"And to think she thought you were the better man to hold this keep," he shot out in disgust. "Caught by the oldest trick in the book."

Galeron's voice was calm. "It was impossible to anticipate this," he retorted. "How could any help have made it in past our defenses tonight? The odds of that were astronomical!"

Jack rolled his shoulders, settling deeper into his stance. "Your damned lists cannot account for everything," he snapped. "And I will not be coming quietly. If you men want me, you will have to come get me."

Reese's voice was quiet, but it rang across the room with certainty.

"Jack is mine."

Jack's grin turned wolfish, and a low chuckle dredged from his throat. "Still feeling upset about that little love pat I gave to your girlfriend?" he asked, his eyes sharp. "Once I am done with you, believe me, she will get what she really deserves."

Reese's face stilled, and he nodded to the trio of men. In a moment Leland and Eric had moved to stand protectively before Kay. Jevan placed his own dagger at Galeron's throat, pulling him back, forcing him to his knees to minimize his threat.

Kay's heart thudded against her chest as she watched Jack and Reese circle each other in the darkened room, moving from streaming moonlight to darkest shadow and back again. Each man held his blade surely in his grip, their eyes intent on each other. Each watched the placement of the foot, the tilt of the shoulders, the sliding of the gaze ...

Jack's attack was as swift as a viper, Reese spun beneath it, countering, and the fight was on. Jack moved with lightning speed, swinging his sword down over his head toward Reese's right shoulder. Reese dodged further to the right, letting the sword skitter down his own sword's length, whipping the tip around to spin toward Jack's ear.

Jack threw his sword up and right, catching Reese's blade on his own, twisting the hilt to send the edge at Reese's neck. Reese ducked under the swing, pulling the blade hard toward Jack's stomach. Then they were in the shadows again, and it was a blur of steel on steel, the stamp of landing feet, the grunts of hard exertion as each man battled for his life.

It took every ounce of control for Kay not to run forward, not to try to help in some way, to instead remain frozen by Leland. She knew if she made one tiny motion toward the fray that his strong arms would easily overpower her, force her to watch in fear … in hope …

The combatants spun into the light again, the dust motes sparkling in the glow. There was a red slash across Reese's arm; a matching one ripped raggedly across Jack's stomach, streaming blood. Both men were breathing heavily.

All at once Jack took a step back, drawing his hand to his stomach almost involuntarily. He cursed in a guttural snarl, his hand becoming instantly wet. A long moment passed before he spoke.

"I concede," he bit out in a growl. "Here, take my sword." He turned his sword around so it was hilt first and offered it to Reese with a cold stare.

Everything in the room went into slow motion. Reese reached forward with his left hand to take the hilt as Jack began to spin with the dagger in his own left hand. Kay drove toward him in a panic. Leland grabbed at her arm, dragging her down onto her knees with a sharp yank. Her two damaged legs slammed onto the wooden planks, and she screamed in agony. Reese intercepted the dagger with his left hand, driving his sword hard, straight through Jack's center.

As Kay fell sideways, Jack fell in the same direction. They both landed with a heavy thud, facing each other, Jack's cold, lifeless eyes gazing into her own.

The distant ring of battle sounded from deep beneath them, but Kay could barely draw in a breath, so overwhelming was the agony cascading over her from both of her legs. Reese was at her side in a moment, and she moved her hand shakily to his arm, to the wound which opened up his tricep.

"Are you all right?" she managed to gasp through the pain.

He shook his head in gentle amusement, leaning forward to kiss her tenderly on her forehead. He carefully helped her back up to her unsteady feet, then nodded at the other three. Jevan went first, ushering his hostage down the stairs, then Leland and Eric followed, with Kay and Reese bringing up the rear.

By the time they made their way down to the barracks, the brief flare of combat had already been brought under control. The soldiers' hands were tied with sturdy rope and they were being ushered down into the basement tunnels. The main doors to the keep remained sturdily shut, and there was no sense that the troops outside had heard anything.

Eli nodded as the group came into the room. "That was easier than we could have hoped for," he reported. "They didn't budge an inch until that yell came from above, and even then their responses were sluggish. It was an easy enough task to keep them from mounting much of a fight. Most never even made it to their feet."

Jevan looked around the barracks area, allowing himself a low chuckle. "I certainly would expect much more from my own soldiers," he mused.

Galeron shrugged in acceptance. "It is hard to get good help nowadays," he agreed. His eyes moved down the length of the barracks, and then stared in surprise at the open cellar door, at the remaining soldiers who were being escorted down into its depths.

"The cellar ..." he stated slowly, his eyes sharpening. "Do not tell me there are tunnels that I missed?"

Kay's mouth drew into a smile. "Your lists cannot hold everything, after all," she countered sweetly. "Now it is time to finish reclaiming what is mine."

She turned to Reese, and he moved over to the main doors, pressing them open. Together the group moved to the top steps, standing in the bright moonlight, their soldiers moving to fill in behind them. The movement on the wall stuttered to a stop as the men guarding it took in the situation and turned to face their new threat.

Jevan pulled his knife blade closer against Galeron's throat. "You threatened my young boys and the people I hold most dear," he reminded Galeron in a low growl. "Do not think I have any compunction about gutting you from nose to tail."

Galeron did not hesitate. "Put down your arms," he called out to the remaining solders. "They have taken the keep, and we need to regroup. Drop your weapons and come down peacefully."

There was a long moment of hesitation. Reese stepped forward, his voice carrying across the courtyard. "We have the gold, too," he pointed out evenly. "We will let you go without harm, if you come down now. Otherwise you will be slain where you stand, and with no chance of being paid either."

That seemed to settle it for most of them. One by one their swords fell clanging onto the stone or wood, and they filed down the narrow steps. They allowed their hands to be tied behind their back by the soldiers of Weston's forces.

There was a soft golden glow in the sky, and Kay's heart swelled with a wave of joy. She had done it. Her keep had been saved. It was all over.

Eric mounted the ramparts, and his voice came short and sharp down to them. "The mercenaries are coming," he warned.

Kay started to run toward the stairs. Bolts of pain shot through her legs, and they gave way almost immediately. She bit back the scream that welled up within her. Reese was at her side catching her; holding her up. He swept her into his arms, and in a moment he was carrying her up the stairs, Leland close behind them. Jevan prodded Galeron along to stand nearby.

Kay had to admit that the mercenaries' forces were more than impressive. The troop moved with well-practiced precision and was amply provisioned.

Eric glanced at the small group of troops which had remained by the camp to watch over his wife and father-in-law. The muscles in his jaw clenched.

Kay gave him a gentle pat on the shoulder. "The mercenaries will be gone in a moment," she promised in a low voice. "I will never see my sister or father hurt."

She leant forward. "You there! Who is the commander of your troop?"

A tall bear of a man rode to the front, looking up at the group on the wall, his eyes running over each in turn. "I am Joshua," he responded in a commanding voice. "And who might you be?"

Kay stood tall, giving herself as strong a presence as she could gather. "I am Keren-happuch," she announced, "Owner and protector of this keep." She glanced sideways at Galeron. "The man who thought to be my husband, and co-owner of these lands, has lost his bet. He has also lost the gold that is my dowry." Her mouth turned up into a smile. "I am afraid he can no longer pay for your services."

Joshua gazed at her evenly for a long moment, then turned his gaze on Galeron. His eyes went to the knife held at Galeron's throat; to the men who stood in fierce resolve at Kay's side.

There was a long breath where a breeze moved through the open landscape, causing the leaves on the ring of trees to rustle and flutter.

Then, with the pull of a rein, Joshua turned. His group circled. Without another word the troop of men moved off toward the south at a steady trot. The noise echoed as the force became more distant, moved along a ridge, and then faded completely from sight.

A cheer rang out from her father's camp, echoed heartily by the soldiers within the keep. In a moment the drawbridge rattled its way down to an open position. It was only minutes before Em was riding in with an escort of soldiers, Eric was running to help her down, and they were entwined in a laughing embrace.

Leland strode down the stairs, mounting and riding out toward the remaining troops. By the time Reese had carefully assisted Kay in moving down the steps and over to her sister, her father's forces were already consolidating around her in the courtyard. The remnants hurriedly scrambled across the drawbridge, and the large, wooden beams were lifted up, securely closing with a muffled thud.

The prisoners were herded into the stables under close guard. Leland rolled his shoulders in relief as he came over to Kay and Reese. "That is everyone," he reported. "There is no person – friendly or enemy - left outside the keep walls."

Em's arms came close around Kay, drawing her in, and for the first time in days Kay's pains melted away.

Em pressed her forehead against Kay's. "I am so proud of you," she whispered with a smile. "You did it. You saved your keep."

Leland's eyes went up to Reese who was standing at Kay's side. "It was both of them," he pointed out with an understanding nod. "Their teamwork was what turned the tide in this situation."

Reese stepped forward to slide his arm around Kay's waist, his fingers tenderly cinching him to her side. A warm glow infused her. She leant against him, and it was as if the sky had become brushed with golden light.

Jevan's voice cut into her blissful world. "So, what do we do with this traitor?" he snapped, giving a prod to Galeron. He still held his knife's blade at Galeron's neck, and Kay could see a thin line of blood forming along its length.

She let out a deep breath. Everything had worked out quite well. She had Reese by her side. Em and Eric were safe and together. And, after all, Galeron had strove to ensure his aims were achieved without anyone being hurt. He had been an enemy, yes, but he had worked in a logical manner. He had treated them with respect. Even when he had the upper hand, he had ensured innocents were kept safe.

She gently separated herself from Reese, then walked to stand in front of Jevan and Galeron. She looked up into Galeron's dark eyes for a long moment, then nodded to Jevan.

"Let him go," she requested, her voice sure and serene.

There was a chorus of grumbles from the circle around her, and Jevan harshly shook his head. "The man deserves to be hung," he snapped in anger.

Kay drew her eyes to Jevan, remaining still. "He treated your boys well, Jevan," she pointed out. "There was food and drink for all. No person was mistreated while he stayed with us." Her eyes moved back to Galeron's. "His crime was to crave ownership of Serenor a bit too strongly. It is hard for me to fault him in that."

Leland's voice rang out behind her. "And what if he comes back, now that he knows our layout inside and out, and launches a fresh attack?"

Kay steadily held Galeron's gaze. "Would you vow never to return to Serenor, once you departed our walls?"

Galeron immediately nodded, his neck stretched against the blade. "I vow to never return to Serenor on my honor and life," he agreed, his eyes clear and sure. "It would not be logical for me to try again. I made my best attempt and failed. It is time for me to move on to other priorities."

Kay searched for any sign of deception within Galeron's gaze, but he seemed to be completely honest in his statement. She looked again at Jevan. There was a long moment of hesitation as the soldier looked across the men standing around the open courtyard.

Then, with a movement half of frustration, he removed the knife from Galeron's neck.

Galeron allowed himself to smile, bringing his hand to his neck and wiping offhandedly at the streak of blood. He then gave a long stretch, rubbing his hands on his lower back to relieve the strain there, before standing straight again.

"Thank you, Kay," he sighed in relief. "I knew I would be able to count on your honorable nature." He offered his hand to her.

Kay stepped forward to take it.

Her world spun as he gave a hard, forward yank. The thrust threw her off balance on her pain-lanced legs, wrapped her around, and in a heartbeat she was pinned hard against his chest, a knife held sharp against her throat. His other hand wrapped firmly around her waist. Her legs throbbed in agony at the twisting movement, and she could barely hold herself upright.

The men surrounding her froze in a tableau of shock, hands partway to their weapons. They were locked in place by the blade against her throat.

Kay choked against the pressure of the knife. "Galeron …?"

He chuckled down at her, his eyes not leaving the ring of furious men. He slowly took a step back to separate from them, then two. "Serenor is a castle of stone, and many others like it exist out there in the world," he mused in a calm, logical tone. "However, you, my dear, you are quite unique. My new priority is to have you by my side. With our combined efforts, no future project will end in failure. Your escapades last night have proven that beyond any shadow of a doubt."

Reese's voice was steely and rang with iron promise. "Let her go, and your death might be swift rather than long," he vowed.

Galeron gave a twist to his blade, and Kay felt a trickle of warm blood trail down her neck. Reese froze in place, his jaw clenching, and Galeron gave a low laugh. "I have the upper hand here," he reminded Reese. "I could torture her with every step and still end up with a live hostage at the end. But you – you never know when my wrist might bite a little too deep."

He pulled Kay back toward the keep, and she stumbled, her legs screaming out their resistance at every step. She struggled to draw a breath, to make some sense of the situation.

"Galeron, this is madness. You could have left on your own, free and clear. Is it logical to burden yourself with an injured hostage? Let me go, and you can escape to wherever you wish!"

Galeron worked his way up the keep steps, his knife steady at her throat, moving into the entryway and then into the deserted barracks area. Reese and the others followed at a safe distance, their eyes alert on every movement.

"Ah, my dear, but this is exactly what my backup plan entailed. If I could not have the keep, I would never leave empty-handed. With you at my side, we can take on any keep we wish and rule it together."

He tugged her along in front of the cellar door, and then moved into the archway, stepping back onto the landing. He pressed the knife into her throat and she froze in place. She balanced carefully as he released the hand from around her waist. Kay's heart sank in panic as Galeron brought the large iron grate closed, separating her from Reese. Galeron carefully withdrew the key from his pouch and sealed the lock from within with a loud CLICK.

Her voice nearly broke. "I could never love you, never love any keep the way I love Serenor," she protested, shaking her head. "Your plan cannot work."

He smiled paternally at her, tucking the key back into its pouch. "You would be surprised what a person can get used to," he countered. "Certainly, for a while you would be upset; would hold to your beliefs. But over time you would come to accept your new situation in life. You would come to look on me first as a friend and then as a loved one. The human mind adjusts to the world it is in. Just wait and see."

Kay's eyes moved to meet Reese's and she saw the glow of determination in them. She knew with absolute certainty that the moment it was safe he would come barreling through that gate by whatever means necessary.

His eyes held Kay's with resolve. "You stay alive," he murmured. "We will find you, no matter what it takes. You just do what you have to do."

She drew in a long breath, then nodded at him, sending him every ounce of her love, belief, and resolution.

"I will wait for you," she promised with quiet determination. "No matter how long it takes."

Galeron chuckled, shaking his head. "Passion is always hot to start. We will see how it cools, once the separation is begun."

His eyes swung to look at Reese. "Speaking of which, let me remind you of the terms of *my* game. I see one flicker of light behind me, and Kay receives a cut. I smell one hint of torch pitch, and Kay receives a cut. I hear any sound of footstep - you know the consequences. If you want Kay to make it out of here alive, you will allow us unfettered conduct through these tunnels and out to sea." His eyes swept the group calmly. "Kay's fate is in your hands, gentlemen. See that you care for it properly."

He closed the wooden door in their faces.

He backed his way down the stairway with Kay, taking each torch that he passed and tossing it back into the depths. Only the one lit one remained as he reached the gaping hole in the wall. That one he took in his hand, finally turning his back on the door.

He drew the knife away from Kay's throat, holding the torch close to her face while he quickly sheathed it. Then he latched a firm grip on her wrist.

"Do not think I would be above adding a burn or two to your repertoire, should you fail to be anything but docile," he warned her in a calm tone. "The better you behave, the quicker we get through this next part of our journey.

He ran his eyes down her body, and a smile flitted on his lips. "Think of this as your endurance test, to see if you are worthy to stand by my side," he added.

Then he was plunging into the darkness, dragging her alongside him. The world narrowed down to the flickering sphere of torchlight, with nothing else existing beyond it.

Chapter 19

Kay's world was reduced to hesitant footfalls, the pained intakes of each breath, and the darkness that pressed in from every side. She had lost track of time and space. The torch created a flickering sphere of visibility immediately around them, but beyond that was a twisted, dream-like world of dripping water, fluttering bats, falling rocks, and musty, rank smells. The tunnels seemed to twist and turn without logic. She could have sworn that they doubled back enough times to be directly beneath the keep on at least five separate occasions.

There was never a glimpse of light, never the sound of pursuit. Never the remotest sense that saviors were coming to draw her away from her captor.

She tripped over an outcropping for what must have been the hundredth time. She turned her head toward Galeron's in the gloom.

"Please, can we rest for just -"

His left hand crushed down firmly on her arm, jerking her against him, and the torch flamed toward her face in a threatening gesture. She bit off her request with a quick intake of breath, turning her head from the glare and heat. He continued the forward trudge as quickly as they could manage across the rocky terrain.

A flutter of panic swirled through her heart. Until now Galeron had been many things, but a calm current of logic had always underpinned each of his actions. In this maze of inky tunnels and chaotic turns, however, his demeanor has begun to drastically change. He had taken to muttering to himself at intersections, cursing the uselessness of his lists and charts. His clutching grip on her arm had long since cut off the feeling in her hand. His movements had become short, furtive - the penned-in actions of a caged rat.

He stumbled to a stop before yet another separation of the tunnels, and Kay wearily looked around her. The combination of the strength of his grip, the heat of the flame, and the jagged pain in her legs meant that escape was the furthest thing from her mind. She was barely able to focus on staying upright, on remaining by his side in the labyrinth of stagnant pools and slimy slabs of stone. Kay knew these networks ran for miles and featured deep drop-offs and jagged pits. Every footfall was a risky proposition.

Galeron yanked her into motion, taking the left-hand tunnel, and her arm scraped a sharp-edged protuberance as she made the turn. She hissed in sharply, biting down on her pain, feeling yet another raw wound open up and trickle blood. She almost wished that she could spot a glimmer of light behind them, even if it meant she was injured as a result. At least then she would feel these red path markers she was leaving behind were acting as clues for any who followed.

She chuckled wryly. Unfortunately, she was the one who had the sharp vision. Reese was the one who -

She drew in a quick breath, the thought coming to her. Reese's talents were in his ability to pick sounds out of chaos, to hear the slightest murmur of information in a sea of noise. If she could just …

Her legs were dragging as she desperately struggled to keep up with Galeron, and she now paid focused attention

to what she was doing with them. Galeron had already
come to accept that she was less than stealthy in how she
was able to move. Perhaps she could use that to her
advantage.

The next time she moved her right foot, she let it hop
along the surface of the floor, giving out an even rhythm.

Tap. Tap. Tap.

She glanced up at Galeron, her breath caught in her
throat, but he did not hesitate a moment in his forward
progress. He did not show even the slightest break in his
wandering gaze as he pushed forward.

Her heart soared. Perhaps she could do some small part
in helping Reese to find her. She knew with absolute
certainty that he was behind them; was tracking them. He
would rescue her, if only she showed him the way.

Another turn, another slab of pebbled rock, and Kay's
left leg was dragging.

Tap. Tap. Tap.

Kay was careful to wait a long minute before her next
signal, to give Galeron time to move them forward, to pick
out a path amongst the rubble. He stared intently into the
darkness between a pair of forks, choosing the one most
likely to bring him out to his chosen destination, whatever
that might be. Kay did not care any more. Her entire focus,
her reason for being in this God-forsaken, dripping, guano-
infested tube was to send her signals back to Reese. To
draw him in to her.

Tap. Tap. Tap.

Galeron pulled up short, skirting them around the edge
of a pit at least five feet on a side. Kay glanced down as
they eased around its circumference and her heart
plummeted. If Reese were to take one step too many in the
pitch black he could easily tumble forward into its depths,
could be mangled on its sharp-edged bottom ... she forced

the thoughts out of her mind. Reese would manage it, even in the darkest night, even in the inkiest state of blindness.

He would come for her.

Another eternity passed, another endless series of tripping over ridges in the floor and slamming her head into low jutting outcrops. She had scraped her elbows, knees, and temples on every manner of rock she could imagine. She began to wonder if they would ever leave this purgatory of granite. Perhaps they were doomed to wander in the flickering dusk for an eternity.

Galeron suddenly stopped, and her eyes dropped down in automatic concern, looking for another gaping chasm. The cavern floor was a sturdy, rough surface of layers of rock and loose debris. She glanced over at Galeron in weary confusion. To her surprise his gaze was sharply forward, and, following his stare, she drew in a breath. There was the slightest hint of light from up ahead. A wavering of less-than-pitch-black which drew her heart with the strong allure of the wafting smell of fresh baked bread.

They were reaching escape.

She didn't care that Galeron clutched her arm with an iron-firm grip or that her legs were throbbing with pain. All that mattered was that they got out of these claustrophobic tunnels and reached the safety of fresh air. She needed to sprawl, just for a moment, on soft sand.

He was in motion again, and for once she was coursing with fresh energy at his side, pressing toward the light which grew in luminescence with every step. Soon it was throwing the faintest of shadows against the rock, and then they rounded the corner.

Kay's heart plunged into the hollow depths. Open before them was a sinkhole at least six feet across, its darkness stretching further than her eye could fathom. She gave a kick to a small stone. It skittered, bouncing, along the length of its depths before releasing a tinny clank from the floor far below.

Galeron's voice squeaked with stress. "Our last hurdle to freedom," he croaked.

Kay turned in astonishment. "You cannot be serious," she gasped, looking again at the open space. "There is no way I can make it across that - not in my state!"

Galeron's eyes sharpened on her own. "There is one way out," he stated, his fingers twitching. "No other plan, no other lists." His shoulder gave a spasmodic jerk. "Either you make it across that or you fail trying. One choice or the other."

Kay's heart thudded against her chest, and she looked out over the expanse. Her legs were shooting daggers of agonizing pain with each movement, and her body was on the verge of collapse. "I have not slept in thirty hours," she protested.

Galeron shook his head. "This is completely logical. There is the way out. Now we reach it." He released her arm with a push, taking a step back from her. "Only thing to do is run at it. Run, and jump. That's the sensible thing. The way out." His voice had gotten short and sharp, and he sounded as if he was trying to convince himself as much as her.

Kay thought of refusing, but looking again at the wild swirl in his eyes, she knew there would be no hope there. His mind was a logical machine which was going haywire. He saw this route as his best way to safety. While he wanted to bring her along with him, in the end his survival was the most important factor.

She had to make the jump.

She took a few steps back, forcing herself to block her exhaustion from her mind, to shut down every nerve ending to her legs. She narrowed her focus on the ledge, on the other side of the pit. She had to make it there. No matter what it took, she had to land safely on the other side.

She visualized the leap, visualized the strong spring of her legs, and visualized the thrill of reaching the firm ground beyond.

Then, with a deep breath, she ran.

Her feet were pounding into the ground, and somewhere beyond her was excruciating pain, but not within her world, not in her realm. Then she was launching, flying, the slow motion of the fall into the leaves, the suspension of time from the dropping into Reese's arms, and she felt the warmth of his love, the caress of his embrace …

SLAM.

Her chest collided with the far edge of the cliff face. The wind was knocked out of her; her world went twisty, fuzzy, and nearly faded into black. She scrambled with her arms for purchase and dug her feet in scrabbling agony. Her fingers clutched at a fault line in the floor in front of her, and her boots found purchase on a thin ledge perhaps five feet down the rocky edge. Her breath came in long, deep heaves. Her world rocked in jumpy waves, but her body did not slip further.

She had made it.

Her cheek pressed against the edge of the pit. She could just see over its top to the open cave mouth beyond, to the stretch of sand and the ocean beyond. The crashing waves were the sweetest sound she had heard in her entire lifetime. She drew in another staggering breath. She did not even try to drag herself up from the ledge she stood on. She could feel in every tendon of her body that simply holding in place would be the most she could manage. She would have to wait for Galeron to make the leap and pull her to safety.

She carefully turned her head, looking back to where he stood in the half-light of the incoming daylight. He tossed the torch down into the pit, and she watched it descend, falling its way down until the light winked out of sight.

He turned then, drawing his sword out of its scabbard, looking with wild eyes back into the darkness of the cave network. "I know you are in there, Reese," he cried out, his voice sharp with suspicion. "Come out and show yourself. Or do you fear you cannot best me?"

There was no response, and Kay wondered if Galeron's mind had finally become overwrought with the strain. Was Reese truly only a short distance away from them? Had he been able to track them through that pitch-black maze of rock and chasm?

Galeron bent down with his left hand, picked up a rock the size of a chick, and turned partially toward Kay. "Step out now, Reese," he warned, his voice cooling. "Do not make me prove the soundness of my logic by dislodging one of her hands, so you are forced to act." He drew back his arm, and Kay's heart thundered against her ribs. Surely he would not -

There was a footstep, and from the darkness Reese emerged with his sword in hand. A wave of relief engulfed Kay. Tears streamed down her face as he held her gaze for a long moment, then turned to face Galeron head on.

Galeron's laugh seemed to border on hysteria. "I knew it," he announced, holding his position between Reese and Kay. "It was the logical answer. Of course you would be back there. You could not resist her, of course. You had to follow. And now I can ensure that you do not bother either of us any more."

Reese's eyes remained on Galeron, watching his every motion, but his voice carried clearly to Kay. "Are you all right? Is your ledge sturdy?" His voice was tight with concern.

Kay took in a long, deep breath, forcing herself to wipe all thought of pain and weakness from her mind. Reese was undoubtedly injured and exhausted – and he was preparing for a swordfight with a master. Every ounce of his focus had to be on Galeron's prodigious talents. She could not distract him in even the slightest way.

"I am perfectly fine," she assured him with the most steady voice she could manage. "My hands have a solid grip, and my feet are planted. You do what you need to do."

Reese's shoulders visibly relaxed at that. He swung his sword into a high guard, dropping down lower into a balanced stance.

His challenge rang down the rocky walls.

"Let us begin."

Galeron flashed into motion, driving hard at Reese, swinging his sword in a glittering arc and aiming for his right shoulder. Reese turned against the motion, catching the blade high, letting Galeron's momentum carry him down and past. He spun on the ball of his foot, whipping the tip around to drive into Galeron's side, but Galeron had already leapt back a half step, moving out of range and resetting his guard across the front of his torso.

Galeron's voice was reedy and tight as he jabbed again, keeping a distance between him and his attacker. "Of course she claims she is all right," he taunted Reese, his eyes wild. "She is a consummate liar," - *slash* – "and she wants you to be distracted" – *slash* – "from the danger she is in."

He whirled, and Reese leapt back, the blade missing him by mere inches. Galeron's eyes glowed. "Kay's legs are barely able to hold her up," – *stab* – "and she fought against nearly overwhelming pain these last few miles." Their blades rang against each other. Galeron gave a low laugh. "Look, she's slipping. I imagine she has only a few seconds left."

Reese's eyes flashed with concern, darting for a moment to Kay. Galeron spun at him, drawing his sword across Reese's arm and leaving a red stripe as Reese's dodge was a hair too late.

Kay's heart leapt. "Reese!" she cried out in anguish. "I am fine, Reese," she insisted, pleading. "Focus on Galeron."

Kay could barely breathe. Both men were consummate swordsmen – and both would give their lives before abandoning this fight. Both were exhausted, injured, and deadly focused.

They could easily both die.

Reese had to do something to tip the odds – but what?

Galeron chortled again. "She's slipping …"

Insight struck Kay.

It wasn't just that Galeron was a superb swordsman, equal to Reese. It was his psychological manipulations that were giving him an edge. He was riling Reese, distracting him from his ability to stay focused on the battle at hand.

And two could play that game.

She forced her voice to be calm and sure. To mask any sense that she was injured. "Reese, I knew from that very first time we spoke, that there was something special about you. That your respect for me, your care for me as a person, was far beyond any other suitor."

She heard the clangs, the steely swish of a sword through air. She focused on her words.

"When you held me, in the chapel, after Uther's attack, I knew. When you stood beneath me, at the cliff, and held out your arms, I knew. When you offered to challenge Jack, I knew."

Galeron's attacks had gotten more jagged with each passing word. His next swing went wild, and Reese's counter drove him back a half-step, nearer to the edge.

Galeron blew out his breath, clearly exhausted. He wove on his feet. Then bright focus lit his eyes. "She's suddenly good with words," he sneered. "When has that woman ever told you the truth about anything? About her name, who she was, anything at all. She has a forked tongue!"

The pain of the charge stabbed through Kay's heart, ripped through her soul, and her vision swam from the tears that welled up in her eyes. It was all true. She had lied for so long …

She called out the one thought which sustained her, which kept each foot placed after the last, which glowed through her soul.

"Reese – I love you. What I say now, I say it because I mean it. Because I want you to live. I want both of us to live, and love, and be together. Forever."

Reese blinked, and awareness came into his gaze. It was as if his body shimmered into new life. As if every muscle relaxed, realigned, came back into cohesion again. His eyes focused in on Galeron, but now they held a quiet determination; an inner calm.

Kay could see him deliberately push down the soul-deep weariness which must be soaking him through.

He pulled his sword hilt back toward his hip, expertly pointing the tip between Galeron's eyes. "She may have lied to me about details, as part of the process," he agreed, his gaze carefully reviewing Galeron's stance, his labored breathing, and his shaky balance. "However, I was the one who hid my true feelings from her, who continued with the façade of the competition with the Curtain Lady when all I wanted was to be by Kay's side."

Galeron snarled. He lashed out in anger, driving a wild blow high and right. Reese neatly caught it on the edge of his blade, tossed the thrust off to the left, and returned to his guard.

Reese continued, his voice growing stronger. "I am the one who left Kay in peril, who nearly saw her raped by Uther, who watched as she was callously abused by Jack, all because I would not speak out about the growing feelings in my heart."

Kay's heart thundered against her ribs. She could see what Reese was doing. He was drawing Galeron's rage – dissolving away the remnants of that logical mind and leaving behind a disjointed cacophony of emotion. And, at the same time he was imbuing her with strength. A glowing, powerful, all-encompassing strength which would see her through anything.

Galeron's face flushed with fury, and he lunged toward Reese's thigh, looking to rip open the leg with a pointed thrust. Again Reese drove the blow aside with a ringing swing, causing Galeron to stagger back. Galeron swung his head from side to side, pausing to gather his breath in long draws.

Reese's face became firmer, steadier.

"I was the one who could not face her that last day. I knew if I stood before her, if her soulful eyes looked into mine, that I could never leave her even for a week. I would not honor my vow - not return my mother's necklace to my brother as I had sworn I would do. It was my weakness that led to this current situation. It is high time I ceased my own lack of being fully, openly truthful."

His eyes sought out Kay's. Her heart stopped, her body resonated with the power of his emotions as a physical force coursing through her.

Reese's voice was rich with emotion. "I love you, Kay," he vowed. "I would be blessed beyond all imagination if you would allow me the honor of being your husband."

Galeron's scream of outrage shook the walls of the cave, and he threw himself bodily at Reese, slicing down his sword with both hands. Reese was thrown back onto one knee with the force behind the blow. Galeron crowed in triumph, spinning in a long arc to whip the blade around to decapitate Reese in a vicious sweep. Reese launched himself forward, leading with his shoulder, driving hard into the center of Galeron's chest.

Galeron flew back into space, arced into the center of the pit, and with arms and legs flailing, he began descending into the darkness.

His voice flared with hysterical fury as he realized what had happened. "She belongs to me!" he screamed, twisting mid-flight. He reached out with his blade, sending the flat of it hard against her right leg as he fell. Then he was past her. There were bumps, and cracks, and he was lost to the depths below.

Kay screamed in panic as her leg caved in, as her other leg failed to support her weight. Her fingers scrambled to hold her body against the cliff face. She kicked desperately with her boots, her weight slamming down on her already exhausted arms, raining a shower of pebbles down against her face.

"Reese!"

The deluge of rocks scattered beneath her feet. Her fingers lost their grip – regained - lost again. She was slipping, her leg was giving way, and she was falling … falling …

A sturdy grip, as steady as the strongest oak tree, caught hold of her arm, holding her in place suspended above the pit. Reese was there hanging on the edge of the pit by one arm, the other arm drawing her up again. Her feet found the ledge. The arm continued raising her up, inexorably. Soon her chest was safely over the lip of the pit. Another pull, and her body was being pressed forward until she could roll over, exhausted, sprawled in utter exhaustion spread eagle in the mouth of the cave. Her breath came in long, lung-emptying draws as reality finally began to sink in.

She was safe. Reese had come for her, and she was finally safe.

There was a movement beside her, and Reese had rolled up onto the ledge, propping himself up on one elbow, gazing down at her in tense concern.

"Are you all right?" he asked, his own voice rough, his breathing slowly coming under control.

Kay looked into his warm eyes, lost in their depths. The world coalesced around him and her, as if nothing else mattered, as if this moment in time could go on forever.

"I am just perfect," she reassured him with a weak smile. "What did you have planned for us tomorrow?"

Reese let out his breath with a chuckle, looking down her dust-coated body, the bleeding cuts and swollen bruises visible on every surface of her skin. He tenderly lowered a hand to rest against her cheek, and she nuzzled softly against it.

"I thought we might become man and wife," he murmured, his eyes held on hers.

Kay brought her hand up to run through his hair, and her voice softened.

"I would like that," she agreed heartily.

Reese gave a low groan, and then he was pressed down against her length, kissing her, holding her against him. It seemed that time whirled, slowed, and created a shimmering sphere around them which would last an eternity.

Chapter 20

Kay stood on the keep's front steps, her heart thundering in nervousness, soaking in the warmth of the brilliant afternoon sunshine. The keep's main doors, freshly hung and sturdy, stood open and glowed on either side of her. Her hand moved for the twentieth time to the beautifully carved golden heart which hung at her neck. Reese's only memento from his beloved mother was now entrusted to her care. She ran her fingers along its etchings, gazing across the sun-drenched courtyard. She took in the crowds of smiling faces, the bouquets of fragrant flowers, and the scattering of rose petals that Molly was releasing along the central path. Her eyes moved across to the drawbridge, freshly replaced, the chain links glittering in the sun.

Her heart sang at the beauty and the wonder of it all. The day was absolutely perfect. Her keep was breathtakingly glorious. And Reese ....

Her father moved with slow steps to come to her side. She snugged her hand on her father's arm, and he gave it a gentle pat in return, his eyes creasing in fondness. Then they set into measured motion, moving step-by-step down the polished steps, across the open courtyard through the throngs. Kay's eyes found the smiling encouragement of Jevan, his arms wrapped around each of his sons at his side. Anne and Jessica were decked out in their finest dresses, their faces beaming with delight. Leland and Eli had polished their leather and shined their swords until they gleamed. Eric had his arm nestled closely around Em's waist, and Kay could only hope that she could find the happiness that glowed from their faces.

Her eyes came to the worn wooden doors, to the entryway of the quiet chapel she loved and adored. There stood Reese, his tawny mane glowing in the autumn light, his green-grey eyes holding hers with love, pride, and deep respect. He reached his hand out to her, and Kay's father gently placed her hand in Reese's, giving her a soft kiss on the cheek before stepping back to take his place in the front of the gathered crowd.

Kay found she could not draw her eyes away from Reese's. Her fingers twined into his, so warm and alive, and she drew them to her chest, to the heart that lay there, to the center of her being.

He smiled tenderly at that. "I think you should see something," he offered in a hoarse voice. His fingers gave a gentle twist. She looking down and saw that the heart had opened into a locket. Within was inscribed a delicate sword.

"When my brother and I were very young," explained Reese, "my mother was returning from a faire with us, and we were attacked by a pair of bandits. My mother was well versed in self-defense, and she held them off with her sword until help could come. My father gave her this necklace to commemorate her bravery and skill. She wore it until she died."

Kay's breath caught. "But when the others would talk about female swordswomen …"

The corner of Reese's mouth quirked. "I was amused by their ignorance," he gently reassured her. "I was thinking how little they knew of the real world, of the value in a woman of strength and honor."

With infinite care he resealed the locket, settling it down against her chest and looking back up into her eyes.

Kay felt as if a golden light were streaming out from the core of her being, filling every last corner of her. He was everything she could want, was all she had ever dreamt of.

"I love you," she whispered, putting every last drop of her soul and being into those simple words. She released all she had into his tender care.

The edge of his finger gently traced against the golden heart which adorned her, and when he smiled, Kay felt as if her soul would explode from joy and fullness.

"I love you, adore you, and treasure you, now, and forever," he vowed, his voice ringing with the simple truth of it.

Together they turned toward the priest, their hands never parting, their souls forever joined.

Epilogue

Kay twined her fingers into Reese's, looking out into the moonlit night to where, only a day ago, an overwhelming force had stood. Now the grasses rippled in the breeze, an owl called from a nearby tree, and behind them the sounds of celebration rang out from the keep.

Reese pressed a gentle kiss on her forehead. "How are you feeling?"

She leaned into him. "Happy. Tired, exhausted, sore, but happy." Her eyes went up to his. "I never dreamt that it could be like this. That contentment could be so powerful."

He traced his hand down her cheek.

A shooting star arced high above them. As Kay followed its movements, her eyes were caught by something. A shadow staggered across the field, its head down. Long, dark hair lifted in the breeze.

Her voice caught. "A woman's out there."

She moved quickly down the steps, Reese right behind her. In a moment the drawbridge had been lowered and they were striding, side by side, toward the figure.

The woman's head snapped up as they drew near, and her hand swept her side, as if reaching for a sword. But there was nothing there, and a low curse sprung from her lips.

Kay could see now that the woman was about her age, with toned muscles as if she led an active life. Her brown eyes matched her auburn hair, and there was a hint of a brown dress showing beneath her dark cloak.

The woman faced them with wary attention. "If you are bandits, it's too late. Someone came across me last night while I slept and stole everything of value." Her brow darkened. "Including my sword."

Kay glanced at Reese. "Might have been the MacDouglas, as they left our lands." She turned back to the woman. "I am so sorry to hear that. My name is Kay, and this is Reese. We own Serenor - the keep behind us."

We. The word sang through her heart with joy.

The woman nodded. "My name is Elizabeth. And it is not your fault. I should not have slept as deeply. I knew better than that."

Reese's voice held compassion. "Why are you out here on your own?"

She gave a low laugh. "My father was disappointed in me when I failed to win a tournament. He expressed his disappointment by locking me in the dungeon until I showed remorse for my faults." She gave a tense shrug. "I decided on another option."

Kay's heart went out to Elizabeth. "Don't you have any other family you could turn to?"

For a moment, Elizabeth's eyes grew distant, and they shimmered with deep emotion. When she spoke again, her voice was rough. "My brother is dead."

Kay's throat tightened. "I am so sorry."

Elizabeth ran a hand through her hair. "If I had only … but it does not matter. I have decided to head east. A friend of mine heads a nunnery there, and she has asked for my help. It seems I might be useful in keeping them safe."

She looked down at the empty spot at her hip, and shadows came across her face. "Well, I would have been."

A tingle shimmered at Kay's hip.

She looked down at her sword.

Suddenly, the mysterious woman's words came back to her, from when Kay was given the sword, all those nights ago in her chapel.

Do not become too fond of Andetnes. When you have at last found contentment, there will be another whose fate balances on the point of a pin. You will know when it is right. And the sword will have a new mistress.

She smiled. "Elizabeth, come in and join us. There is plenty of room at the celebration for all. And I think we can find a way to ensure your path goes the way you wish.

Reese looked to Kay, his gaze shining with respect. He twined his fingers into hers.

And Kay knew everything would be all right.

The Sword of Glastonbury series continues with Book 2, *Finding Peace* –

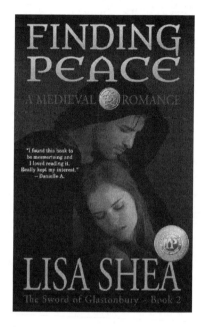

http://www.amazon.com/Finding-Peace-Medieval-Lisa-Shea-ebook/dp/B008FQZ8JY/

If you enjoyed *Knowing Yourself*, please leave feedback on Amazon, Goodreads, and any other systems you use. Together we can help make a difference!

https://www.amazon.com/review/create-review?ie=UTF8&asin=B006JDEK0I#

Be sure to sign up for my free newsletter! You'll get alerts of free books, discounts, and new releases. I run my own newsletter server – nobody else will ever see your email address. I promise!

http://www.lisashea.com/lisabase/subscribe.html

Join my online groups to get news of free giveaways, upcoming stories, and fascinating trivia!

Facebook
https://www.facebook.com/LisaSheaAuthor

Twitter
https://twitter.com/LisaSheaAuthor

Google+
https://plus.google.com/+LisaSheaAuthor/posts

GoodReads
https://www.goodreads.com/lisashea/

Blog
http://www.lisashea.com/lisabase/blog/

Be sure to download all of my FREE books! Each of these is completely free and available on Kindle.

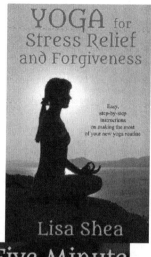

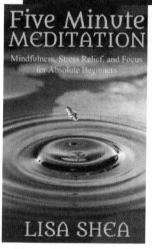

COCKTAILS

Low Carb Recipes Series

Delicious recipes
perfect for unwinding,
relaxing, and enjoying!

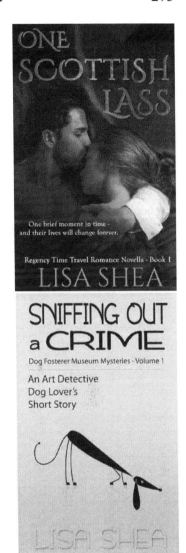

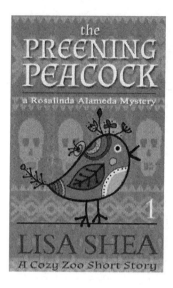

Medieval Dialogue

I've been fascinated by medieval languages since I was quite young. I grew up studying Spanish, English, and Latin, and loved the sound of reading Beowulf and the Canterbury Tales in their original languages. I adore the richness of medieval languages. How did medieval English people speak?

There are three aspects to this. The first is the difference between written records and spoken language. The second is the rich, multi-cultural aspect of medieval life. And the third is how to convey this to a modern-language audience.

Let's take the first. Sometimes modern people equate the way medieval folk would talk, hanging around a rustic tavern, with the way Chaucer wrote his famous *Canterbury Tales*. Something along the lines of this (note this is a modern translation, not the original Middle English version):

"Of weeping and wailing, care and other sorrow
I know enough, at eventide and morrow,"
The merchant said, "and so do many more
Of married folk, I think, who this deplore,
For well I know that it is so with me.
I have a wife, the worst one that can be;
For though the foul Fiend to her wedded were,
She'd overmatch him, this I dare to swear."

Sure, it seems elegant and rich. But did worn-down farmers sitting around a fireplace with mugs of ale really talk like this?

Do we think the London street-dwellers in the 1600s skulked down the dark alleys emoting like Shakespeare –

Two households, both alike in dignity
In fair Verona, where we lay our scene
From ancient grudge break to new mutiny
Where civil blood makes civil hands unclean.

And, in the 1920s in Vermont, did farmers really wander down their snowy lanes murmuring to their farming friends, a la Robert Frost:

Whose woods these are I think I know.
His house is in the village though;
He will not see me stopping here
To watch his woods fill up with snow.

As someone who lives in New England, I can pretty resolutely say "no" to that last one. And, given my research, I'm equally content saying "no" to the previous two. There is a big difference between poetry written with deliberate effort and the way "normal people" talked, flirted, cajoled, and laughed day in and day out. People simply did not talk in iambic pentameter. I'm a poet and even I don't talk in iambic pentameter :).

Modern people sometimes think of the medieval period in terms of the plays we see. We imagine actors on a stage, speaking in formal, stilted language, carefully moving from scene to scene. But medieval life wasn't like that. It was a rich cacophony of people struggling hard to survive amongst plagues and crusades, with strong pagan influences and the church trying to instill order. People fought off robbers and drove away wolves. They laughed and loved in multi-generational homes. It was a time of great flux.

England - A Melting Pot

England wasn't an isolated, walled-off island. It was continually experiencing influxes of new words and sounds. The Romans came and went. The Vikings came and went. The French invaded. Nearly all of the English men headed off to the Crusades, leaving behind women to gain strength and position.

The men returned with even more languages. Pilgrims went to Jerusalem. Merchants arrived from all over. This was a true melting pot.

So, in part because of this, Middle English was a rich, fascinating language. People in this time period had a wealth of contractions, nicknames, abbreviations, and combinations of words they used. Often people could speak multiple languages - their old English, the incoming Norman language, Latin from church, and random other words from tinkers, merchants, and pilgrims they encountered. Medieval people had all sorts of words for drinking, for fighting, for prostitutes, you name it. They had slang and shortcuts just like any other language does. After all, these are the people who turned "forecastle" (on a ship) to "foc's'le" and who pronounce the word "Worcester" as "Woostah."

But, here's the trick. With the medieval language being so rich, varied, intricate, and full of fascinating words, how can we bring that to life for a modern audience?

Centuries of Change

Let's start with a basic issue - most modern readers simply cannot understand authentic medieval dialogue. They don't have the grounding in Middle English, French, and Latin that would be required. Even the fairly straightforward, basic Chaucer works look like this:

And Saluces this noble contree highte.

Modern readers generally wouldn't know that "highte" meant "was called" as in "And Saluces this noble country was called."

This happens over and over again. Words change meaning. In the Middle Ages, if you *abandoned* your wife it means you subjugated her. You got her under your thumb. It didn't mean you left her - quite the opposite. Awful meant *awe-ful* - as in stunning and wonderful. It had a positive connotation. Fantastic wasn't great - it was a fantasy; something that didn't exist.

Nervous didn't mean worried or agitated - it meant strong and full of energy. Nice meant silly, and so on.

If a book was written with proper medieval words and meanings, first, even if the words are reasonably close to what we use now, modern readers would have to struggle with the spelling -

By that the Maunciple hadde his tale al ended,
The sonne fro the south lyne was descended
So lowe, that he nas nat to my sighte
Degrees nyne and twenty as in highte.

But, again, that is just the tip of the issue with medieval language. The word "bracelet" didn't exist until the 1400s. Necklace wasn't a word until 1590. The word "hug" wasn't around until the mid-1500s. We also didn't have the words tragedy, crisis, area, explain, fact, illicit, rogue, or even disagree! Shakespeare invented the words "baseless" and "dwindle" in the 1600s. Staircase is from 1620. A story written solely with words that existed in the year 1200 - and that still retain their modern meaning so modern readers could understand them - would be fairly basic.

(Speaking of which, the word "basic" didn't exist until the mid 1800s.)

Conversely, some words we might think of as thoroughly modern, like "puke", were also used in Shakespeare's time. "Booze" traces back to the 1500s. And these are just the proofs we have. While "shiner" for a black eye can be traced definitively to the 1700s, it could easily have been used for centuries before then and we just don't happen to have a letter or newspaper article which mentions it.

It's fair to say that people in medieval days did get black eyes and had a wealth of interesting terms for that situation. After all, it could be a rough life back then. Was one of the terms used "shiner"? Maybe, maybe not. Out of the ten fun phrases they used, probably nine of them would make zero sense to a modern reading audience. So authors strive to find phrases that provide meaning to a modern audience without being too *l33t* and techno-speak. It doesn't make sense to completely avoid the word "bracelet" simply because it technically didn't exist in the 1200s. Surely people in the 1200s had several words for "bracelet" and we are simply using the word modern readers understand. Similarly, people in medieval times hugged! They just called that action something else.

Medieval people loved playing with words. They called their kids "dillydowns" and "mitings" (little mites). They called sweethearts "my sweeting" and "my honey. They loved snapping out insults, from "dunce" to "idiot" to "pig filth" and "maggot pie." And, again, these are just the ones that happened to get recorded.

Medieval people loved contractions. There's a phrase "ne woot," meaning *knows not*. They'd simply say "noot". They did this with all sorts of words.

So writing in modern English should have this same sort of loose, fun sense to the writing. It's important to remember that even the kings, in this era, were rough fighters. They were out with soldiers, crossing multiple countries, and experiencing a range of languages. They weren't necessarily concerned about speaking in iambic pentameter. They were more concerned about breaking down their enemy's walls to plunder what lay within and then drinking themselves under the table to celebrate.

So, certainly, treasure the poetry and prose of the time. As a poet, I appreciate that immensely. But also keep in mind that people did not talk in poetry. They did not speak in fantasy-speak of *Lord of the Rings* or *Game of Thrones*. They talked and laughed, flirted and cursed, gossiped and cajoled in a rich, multi-lingual, contraction-filled, sobriquet-laden dialogue which mirrors how we talk in modern times.

About Medieval Life

When many of us think of medieval times, we bring to mind a drab reality-documentary image. We imagine people scrounging around in the mud, eating dirt. The people were under five feet tall and barely survived to age thirty. These poor, unfortunate souls had rotted teeth and never bathed.

Then you have the opposite, Hollywood Technicolor extreme. In the romantic version of medieval times, men were always strong and chivalrous. Women were dainty and sat around staring out the window all day, waiting for their knight to come riding in. Everybody wore purple robes or green tights.

The truth, of course, lies somewhere in the middle.

Living in Medieval Times

The years in the early medieval ages held a warm, pleasant climate. Crops grew exceedingly well, and there was plenty of food. As a result, their average height was on par with modern times. It's amazing how much nutrition influences our health!

The abundance of food also had an effect on the longevity of people. Chaucer (born 1340) lived to be 60. Petrarch (born 1304) died a day shy of 70. Eleanor of Aquitaine (born 1122) was 82 when she died. People could and did lead long lives. The average age of someone who survived childhood was 65.

What about their living conditions? The Romans adored baths and set up many in Britain. When they left, the natives could not keep them going, and it is true they then bathed less. However, by the Middle Ages, with the crusades and interaction with the Muslims, there was a renewed interest both in hygiene and medicine. Returning soldiers and those who took pilgrimages brought back with them an interest in regular bathing and cleanliness. This spread across the culture.

While people during other periods of English history ate poorly, often due to war conditions or climatic changes, the middle ages were a time of relative bounty. Villagers would grow fresh fruit and vegetables behind their homes, and had an array of herbs for seasoning. The local baker would bake bread for the village - most homes did not hold an oven, only an open fire. Villagers had easy access to fish, chicken, geese, and eggs. Pork was enjoyed at special meals like Easter.

Upper classes of course had a much wider range of foods - all game animals (rabbits, deer, and so on) belonged to them. The wealthy ate peacocks, veal, lamb, and even bear. Meals for all classes could be flavorful and well enjoyed.

Medieval Relationships

Some movies present a skewed version of life in the Middle Ages. They make it seem that women were meek, mild, and obediently did whatever their father or husband commanded.

This was *far* from the truth!

Medieval times were times of immense change. Men were off at the Crusades, leaving the women to run things. Christianity was trying to get a foothold, but many areas of Britain were still primarily pagan, with all the Goddess worship and female empowerment which had been tradition for centuries. The vast majority of brewers were female. Most innkeepers were female. Women's knowledge about herbs, health, and food was respected. Healthy women were treasured as the key to a child-rich partnership.

Medieval life was heavily focused on fertility. Farm animals had to be fertile in order to create meat to feed the family. Women had to be fertile to create helpers for the farm and household. Celebration after celebration in medieval times focused on fertility. These people weren't shy about the topic. They watched their horses, cows, and dogs continually engage in these activities. Their festivals focused on the topic with bawdy delight. Their songs lusted about it.

The church tried, again and again, to squelch this behavior so that all aspects of relationships could be regulated by the church. However, half of all medieval couples were together outside of a church marriage and, for those sanctified by the church, a large proportion were "sealing the deal" for a couple already pregnant.

This was the way the medieval people looked at it: they needed to know their partner could create children. This was a key consideration for a relationship.

The Medieval period was far from an era of Victorian prudity. Quite the opposite. People of this era celebrated fertility, felt it was wholly natural, and even felt it was unhealthy for a man or woman to go for too long without sex. The celibacy would block critical flows of the body.

It was considered natural that a male noble might take on mistresses and that unmarried couples might seek out partners. It was the same as someone needing food if they were hungry. It was a bodily function which had to be tended to for the health of the person.

So where does marriage fit in with this mindset?

Medieval Marriage

In medieval times, marriage was primarily about inheritance. It was almost separate from sexuality. Sexuality was an important part of bodily health, like eating well and getting enough exercise. Marriage, on the other hand, was about ensuring one's lands and chattel were cared for from generation to generation. Sex, within a marriage, was focused on creating family-line children to then tend to that wealth.

For this reason, wealthy families would put immense energy into arranging optimal marriages for their children. This was about the transfer of land far more than a love match. Parents wanted to ensure their land went to a family worthy of ownership - one with the resources to defend it from attack. It was not only their own family members they were concerned with. Each block of land had on it both free men and serfs. These people all depended on the nobles – with their skill, connections, and soldiers – to keep them safe from bandits and harm.

That being said, both the woman and man would be consulted about the match. Their input was a critical aspect of the decision. Choices were often made with intricate selection processes. Keep in mind that the woman and her suitors would have been raised from birth to think of this process as natural. They would participate in that choice-making with an eye as to how it would secure the stability of their future family.

Yes, villagers sometimes married for love. Even a few nobles would run off and follow their hearts. Even so, they would have first seriously considered the potentially catastrophic risks which could result from their actions.

Here is a modern example. Imagine you took over the family business which employed a hundred loyal workers. Those workers depend on your careful guidance of the company to ensure the income for their families. You might dream about running off to Bermuda and drinking martinis. But would you just sell your company to any random investor who came along? Would you risk all of those peoples' lives, people who had served you loyally for decades, to satisfy a whim of pleasure? It is more likely that you would research your options, map out a plan, and made a choice with suited both you and your responsibilities.

Medieval Women

In pagan days women held many rights and responsibilities. During the crusades, especially, with many men off at war, women ran the taverns, made the ale, and ran the government. In later years, as men returned home and Christianity rose in power, women were relegated to a more subservient role.

Still, women in medieval times were not meek and mild. That stereotype came in with the Victorian era, many centuries later. Back in medieval days, women had to be hearty and hard working. There were fields to tend, homes to maintain, and children to raise!

Women strove to be as healthy as they could because they faced a serious threat - a fifth of all women died during or just after childbirth. The church said that childbirth was the "pain of Eve" and instructed women to bear it without medicine or follow-up care. Of course, midwives did their best to skirt these rules, but childbirth still took an immense toll.

Childhood was rough in the Middle Ages – only forty percent of children survived the gauntlet of illnesses to adulthood. A woman who reached her marriageable years was a sturdy woman indeed.

You can see why fertility was so important to medieval people!

To summarize, in medieval days a woman could live a long, happy life, even into her eighties – as long as she was of the sturdy stock that made it through the challenges of childhood. She would be expected to be fertile and to have multiple children, which again weeded out the weaker ones. This was very much a time of 'survival of the fittest.' Medieval life quickly separated out the weak and frail. Those women who ran that gauntlet and survived were respected for that strength and for their wisdom in many areas of life.

So medieval women were strong - very strong. They had to be. They were respected. Still, would they fight?

Women and Weapons

Queen Boudicia, from Norwalk, was born around AD60. She personally – and successfully - led her troops against the Roman Empire. She had been flogged - and her daughters raped - spurring her to revenge. She was extremely intelligent and quite strategic. Her daughters rode in her chariot at her side.

Eleanor of Aquitaine, born in 1122, was brilliant and married first to a King of France and then to a King of England. She went on the Second Crusades as the leader of her troops - reportedly riding bare-breasted as an Amazon. At times she marched with her troops far ahead of her husband. When she divorced the King of France, she immediately married Henry II, who she passionately adored. He was eleven years her junior. When things went sour, Eleanor separated from him and actively led revolts against him.

Many historical accounts talk of women taking up arms to defend their villages and towns. Women would not passively let their children be slain or their homes burned. They were able and strong bodied from their daily work. They were well skilled with farm implements and knives, and used them with great talent against invaders.

Many of these defenses were successful, and the victories were celebrated as brave and proper, rather than dismissed as an unusual act for a woman. A mother was expected to defend her brood and to keep her home safe, just as a wolf mother protects her cubs.

Numerous women took their martial skills to a higher level. In 1301 a group of Italian women joined up to fight the crusade against the Turks. In 1348 at a tournament there were at least thirty women who participated, dressed as men.

This is not as unusual as you might think. In medieval times, all adults carried a knife at their belt for daily use in eating, chores, and defense. All knew how to use it. Being strong and safe was a necessary part of daily life.

Here is an interesting comparison. In modern times most women know how to drive, but few choose to invest themselves in the time and training to become race car drivers. In medieval times, most women knew how to defend themselves with a weapon. They had to. Few, though, actively sought the training to be swordswomen. Still, these women did exist, and did thrive as valued members of their communities.

So women in medieval times were far from shrinking violets. They were not mud-encrusted wretches huddling in straw huts. They were not pale damsels locked away in towers. They were strong, sturdy, and well versed in the use of knives. Many ran taverns, and most handled the brewing of ale. Those who made it through childhood and childbirth could expect to enjoy long, rich lives.

I hope you enjoy my tales of authentic, inspiring heroines!

Glossary

Ale - A style of beer which is made from barley and does not use hops. Ale was the common drink in medieval days. In the 1300s, 92% of brewers were female, and the women were known as "alewives". It was common for a tavern to be run by a widow and her children.

Blade - The metal slicing part of the sword.

Chemise - In medieval days, most people had only a few outfits. They would not want to wash their heavy main dress every time they wore it, just as in modern times we don't wash our jackets after each wearing. In order to keep the sweaty skin away from the dress, women wore a light, white under-dress which could then be washed more regularly. This was often slept in as well.

Drinking - In general, medieval sanitation was not great. People who drank milk had to drink it "raw" - pasteurization was not well known before the 1700s. Water was often unsafe to drink. For these reasons, all ages of medieval folk drank liquid with alcohol in it. The alcohol served as a natural sanitizer. This was even true as recently as colonial American times.

God's Teeth / God's Blood – Common oaths in the middle ages.

Grip - The part of the sword one holds, usually wrapped in leather or another substance to keep it firmly in the wielder's hand.

Guard - The crossed top of the sword's hilt which keeps the enemy's sword from sliding down and chopping off the wielder's fingers.

Hilt - The entire handle part of the sword; everything that is not blade.

Mead - A fermented beverage made from honey. Mead has been enjoyed for thousands of years and is mentioned in Beowulf.

Pommel - The bottom end of the sword, where the hilt ends.

Tip - The very end of the sword

Wolf's Head – a term for a bandit. The Latin legal term *caput gerat lupinum* meant they could be hunted and killed as legally as any dangerous wolf or wild animal that threatened the area.

Parts of a Sword

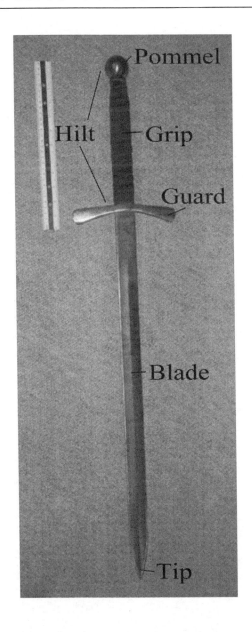

Medieval Clothing

Medieval people - despite modern stereotypes - did have noses and did like to stay clean. Public baths were popular, and people liked to swim as well. However, they did not have the luxury of bathing daily. Also, in medieval times people were often cold. Castles were damp and drafty. Fireplaces were not kept blazingly hot all night long. There is a reason that people wore many heavy layers including cloaks. That way they could add or remove layers as necessary to keep warm.

The basic under-layer was a chemise. This thin nightgown would be worn at night as well as during the day. Because it was against the body it kept the actual clothes clean from sweat. That way you could wash the chemise regularly and not have to wash your actual dress every day. Think of it like when you wear a turtleneck and a wool sweater. At the end of the day you would wash the turtleneck, but you would not wash the wool sweater after every wearing. If you wear a t-shirt under a jacket, you would toss the t-shirt into the washing machine but just hang the jacket on a hook again. The same is true for medieval outfits. The inner layer would be washed, while the other layer would be reused multiple days before it had to be washed.

The chemise was generally not meant to be seen, especially in colder months. It was underwear. There would always be an over-dress with a floor-length hem on top of that. Perhaps a glimpse of the chemise would show at the neckline or at the end-of-sleeve area. In hotter months the chemise might be more visible as the outer dress had short sleeves or no sleeves.

Men would typically wear a tunic over leggings. Men working in summer heat would sometimes wear simple linen "shorts" without anything else. Their chest and lower legs would be bare. This is a stark difference from how covered up women would be.

Both sexes would wear boots or shoes. There as no "left" or "right" - both halves would be made in the same oval shape.

Cloaks would be worn when going out into poor weather, to help keep you warm. These cloaks could be quite heavy if they were full circle cloaks, and incredibly warm.

Monks would wear similar clothing to non-religious men, but the monk's hair would be cut short and have a "tonsure" - or bald spot - shaved out of its center. The tonsure was a sign of their humility. This illuminated image is from a 12th century manuscript at the library at Cambridge University.

Women's Clothing

A number of readers had specific questions about women's medieval clothing so I created this page with those specific details. To illustrate it, I have included a drawing done by Andreas Muller, a famous German artist known for his work restoring ancient paintings. This drawing was published back in 1861, so it's now out of copyright. As you might expect the drawing shows German people, not English, but the fashions are from the 1200s and are quite similar in style.

So, the basics. Women wore at least two layers of long dress. The bottom layer, or "chemise," was often plain white but could be fancier with nobles. This was what was against the skin, got sweaty, and would be washed. The chemise was often slept in, again especially if the person was poor.

The outer layer, what we would call the "dress," was the prettier layer. This would have the nicer stitching and designs. It could have embroidery or different fabrics stitched together to create designs. The outer dress could have long sleeves, short sleeves, or no sleeves, depending on how hot the weather was. In general, though, a woman's arms and legs were covered by the inner chemise and perhaps also by the outer dress as well. Women in medieval times did not tend to show skin from those parts of the body.

You might see images on the web with medieval women wearing long "trumpet" sleeves which made housework impractical. These were sometimes worn by French nobles who were showing off that they did not have to do menial labor. They were not a normal fashion in England or most other areas.

By the same token, women who had to work hard would wear shorter dresses - ending above the ankle rather than dragging on the floor. That was so their dresses did not catch or drag while they went about their work. Noblewomen who had a quiet day planned or a formal event would wear longer, floor-dragging dresses. These subtle differences helped to show off their status.

If it got even colder women would wear cloaks. These range from light, like the woman in the middle is wearing here, to heavy and full-circle, which could be amazingly warm. I have one of those.

Here is an illuminated image done between 1285 and 1292 which shows the famous poet Marie de France. Marie primarily wrote between 1160 to 1190 and was well known by nobility in France and England. Again, you can see how her outer long dress goes to the floor and the inner dress is visible at the arms. This copyright-free image comes via the National Library of France.

Women had an immense array of colorful dyes to choose from, some more expensive, some less expensive. So clothing could be quite bright and cheery. Just as in modern times, practicality had an aspect here. If someone was going to work in the pig pen all day long they'd probably wear something brown and old. If they were going to church they'd wear their best outfit they had.

In modern times we can sometimes think of dresses as "fancy" items we wear to "dress up" that are hard to move in. In medieval times, a dress was normal and natural! These were the outfits they wore every single day. Women made their dresses so they could do all their normal activities in them. To them a dress was like our modern t-shirt and sweatpants. So they're no question about "could they do chores in a dress" or "could they ride a horse in a dress." Of course they could - that's what the clothing was made for. Medieval women didn't generally hide out in tower rooms. Noblewomen would do archery and horseback riding for fun. Working women would scythe hay, ride to the market, and do a myriad of other chores in their dresses. It was what one wore. So those outfits absolutely were made to easily let them do those tasks. Dresses were loose to allow all of that. Women didn't ride side-saddle in medieval days - they simply put their legs on either side for stability. And their clothing was made for that. To ride, a woman could either tuck the skirt beneath her, like when one sits on a chair, or let it flow behind her. Either way works!

In terms of underclothes, most medieval women did not wear a bra. Their simple, straight dresses were meant to keep the body hidden rather than emphasized. A large breasted woman might wear a "binder" to keep the breasts from jiggling around while they tried to work. Current thought is that women didn't wear "underwear" (underpants) either. With their long multi-layer dresses it would be a challenge for underwear-wearing women to go to the bathroom. Instead, they would just move to a section of the field, fluff out their dresses, and go. Then they could get back to work. The same in the outhouses.

Even during the time of their periods, many researchers feel that the philosophy of the time was that binding or constricting a woman's flow would damage her fertility. So she simply bled into her underdress and that was washed. This free-flow practice continued long after medieval times. It was mentioned in doctors' journals in the 1800s. Even as recent as the 1900s there were cotton mills in the United States that had straw-strewn floors to absorb female workers' blood, so again this was not a short-term trend. And given that tampons can cause toxic shock syndrome, maybe those medieval women knew what they were doing :).

Let me know if you have any other questions about medieval women's clothing! I have a library of books here to help with research.

Dedication

To my mom, dad, siblings, and family members who encouraged me to indulge myself in medieval fantasies. I spent many long car rides creating epic tales of sword-wielding heroines and the strong men who stood by their sides. Jenn, Uncle Blake, and Dad were awesome proofers.

To Peter and Elizabeth May, who patiently toured me around England, Scotland, and France on three separate occasions. Elizabeth offered valuable tips on creating authentic scenes. Visiting the Berkhamsted motte and bailey was priceless.

To Jody, Leslie, Liz, Sarah, and Jenny, my friends who enjoy my eclectic ways and provide great suggestions. Becky was my first ever web-fan and her enthusiasm kept me going!

To the editors at BellaOnline, who inspire me daily to reach for my dreams and to aim for the stars. Lisa, Cheryll, Jeanne, Lizzie, Moe, Terrie, Ian, and Jilly provided insightful feedback to help my polishing efforts.

To the Massachusetts Mensa Writing Group for their feedback and enthusiastic support. Lynn, Tom, Ruth, Carmen, Al, and Dean all offered detailed, helpful advice!

To the Geek Girls, with their unflagging support for my expanding list of projects and enterprises. Debi's design talents are amazing. I simply adore the covers she created for me.

To the Academy of Knightly Arts for several years of in-depth training and combat experience with medieval swords and knives. I loved sparring with Nikki and Jo-Ann!

To B&R Stables who renewed my love of horseback riding and quiet forest trails.

To my son, James, whose insights into psychology help ground my characters in authentic behavior.

To Bob See, my partner in love for over 19 years and counting. He enthusiastically supports all of my new projects.

About the Author

Lisa Shea is a fervent fan of honor, loyalty, and chivalry. She brings to life worlds where men and women stand shoulder to shoulder, steady in their desire to make the world a better place for all. While her medieval heroines often wield a sword, they equally value the skilled use of their intelligence, wisdom, courage, and compassion.

Lisa has studied the Middle Ages since she was quite young. She has trained in medieval swordfighting for several years. She studied medieval dance and music with the SCA. She has been to England numerous times and loves exploring old castles and churches.

Please visit Lisa at LisaShea.com to learn more about her background and interests. Feedback is always appreciated!

As a special treat, as a warm thank-you for reading this book and supporting the cause of battered women, here's a sneak peek at the first chapter of *Finding Peace*.

Finding Peace Chapter 1

England, 1174

"Anger is short-lived madness."
-- Horace

"God's Teeth, next the badgers and wolves will march by two-by-two," scowled Elizabeth with vehemence as she lugged the soaked saddle off her roan and dropped it in a sodden heap on the cracked bench. The fierce November storm crashed down all around her, hammering off the thin roof, reverberating through the small stable's walls. The lantern hanging in the corner guttered out dense smoke, barely holding off the deep gloom of the late hour.

She worked quickly in the flickering dark to bed down her horse, the familiar routine doing little to soothe her foul mood. She was drenched to the bone – her heavy cloak and hood had done little to shield her after the first ten minutes in the torrent. Her stomach was twisting into knots with hunger. Exhaustion and cold caused her fingers to fumble as she finished with the bridle. She hung it on the wooden peg, then turned to walk the few short steps toward the stable entrance.

The small inn's door was only ten steps away, but it seemed like ten miles through the deluge. Elizabeth took in a deep breath, pulled her hood up over her head, tucked in her glossy auburn curls, then sprinted across the dark cobblestones. It felt as if she were diving into a frigid stream, struggling against its strong current, and she reached out a hand for the thick, wooden door. In another second she had pulled open the latch, spun through the door, and slammed it heavily behind her.

The inn looked like every other hell hole she had stayed in during this long, tiring trip. Six or seven food-strewn oak tables filled the small space, about half occupied by aging farmers and rheumatic merchants. A doddering, wispy-haired barkeep poured ale behind a wood plank counter. The only two women in the room were a pair of buxom barmaids, one blonde, one redhead, laughing at a round table in the back with a trio of men. Two of the men appeared to be in their early twenties and were alike enough to be twins. Their dusty brown hair was the exact same color, the same periwinkle blue eyes gazed out from square faces. Like every other pair in the room, they swept up to stare at her the moment she came to rest, dripping from every seam, against the interior side of the door. After a moment of halfhearted interest, the farmers, merchants, and twins turned back to their pints of ale and their conversations on turnips and wool prices.

All except one. The third man, sitting somewhat apart from the preening twins and the flirtatious waitresses, held her gaze with steady interest. Her world slowed down, her skin tingled as a drip of water slid its way down her neck, tracing along every inch of her spine.

He was in his late twenties, a dark brown mane of hair curling just at his shoulders. He was well built, with the toned shoulders of a man who led an active life. It was his eyes that caught her and held her pinned against the wall. They were a rich moss green, a verdant color she remembered so strongly that her breath caught, her left hand almost swung down toward her hilt of its own accord.

She shook herself, turning to the row of wooden pegs running in an uneven line next to the door. That man was in the past, and by God, he would stay there. Why did she have to keep seeing that foul bastard's eyes everywhere, in every tavern, in every stranger she passed on the road? She pushed the hood of her cloak back, then shook its damp embrace off her body, revealing the simple, burnt-orange dress she wore beneath and the well-used sword hanging on her right hip.

Now, to get some stew, or gruel, or whatever mystery meat this cook had to offer, and get some sleep.

"You, woman!" came the growled order, plunging the room into immediate silence.

Elizabeth blew out her breath in an exasperated huff. Just for once she would like to have her food and rest without going through this ordeal. Sometimes it was just a snide comment, a mention of the dangers of a young woman traveling alone, or a sly joke about the "oldest profession". Sometimes the greeting cut with its chill edge. One solemn innkeeper had served her meal brusquely, informing her that she would have to find somewhere else to sleep.

All she wanted was food and a bed. She took in a deep breath and closed her eyes for a moment. If she could just rein in her temper she could get through this and snatch a few hours' reprieve from the torrential deluge.

She turned around slowly, holding her features in what she hoped was a neutral gaze. The twins were on their feet, their eyes sharp on her, their faces twisted in anger. They wore matching outfits of fine leather jerkins. Behind them the green-eyed man stood more slowly, his eyes scanning her with careful attention.

Twin number one shouted in rage. "You! Woman! I cannot believe you simply strolled in here and expect to be fed and cared for!" His eyes nearly bulged from their sockets. "What, did you expect a pint of ale?"

Elizabeth blinked in surprise. She had certainly encountered people in rural towns who thought little of her traveling alone – but she had reached new lows in hospitality with this outpost from Hades. Still, the hammering of the torrential downpour just outside the door encouraged her to press her case.

"Please," she bit out, her rising anger sharpening the edges of her attempted civility, "all I want is something hot to eat and a place to sleep. In the morning I will be out of your town and on my way."

Twin number two took a step forward. "Maybe you did not hear my brother, John," he snarled, his voice perhaps even a few notes higher than his double. "I think we should step outside."

His brother's voice was almost like hearing an echo. "Absolutely, Ron," agreed the clone with heat.

Elizabeth couldn't help herself. John and Ron. Twins. The rhyming duo. Her laughter bubbled up within her, emerging from her exhaustion, her frustration, her hunger and weariness with the world. It was the final straw in the long carnival which had made up these past few weeks.

The brothers glanced at each other, fury boiled their faces crimson, and her left hand dropped to her hip, doing the twist – latch – release to free her sword hilt from its clasp in one smooth movement. She had her weapon sliding smoothly from its sheath in the same moment that the pair launched themselves across the spellbound tavern toward her. Her steel rose in an arcing block as John brought a haymaker drive down toward her skull. She deflected his blow easily, sliding it off to her left, turning and whipping the sword – flat first – against his kidney with the full force of her momentum. He screamed in pain and sprawled back on the rough wooden floor, his face contorted in agony.

She continued her spin, remaining low, the whistle of Ron's blade skimming over her head. She kicked her boot hard against his kneecap. He buckled backwards, screaming in fury, and she rose, whirling her sword in a circular motion, preparing to give him a welt to remember her by.

There was a dark figure before her. Her moving blade slammed into a block, was held, and she looked up into moss green eyes. Her breath caught, and she leant her sword against the tension. Her blade pressed in an X against his, their hands nearly touching, his body presenting a barrier now between her and the two young men.

"My name is Richard." His voice rumbled out deep, steady, serious. He gazed at her face for a long minute. "I would call your eyes a deep brown, would you agree?"

Elizabeth shook her head in confusion. "What? I suppose," she ground out, continuing her press against his sword. The man had excellent balance; his arm did not move one breath.

Richard turned his head slightly, calling down to the two at his feet. "Certainly not ice blue," he informed them calmly.

His focus came back to her. "I apologize for these two impetuous ones, and would ask that you choose to stay at the Traveler's Inn, a scant mile east. To be truthful, they are much cleaner than this location."

A hot flare of fury burst through her. She was attacked, and now she was the one who had to leave? It was the second coming of the Flood out there! She snapped her sword free of his and sidestepped to the right, determined to finish what she had started.

Richard moved easily with her, brought his sword hilt back against his hip, and pointed the tip between her eyes. His body remained evenly between hers and the sprawled men. "I will defend them," he added in a cool, steady voice. Elizabeth could see the steel settle into his gaze. She remembered being sheltered by that same style of fierce protectiveness, remembered being sprawled, herself, on a cold floor, her guardian angel standing resolutely between her and danger.

God's teeth, she missed her brother.

The burning flame of fury ebbed within her, and she sighed. It was not worth it, not for a flea-bitten mat in this God forsaken hole in the ground.

She took a step back, slid her sword smoothly back into its sheath, then turned on her heel. She pulled the soaking wet cloak over her shoulders, shivering as its damp caress sucked the warmth out of her body. She half kicked the door open. Outside the rain pummeled the ground as if to beat it into submission, and she nearly turned back, nearly took on all three.

"Here," came a call behind her. She turned, and Richard tossed her two golden coins. She caught them easily as they came near her, and the corner of his mouth twitched up in appreciation.

Now she was being paid to leave. She turned back toward the rain, took a deep breath, and walked steadfastly into the torrent, leaving the door wide open behind her.

Here's where to read Elizabeth's full story!

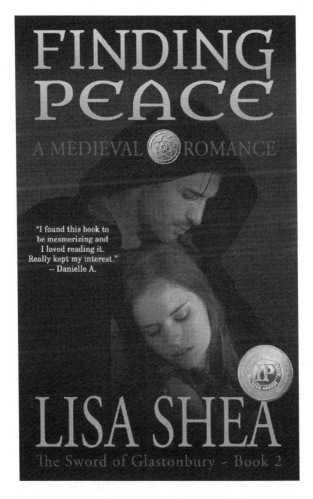

http://www.amazon.com/Finding-Peace-Medieval-Lisa-Shea-ebook/dp/B008FQZ8JY/

Made in the USA
Middletown, DE
06 June 2016